COMES A HORSEMAN

ANNE BARWELL

ECHOES RISING, BOOK 3

A game of cat and mouse across war-torn Europe.

Copyright © 2021 Anne Barwell

All rights reserved. No part of this story may be used, reproduced, or transmitted in any form or by any means without written permission of the copyright holder, except in the case of brief quotations embodied within critical reviews and articles.

This book is a work of fiction. All names, characters, places, and events are products of the writer's imagination or have been used factiously and are not to be construed as real. Any resemblance to persons, living or dead, actual events, locale, or organisations is entirely coincidental.

Published by LaceDragon Publishing

All trademarks, brands, and or licensed materials mentioned are registered trademarks of their respective holders/companies.

Cover design: © 2020 T.L. Bland
Publishing logo © 2019 T.L. Bland
http://www.thruterryseyes.com/
Cover art is for illustrative purposes only and any person depicted on the cover is a model

Editing: Desi Chapman
Blue Ink Editing
https://blueinkediting.com/

ISBN: 978-0-9951466-3-1 (epub)
ISBN: 978-0-9951466-4-8 (mobi)
ISBN: 978-0-9951466-5-5 (print)

First Edition published by DSP Publications, 2017

AUTHOR'S NOTE

This is the second edition of Comes a Horseman. The first edition was released by another publishing house. This story has been re-edited, and uses UK spelling to reflect its setting.

Although this story is a world of fiction, it is set against a backdrop of actual places and events. While many of the locations used are real, some liberties have been taken for the sake of a good story.

The village of Cyrville-sur-Mer is not a real place but is based on villages in the Normandy area at the time.

*To all those who were part of the Resistance during WWII.
Lest we forget.*

ACKNOWLEDGMENTS

To Susanne for beta reading and all her help with the German; Reesha and Lou for beta reading; Angela for beta reading and help with the French; Sharon for always commenting on each new bit as I wrote it, and her love for this series; and Bruce for coming on board to help out with the cold read.

To my writing and reading communities for your support and friendship, in particular RWNZ, and my Facebook groups Anne's Books and Brews, Kiwi Authors Rainbow Readers, and Rainbow Readers Club. A special thanks to the New Zealand Rainbow Romance Writers group—you guys rock.

Gillian and Emma for all their support, friendship, and awesome accountability.

T.L. Bland for her wonderful cover art.

Desi for editing.

To my family. Love you

And last, but in no way least my friends at Upper Hutt Science Fiction Club and Hutt City Libraries.

CHAPTER ONE

"Be quiet," Zhou Liang muttered.

He shoved a pillow over his head but couldn't muffle the sound of water from the dripping kitchen tap. The other occupants of the cottage had finally fallen silent—how they could sleep through it, Liang didn't know—leaving him to what he'd hoped would be a decent night's sleep. Then he'd become aware of the tap, which he swore had behaved itself up to now.

Still muttering, he felt around for his coat on the end of the sofa, pulled it around him for extra warmth, and made his way out to the kitchen. If someone had told him a couple of months ago that he'd be happy to leave this safe house and journey into much more dangerous surroundings, he wouldn't have believed them. But after weeks moving around Germany, working the land to help the farmers who had given them refuge, he was definitely ready to move on.

In a few days' time, they'd be crossing the German border into France. Liang hoped it meant they would finally be on the next stage of their journey home, but he'd experienced enough during his extended stay in Germany to not count on it.

He lit the stove and filled the kettle before making sure the offending tap was turned off properly and then pulled out a chair while he waited for the water to boil. Funny how, despite his present situation, he continued to seek comfort in familiar habits. His Chinese grandparents had taught him about the importance of tea, and he'd also adopted the British adage that it solved everything.

So much had happened since the beginning of a supposedly simple mission. He'd been approached by the Special Operations Executive to join a team being sent to Germany to retrieve the plans for a weapon that could potentially change the outcome of the war. As a civilian, Liang's job was to confirm the plans were authentic. However, since one of the scientists from the project—Dr Kristopher Lehrer—had joined them, Liang's presence was no longer necessary.

He glanced up at the ceiling, then shook his head. Did Kristopher and Michel—the French Resistance fighter who had helped Kristopher get out of Berlin—realise Liang had figured out they were more than friends? Six months ago, he might have reacted differently, but now he figured if they'd found love and solace in each other, they might as well enjoy it while they could. There was something to be said for finding love in the middle of all this chaos.

Matt Bryant and Ken Lowe—already good friends—were now also more than that.

None of them talked about it, of course. Two men discovered in a relationship did not have much of a future, if any, to look forward to—and not only in Germany. Their team already had enough problems with Standartenführer Holm after them, without giving him another excuse to arrest them.

Holm didn't need an excuse.

The two couples were very discreet, and if they hadn't all been sharing close quarters for these months, Liang doubted he would have noticed. And, if he was being honest with himself, one of the reasons he'd noticed was that he missed Juliane and wondered if he'd ever see her again. Falling in love with the sister of the SS officer hunting them hadn't been the brightest move, but emotions didn't always follow the path of common sense. Liang and Juliane had promised each other they'd meet after the war, but the small problem of surviving it remained.

Juliane Dunst not only worked for her brother, but also for the German Resistance. If her ties to the Resistance were discovered…

He wasn't going to think about that. Not now and not ever.

Liang stretched as he got up to make his tea. The scars on his back, although mostly healed, irritated him on occasion. Some nights when he closed his eyes, he relived the whipping he'd received at the hands of Holm's second-in-command, Reiniger, yet his memories always stopped at the same point. Excruciating pain had driven him to yelling, "No more," but he couldn't remember anything after that. Not until he'd woken in his cell.

Had he told Holm something he shouldn't? They'd almost been caught, and Liang couldn't help but think it was his fault.

He mentally changed the subject, not needing the reminder of the real reason he wasn't sleeping well. Holm had done more than given the order for Liang to be whipped; he'd also given Liang some information about one of his team that he couldn't stop thinking about.

What if Holm was right about Ken? And if so, did it really matter?

Liang didn't know what to think anymore. He'd told

himself that Ken was a good man who couldn't and shouldn't be judged because of—

A discreet cough from the doorway pulled him back to reality. Kristopher Lehrer stood there, running his hand through sleep-mussed hair. The dye he'd used months ago to darken it had grown out, the colour returning to its natural blond. "I smelt tea. Is there enough for two?" he asked.

"You couldn't sleep either." Liang didn't phrase it as a question. This wasn't the first time he and Kristopher had shared a late-night pot of tea. Despite their different backgrounds, Kristopher and Liang had quickly discovered they had more in common than their love for science. Kristopher had admitted on his thirtieth birthday a couple of months ago that there were times he felt much older after everything they'd been through in the past six months. Liang figured the rest of their team—who were of a similar age—probably felt the same way. However, although they rarely discussed their personal lives, information slipped out unintentionally on occasion. Kristopher, on the other hand, seemed to have a need to talk about such things. Liang sometimes wondered if it was because he'd left it all behind while the rest of them had lives to return to once the mission was over.

"No." Although Kristopher didn't elaborate, he didn't need to. Liang had suspected for a while that Kristopher had nightmares too. It surprised him that they hadn't woken Michel, but it would only be a matter of time before he joined them. He always did.

Liang poured tea for them, and then set the cups down on the table. They drank silently for a few moments.

"The more I think about this situation, the more complicated it becomes," Kristopher said finally.

"I can understand that." Liang sipped his tea and waited for Kristopher to elaborate.

"I still can't believe how naive I was." Kristopher's fingers tightened around his cup. His English was impeccable. "I tell myself I'm not like that anymore, but perhaps I've swapped one naivety for another?"

"It's difficult to push aside what you've been taught to believe most of your life." Liang had his eyes forcibly opened during his time in Germany. He had known about the atrocities humans could inflict on other humans through the stories his grandparents had told him about the family they lost in the Japanese invasion of Nanking. He thought those stories would prepare him, but they were about family he'd only heard about, people he never met. He hadn't seen or endured the horrors they'd experienced.

He shivered, remembering the fire the night the institute in Berlin had been bombed. With the realisation that one of their team—Ed Walker—was still inside when the armoury had gone up, Liang had run after a distraught Trevor Palmer to stop him doing anything stupid, knowing they didn't have time to grieve if they wanted to survive.

Both men were gone now. Walker, dead, and Palmer arrested by Reiniger.

"I was an idiot." Kristopher shrugged. "Am an idiot," he amended.

"You are the last man I would ever call an idiot." Liang had seen the plans and formulae for the atomic device Kristopher had helped design. "You have a brilliant mind. I know enough to verify what you've shown me, but I could have never come up with any of it."

"If I were brilliant, I wouldn't have designed the thing in the first place." Kristopher shrugged again.

"You didn't design the weapon." Liang had heard Kristopher chastising himself like this before. It didn't achieve anything. "They used your ideas for something you didn't intend."

Kristopher snorted. "Yes, and I ignored what they were

doing because I wanted to think it would be used to advance mankind, not wipe it out."

"We all make mistakes. My grandmother also told me that once we think we're perfect, we need to start worrying."

"Your grandmother is a wise woman. I wish I could meet her."

"Perhaps one day you will. She'd enjoy talking with you." Liang put his cup down. He missed his grandparents and wished he could find a way to let them know he was all right. "Have you decided what you're going to do yet?"

Kristopher fidgeted with a loose thread on the cuff on his shirt. "This weapon should not be in the hands of either side. When I escaped from the institute, I thought I'd help the Allies defeat Hitler and his Nazis. But I'm not sure it's that simple anymore."

"Wars are never simple."

"This is still my country. There are good people living in it. No one deserves to die."

"I'm not sure I'd agree with that last bit," Liang muttered. "I can think of at least two people I'd love to see die slowly and painfully."

"You don't really believe that, do you?" Although Kristopher questioned Liang's comment, he didn't look surprised or shocked. "I know Holm and Reiniger hurt you badly, but if you kill them, doesn't that make you as bad as they are?"

"And what if it had been your sister they'd hurt, or—" Liang caught himself in time. "—someone else you care about?"

"For all I know, Clara might be already dead." Kristopher's tone flattened. "Michel said Holm is probably using her as a hostage to get me to give myself up, so there's a good chance she is alive, but…" He shook his head.

"Would you give yourself up for Clara?" Liang had met Dr Clara Lehrer. She'd helped Matt when he'd been injured, and she'd been arrested because of it, along with Trevor Palmer.

"I don't know." Kristopher shook his head. He slipped his hand into his pocket, pulled out a piece of paper, and slid it over the table to Liang.

Liang recognised it immediately. "Leo's letter. I've already read it. I don't need to read it again. We already agreed you should keep it."

"Leo wanted Mary to have it. You'll be able to pass it on to someone who can get it to her." Kristopher traced bubbles of moisture along the rim of his cup with one finger. "He shouldn't have died. He had his life ahead of him before he signed up to fight in this war. He should be home in New Zealand with her. Not blown to pieces trying to save us."

Leo Dawson was—had been—an RAF pilot shot down over the Black Forest. When Reiniger had cornered them at the vineyard at Freiburg, Leo had stayed behind to give them time to get away. Liang hadn't known him as long as Kristopher and Matt had, but he'd liked the young man.

"He told me he didn't want to go back to his sweetheart with one leg," Liang reminded Kristopher quietly. Leo had been injured when his aircraft had crashed, and his leg badly infected. "He made his choice. He was a brave man, and we need to respect that. He died with honour."

"I know that. I sometimes wonder if he was the bravest of all of us. It's easier to run, isn't it?" Kristopher grimaced. "I'm not sure how brave I am, Liang. The more I think about it, the more I come to one conclusion."

"There's only one way to make sure neither side gets your formulae." Liang had a nasty feeling where this conversation was going. The only physical copies of the plans had been destroyed when the institute was bombed, and Kristopher was the only person who could reproduce them.

Kristopher nodded. "Doktor Kristopher Lehrer cannot be

allowed to survive this war," he continued in German. "They won't stop coming after us. Both sides want that weapon. It doesn't matter who builds it. The outcome will be the same. People will die."

"And what if someone else figures out how to build it first?" Liang followed Kristopher's lead and asked his question in German.

"At least it wasn't because of me. I can't let anyone die. I can't." Kristopher looked up at Liang, this time not bothering to hide the pain in his eyes. "This is the only way. I've thought about it and—"

"When were you going to tell me?" Michel interrupted from the doorway. "You *were* going to tell me, weren't you?"

Kristopher pushed his chair out. He spun around. "Michel... I..."

"I'm going back to bed," Liang said quickly. He stood and left the room before either man had a chance to reply. The horrified look on Michel's face was enough for Liang to want to avoid that conversation. "I think you two gentlemen need to talk in private. Good night."

Michel Faber shut the kitchen door as soon as Liang left. "Kit?"

When Kit didn't answer, Michel filled an empty cup with water and drank it slowly in an attempt to calm himself.

It didn't work.

"I woke and you weren't there." Michel had given Kit a few minutes, guessing he had probably found Liang awake and the two men were talking.

"I couldn't sleep," Kit said finally.

"I noticed."

"You're angry." Kit still didn't look at him. "I can hear it in your voice."

"Yes." Michel did feel angry, but it was more than that. He shoved down his fear of losing the man he loved. He'd wake one morning to find Kit gone, and he'd never see him again. "Merde. If you're planning to kill yourself, don't you think you should talk to me about it first? I thought we could talk to each other. Instead I find you… Or did you forget to speak English so I couldn't understand you?"

"What? No." Kit frowned. "Oh. I thought… I didn't realise I'd switched languages. Liang must have followed my lead without thinking. Verdammt, Michel. It's not what you think. I promise."

So they had thought they'd been speaking English.

"You told me you'd stay for as long as you could," Michel reminded him. He shrugged and pulled up a chair but deliberately kept some distance between them. Although he wanted to pull Kit into his arms and hold him, he refused to be distracted until they'd talked about this. "I thought you'd at least tell me when you were planning to leave. I might not like some of these ideas you have, but that doesn't mean I won't listen to them."

"I know, and I'm sorry. I've been thinking about this for a while, but I didn't know how to bring it up. It's not exactly something you casually slip into a conversation."

They both knew they might be lost to each other with no warning. But, unlike this, that was something neither had any control over.

"We can talk about it now." Michel laced his fingers together, his knuckles whitening.

Kit shifted his chair so they were sitting side by side, rather than at opposite ends of the table. "I'm not planning to die," he said evenly. "I said that Doktor Kristopher Lehrer cannot survive this war. I didn't say anything about killing myself." His voice cracked. "I wouldn't do that to you. I don't want to leave you. I…"

"Mon cher," Michel said softly. He took one of Kit's hands in his and caressed it with his thumb. "You *are* Kristopher Lehrer. You're not making sense."

"Yes, I am, but I'm sorry. I should have talked to you about it first." Kit sighed. He pointed to the letter lying on the table. "I'm giving Leo's letter to Liang. He can deliver it. I'm not going to England. I'm not giving the plans or the formulae to the Allies."

"Do you honestly think they'll take no for an answer?" Michel knew both sides could be ruthless when they needed to be. "They know about you, and it's one of the reasons they've helped us to get this far. You're important to the war effort."

"I've put our friends in a terrible position. Matt and Ken are part of the military. Their priority is to follow orders and complete this mission."

"You weren't supposed to be a part of their mission." Michel had taken the place of a dead German soldier and infiltrated the institute where Kit worked. A few months into his assignment, he knew he had to help Kit. Finding him standing over the body of Dr Kluge—the scientist in charge of the German project—had led to them both fleeing the scene. Michel hadn't thought for an instant that Kit was responsible for Kluge's death. He still didn't think Kit was capable of killing. If given the choice between killing someone and sacrificing himself, Michel knew what decision Kit would make.

As much as he loved Kit, Michel also knew Kit was too idealistic for his own good. One day it would literally be the death of him.

But it was one thing to think about it possibly happening

in the future, and quite another to hear Kit actually planning it.

"I'm where I'm meant to be." Kit shook his head when Michel opened his mouth to protest. "If I hadn't left the institute when I did… they'd never have let me go. With Kluge dead, there is no one else. They know I've solved the problem with the formulae. I was stupid enough to tell Reiniger I had."

"You told him because you were trying to save my life." Michel was missing something. "How can you die and not die?" He felt cold inside. Not just because of the words Kit had spoken, but also because he'd spoken to Liang about this, not him. "As I said, it doesn't make sense."

"People disappear and are presumed dead all the time during war. It doesn't mean they are dead."

"You're planning to fake your death?" Michel said slowly. The relief he felt was short-lived as practicality took over. "We'd have to supply a body."

Kit held up his hand. "No," he said firmly. "We're not killing someone to take my place. Holm already knows what identity papers I'm using. We'll leave them on someone who is already dead."

"I'm not suggesting we kill someone, but do you really think a body matching your description will conveniently turn up when we need it?" Michel couldn't help but roll his eyes. "I'm sorry, Kit, but your plan has a few flaws in it."

"It's a work in progress," Kit insisted. "But as long as we can convince both sides I'm dead, that is all that matters."

"And what are you planning to do once you've died? Have you thought that through?"

Kit lowered his gaze. He flushed. "I still want a life with you. I thought… We can't get married, but I could take your name and pass myself off as a relative or something. At least that way I wouldn't have to say goodbye to you. No one on our team knows your last name or much about you. They wouldn't be lying if they tell their superiors they don't know where to find you. And if they can't find you, they wouldn't be able to find me."

"If only it was that easy." Michel wished Kit's words could become reality. He wanted to believe that a future together was possible. He'd found himself dreaming about it, although he didn't dare hope it could come true. "If they know you're alive… I know Matt and Ken are our friends, but as you said, they do have to report back to their superiors."

"Are you suggesting we let them believe I'm dead?" Kit didn't look happy with the idea. "They're our friends. I can't lie to them."

"Not even to protect them?"

"To protect me, you mean." Kit shook his head. "No one can torture information out of someone if they don't possess it in the first place." He took a gulp of what had to be cold tea. "God, what is wrong with me, discussing something so serious as though it's not?"

"There is nothing wrong with you." Michel could tell Kit was more upset than he was letting on. "Look at me, mon cher," he said softly. "You are a good man who has made mistakes. We've all done that, and it's nothing to be ashamed of. You're in an impossible situation, trying to make choices you don't really have."

"I used to believe we make our own choices in life, but now I'm not so sure. I've been thinking about David and the future he wanted." Kit had told Michel about David, a close friend who could have been much more. David had risked his life to convince Kit to listen to his conscience and leave the institute. "He was a doctor like my sister, with a life ahead of him helping people. He always wanted to do that. It was one of the reasons he studied so hard. Now he's either dead or in a work camp somewhere because he's Jewish."

"Not everything in life is fair, but it's better to focus on the situations we can do something about." Michel had lost his brother, Corin, and a man he'd cared about to this war too. "I think the best way we can honour the memory of our friends and loved ones is to try to make a difference where we can."

"You make it sound so easy."

Michel winced. "It's not, and sometimes it's so difficult I struggle to find the strength to keep going. I tell myself if I repeat the words enough times, it will get easier. I owe Corin my life. He died fighting to free France. I can't let his sacrifice be for nothing."

"I know." Kit leaned over and kissed Michel on his cheek. "I've held you while you've cried for the people you've lost."

"Just as I've held you." Michel took a deep breath. He wouldn't think about it now, didn't want to get sucked into the whirlpool that was his grief for Corin and François again. It had taken him too long to break free of it. "So, what are we going to do about all of this? I'm not going to watch you die. If we're going to fake your death, we need some kind of plan. Do you still want to travel with the others until they reach Normandy?"

"Yes, I need to leave Germany. We have more of a chance of disappearing to start a new life in your country than mine. You have contacts in the Resistance, people we could help until this war is over."

Michel raised an eyebrow. "Doesn't that rather negate your being dead? I thought… Never mind."

"You thought what?"

"We've talked about a future together. If we survive all of this, I'd like that. I think your idea of passing yourself off as a relative will be a little problematic, but we'll worry about the details later." More than a *little* problematic. Michel's mother would take one look at the two of them together and figure out they were more than friends. "I want to return to my family when this is over. My parents have already lost one son. I promised Papa I would do everything I could to make sure he and Maman wouldn't lose another. I'm a farmer. You know nothing of that kind of life."

"I've learnt a lot over the last six weeks, and it would be safer than living in the city." Kit looked thoughtful. He was seriously contemplating this. "I'll have to improve my French, though. It's not very good; although it's better than it was."

"My aunt would help." Michel's Uncle Brice had married a German woman. She'd welcome Kit with open arms. So would Michel's parents, or at least his mother. "We're getting ahead of ourselves, though. We have to get out of Germany, and that won't be easy."

"I think it would work better if we travel with Matt, Ken, and Liang for a while longer and then fake my death. You've already told them you aren't crossing the Channel." Kit tipped his cup and studied the tea leaves, using his spoon to swish them around the bottom of it. "I'm not sure you're right about keeping all this from them. They'll know something is wrong. We can trust them."

"I know we can trust them, but it's not them I'm worried about." Michel could tell he wasn't going to easily persuade Kit to change his mind about that part of the plan. "It's Holm and Reiniger."

"They'd torture our friends for the information until they got the answers they wanted. It wouldn't matter whether it was the truth or not." Kit had that stubborn look Michel recognised all too well.

"We won't have to talk about that part of it now. Let's take one step at a time, hmm? Promise me you won't say anything until we've discussed it further?"

"All right, but Liang already knows I'm planning something."

"Yes, but he doesn't know any details."

"That's because we don't have any to share." Kit shrugged. "I'm tired, and we've gone around in circles enough for one night." He stood and held out his hand. "I want to go back to bed with you. Once we leave here, we might not have the opportunity to share a bed again."

No one had commented about them sharing a room and shutting the door. Michel suspected it was because Matt and Ken were also sharing more than a room. However, he wasn't about to voice his suspicions. He had too many secrets of his own to keep safe.

"I'd like that." Michel took Kit's hand and squeezed it tightly before pulling him close and kissing him.

"Je t'aime, Michel," Kit whispered once they broke the kiss. "Whatever happens, never forget that."

"Whatever happens, I never will." Michel buried his head in Kit's shoulder, caressing the skin there with his lips. "Ich liebe dich, Kit."

CHAPTER TWO

"That didn't go well." Ken packed away the radio set. He then placed the suitcase into the hole he'd dug earlier and picked up a spade.

Matt made a noncommittal noise from behind him. "I was expecting worse," he admitted after a few moments' silence. "Do you want any help filling the hole?"

"No, it's fine." Ken began shovelling dirt. He worked in silence, using the time to mull over the messages he'd received from their superiors.

Matt leaned against the wall of the workers' cottage, watching him, his arms folded across his chest. He'd grown his hair longer now they had finished posing as German soldiers, and one light brown strand of hair fell forward across his brow. Matt brushed it back, yet his gaze didn't waver. He smiled, although it didn't quite reach his eyes, a sure sign he wanted to talk about something. Ken knew Matt well enough to know he'd wait until Ken was ready to listen. This was a job that wouldn't be hurried as it needed to be done properly.

Finally, Ken pulled a handkerchief from his pocket and

wiped his brow. As they'd worked their way around various farms over the past few weeks, he'd found he enjoyed the hard labour. It helped him think.

He also felt some relief that the radio set was hidden once more. Since building it, he'd had nightmares about its discovery leading to Matt being captured again. Ken hadn't completely pushed from his mind the memory of the state in which he'd found Matt in that cell at the institute.

"This mission has taken six months longer than it should have." Ken shook off most of the dirt from the spade and threw a pile of branches over the new earth to disguise it. "We've lost two men and acquired another who wasn't part of the initial orders we received. We're also still in Germany, and it's going to take us several weeks to reach the Channel, and that's presuming we aren't caught before we get there."

They hadn't told London about Holm's obsession with finding Ken because of something that was supposed to have happened during the last war. Matt hadn't seen the point, as there was nothing that could be done about it. He wasn't about to give Holm what, or rather, who he wanted. The official story was that Holm was hunting them to find Kristopher.

As the only source of the plans, Kristopher was a very important asset, and as such he should have been safely out of Germany by now. London was not impressed by how long this mission was taking or how complicated it had become.

Ken also suspected if London wanted Kristopher, they'd have to make a deal to ensure Michel's safety or Kristopher wouldn't agree to their terms. Although Michel was now part of their team, he'd told them he would stay in France once the mission was completed.

"As I said, I was expecting worse." Matt touched Ken lightly on his shoulder. "Sit with me awhile? There's something we need to discuss, and it's not something I want to talk about in front of the others."

Ken frowned. "We shouldn't be—"

"Not that." Matt chuckled. He lowered his voice to a whisper only Ken could hear. "That, I'd prefer to explore more of later." He licked his lips once Ken was facing him.

"Is that a promise?" Ken's voice came out hoarser than he'd expected. He swallowed and cleared his throat. Hell, did Matt realise what that—he—did to him? He glanced around nervously.

"Yes." Matt smiled, a proper one this time. His eyes twinkled, their brilliant blue a stark contrast to the piercing black Ken saw when he looked at his own reflection. "Don't worry, we're definitely alone. I'm not about to take any chances." He sat down with his back against the wall of the cottage and patted the ground next to him.

Ken was no fool. Even if he and Matt made it back to America alive, they wouldn't have the future both of them wanted. At best they'd be able to settle somewhere as war buddies sharing a house.

"I'm still thinking about your offer of sharing your home after the war," Ken said cautiously.

"But it's not that simple?" Matt shuffled over when Ken joined him. "Don't worry. When I said I wanted to talk to you about something, it wasn't that. I know it's complicated, and you have your mom to think about too. Let's survive this war first, and then we can work all that out."

"I don't want you to think I don't want the future we've talked about." Ken chose his words carefully, so Matt wouldn't draw the wrong conclusions. "You know how I feel about you."

"And you know how I feel about you." Matt mouthed, "I love you too," but didn't speak the words aloud. Although they were supposed to be alone, he brushed his thumb against Ken's hand, taking care not to linger.

Ken couldn't help but smile.

"I've told you how much I love that smile, right?"

"Several times, but don't feel you have to stop." Ken reserved that particular smile for Matt, and Matt knew it.

"I'm not planning to." Matt cleared his throat. "I've been thinking about your mom." He lowered his voice. "I know someone I can talk to about getting her out of the camp and getting her safely settled somewhere outside the exclusion zone. Then, after the war, we can help her get back on her feet."

Ken's mother was half Japanese and in an internment camp. He'd always thought he'd been lucky in that he took after his American father and maternal grandmother in looks, and his Japanese heritage wasn't obvious, despite his dark hair and slight stature. Cho Tsukino had insisted her son take his father's name, although Ken's father had abandoned them before Ken was born. Ken hadn't seen his mother since she'd entered the internment camp. When the government had begun to round up people of Japanese ancestry, she'd insisted he keep his distance from her. He couldn't risk being identified as part Japanese, and he needed his freedom in order to follow in his father's footsteps and help to fight to end this war.

Unfortunately, that had worked a little too well. While Ken had spent most of his life looking up to the father he'd never met, he now wondered whether Patrick Lowe had been the war hero some claimed him to be.

Despite logic telling him the information Holm had given him about both their fathers was wrong, Ken couldn't help but wonder if there might be something to it.

His and Holm's father had been at the Battle of Belleau

Wood, but that didn't mean Patrick Lowe had murdered Heinz Holm.

They'd been on opposite sides, fighting a war. Men died. It wasn't personal, or at least it wasn't meant to be.

Ken sighed. He couldn't afford to be distracted by all that now. "You've been thinking about this awhile," he said to Matt.

"Yes, since before we got separated looking for Leo's aircraft. I should have spoken to you about it before now, but we've had other things on our minds." Matt stared straight ahead, his eyes unfocused. If he'd noticed Ken had been distracted and the time he'd taken to reply, he didn't show it. Or he'd been lost in his own thoughts. "If something happened to you, I'd make sure your mom was looked after."

"You don't have—"

"I want to." Matt's expression was one Ken knew well. He wasn't stupid enough to try arguing with him. Nor did he want a repeat of the last time they'd quarrelled.

Ken had spent a horrible few days unsure whether Matt was dead or alive and knowing what might have been their last conversation had been an argument.

"We'll do it together," Ken said firmly, "but just in case..." He thought for a moment of the stories his mother had told him about her side of the family. "My grandparents live in Nagasaki, and she has other relatives in Iwaki. I'm certain she'd be happy going to stay with either of them after the war."

"Nagasaki and Iwaki. Got it." Matt nodded, but Ken could tell there was something else on his mind.

"What did you want to talk about?" he asked. "It wasn't only about my mom, was it?"

"No." Matt frowned. "I'm having serious doubts about this mission."

"It's not gone well," Ken agreed.

"It's not just that." Matt paused for a moment. "Kristopher's told us what this weapon—this atomic bomb—is capable of. I've also listened to him and Liang talking about specifics. While I'm not a scientist, I've heard enough to know if either side gets hold of this weapon, lots of people are going to die. I'd like to believe the Allies wouldn't use it, but I don't know anymore."

"I wouldn't have thought they'd round up their own citizens and put them in camps," Ken said. "A lot of those people were born in America, as were their parents. They—we—think of ourselves as American."

"Desperation and paranoia make people do things they wouldn't normally do." Matt shook his head. "Are we doing the right thing in delivering Kristopher to our superiors? If he helps them develop this weapon before the Nazis develop theirs…"

Although their team reported to London, it was a joint mission between the British Special Operations Executive and American Office of Strategic Services.

"London's not going to be impressed if we don't complete the mission," Ken pointed out. "Although—"

"Although?" Matt met Ken's gaze, his brow furrowing into a frown. "You've been thinking about this too, haven't you?"

Ken shrugged. "So far nothing about this mission has gone to plan. They'd be angry, but I doubt they'd suspect anything if the rest of it went the same way." He thought back to a couple of days before when he'd almost walked in on Michel and Kristopher having a very animated conversation. "Michel's worried about Kristopher."

"How can you tell? That guy doesn't give much away."

"Watch the two of them together. He thinks he hides it, but he's worried. I saw the way he reacted in Stuttgart when he thought Kristopher might have been captured. There's something of that in him now."

"Hmm." Matt looked thoughtful. "Have you tried talking to him about it?"

"I don't do that. You do." Ken knew his limitations. He wasn't someone people opened up to, which was ironic, considering he'd gotten the role of wireless operator on this mission. He was good at his job; the makeshift radio he'd built was proof of that. He received the messages. Matt—as the leader of their team—decided what to do with the information and how to follow the orders.

"Kristopher's no fool. I'm sure he's figured out what will happen to him and the information he has if he hands himself over to either side."

"He's had plenty of opportunities to disappear if he wanted to." Ken doubted Kristopher would work with the Nazis. He'd already lost too much getting away from them. "Do you think he's biding his time?"

"And using us to get him out of Germany?" Matt shrugged. "The thought had occurred to me. Michel's planning to contact his old Resistance cell once we're over the border. He also speaks the language. We don't, and neither does Kristopher, although I've heard Michel giving him a few more lessons." Michel and Liang had also coached the rest of their team in basic language skills, although Matt doubted they'd know enough to have, or follow, any more than a very simple conversation. "That gives Kristopher an advantage if they stick together."

"They'll stick together." Of that Ken was sure. He'd wondered once or twice whether Michel and Kristopher were more than friends, but dismissed it. He wasn't about to ask them and figured if he didn't, they wouldn't ask about him and Matt either. It was easier and safer that way.

"So the way I see it, we have two options."

"Oh?" Ken frowned. "I hope your ideas are better than mine. I keep reminding myself they're our friends. Despite what's at stake, I don't want either of them hurt."

Matt narrowed his eyes. "What do you take me for? I know we have a job to do, but there are always options. You didn't leave me behind when I was captured, even though you were ordered to. I've gotten to know Kristopher over the past month or so, and it would surprise me if he's planning to cross the Channel with us."

"As I said," Ken reminded him mildly, "I hope your ideas are better than mine. You're in charge here, not me, and there's a reason for that."

"Because of my ability to follow orders?" Matt laughed bitterly. "I followed enough of your conversation with London to know they don't think either of us are good at that. My knowledge of the code you used isn't as good as yours, but it's not bad."

"I'll keep that in mind for future reports." Not that Ken was about to send anything he hadn't cleared with Matt first, but he couldn't help but make the comment, nevertheless. He sobered. "That doesn't solve our problem, though."

"I was getting to that. I figure we need to help both of them disappear. But more than that, we need to convince London they're dead. Not just London but Holm and his men too. As long as there's any hint Kristopher is still alive, neither side will stop looking."

"You're suggesting we lie to our superiors?" Ken frowned. "What makes you think they're going to believe us?"

"We provide proof."

"Sure, so in the midst of everything that's happening, we pause long enough to take a photo of a convenient dead body that looks like him? Kristopher's not military. He doesn't have dog tags to identify him."

"I'm working on that."

"Do you think it might be a good idea to talk to him about it first? Rather than presuming he'll happily go along with it? People don't always act the way you think they will."

"I'm working on that too." Matt sighed. "I said they were options. I didn't say I had a step-by-step plan. I figure we'll get across the border first, and then worry about the rest of it. Meanwhile keep an eye on them."

"If they disappear, it solves our problem, though, doesn't it?" Ken didn't want to be the one to have that conversation with Kristopher, especially with Michel around. He wasn't in a hurry to get a fist in his face if Michel took what they were suggesting the wrong way. Not to mention that Michel had three inches on him and a hell of a lot more muscles to go with it.

"That's a big if, and there's always the chance they've vanished because Holm's gotten hold of one of them." Matt bit his lip and lowered his voice. "I know what I'd do if he captured you. I'd do whatever it took to get you back."

Was Matt suggesting what Ken thought he was? "But they're not…" He held up his hand before Matt could answer. "I don't think that's something we should discuss, especially if we have no proof. Some secrets need to remain that way."

"Especially as we have one ourselves?"

"Exactly," Ken said finally, although there was no need to answer the question as it was rhetorical. They had other things to worry about without talking about a topic that wouldn't achieve anything. "We should get back to work, especially as we're leaving tomorrow. These people have taken a huge risk in letting us stay here. It's a small way to say thank you."

"The next couple of days are going to be very tiring. We need to make sure we get a good night's sleep as there won't be much chance of that until we reach Haguenau." Matt started to stand.

Although they hadn't seen any of Holm's men since they'd returned to the area, it would be foolish to take any chances. With any luck, Holm still thought they were heading for Switzerland.

The journey to Gernsbach would take two days. Heading directly for Rastatt would take less time, but the detour would be safer. Gernsbach was only a few hours away from where they'd agreed to meet their contact on Friday. They'd cross the Rhine that night, under the cover of darkness, and head for Seltz. It was further north than the bridge at Strasbourg, which was likely to be heavily guarded.

"I still think we should split up."

"And I *still* disagree with you." Matt shook his head and stood. "Considering what happened last time, I think it's safer if we stick together."

"Last time wasn't planned, and this would be," Ken reminded him. He scrambled to his feet, not wanting to let Matt dismiss their conversation yet. "Five of us travelling together... I'm not convinced it's the sensible thing to do."

Matt shrugged. "Perhaps we'll revisit the idea once we meet Michel's contact in Haguenau. We need to get across the Rhine and into France. One problem at a time."

Ken caught his arm. "Are you going to be all right on Friday night?"

Matt flinched. His issues about being in the dark hadn't disappeared, although he hadn't had a really bad nightmare for a few weeks. "Come on, let's get back to work. I promised our hosts I'd finish fixing that section of fence before we leave. Michel's already finished the section he was weeding, and he's showing Kristopher and Liang—"

"Something about bud break and vines bleeding?" Ken asked. "I heard Michel talking about that before too before I came to find you. I swear we'll have to drag him away from all of it tomorrow."

Michel had experience working the land, although as usual, he wasn't forthcoming about any details. When Ken had asked him about it, he'd shrugged and said he knew enough to get by. The rest of them had had to learn quickly, but Ken thought they'd adapted well. Even Liang seemed to be enjoying it on some level, although he would never admit it.

"I suspect it reminds him of home. He's been away from his longer than we have from ours."

A shadow crossed Matt's face. Ken recognised the look. Elise had been Matt's family for years after he'd lost his own as a child, and they'd remained friends even after Matt had realised he couldn't give her the romantic relationship she wanted. Instead of the reunion in Berlin he'd hoped for, he'd been arrested by her killer and tortured for information he refused to reveal. Ken wondered if Matt would be ever truly put it behind him.

"Are you going be all right on Friday night?" Ken repeated. He'd given Matt enough of a chance to answer without prompting. While Ken had thought he'd done the right thing in promising Juliane not to harm her brother, he questioned that decision after learning how badly Holm had hurt Matt. If Ken got his hands on Holm now, he'd—

"I'll have to be," Matt replied.

CHAPTER THREE

"He's late." Matt glanced again at the door leading to the street, his growing nervousness derailing his attempts to appear nonchalant.

Their journey to Gernsbach had been without incident, and that made him edgy as hell. After one night there, he'd suggested they keep moving for a couple more hours until they reached Bischweier. He'd been to Bischweier years ago when he'd lived in Germany before the war. The local priest was an old friend of Father Joseph's, the man who had run the orphanage where Matt had grown up in Pennsylvania after he'd lost his family in a fire.

"Not that late." Michel shrugged. "If we're not back by two, Ken knows not to stay in Bischweier."

Michel and Matt had gone ahead to Rastatt to meet their contact in the back room of a local Kaffeehaus. The owner—a member of the local Resistance—had been kind enough to leave them some coffee while they waited.

"They should be safe if they stay in the chapel." Matt hadn't been surprised to learn that Father Markus was working with the Resistance. Father Joseph had spoken highly of him.

"You didn't trust our contact in Gernsbach. Why?"

"Just a feeling."

Now they were finally heading towards home, he kept expecting Holm or one of his men to turn up. Standartenführer Holm wouldn't give up easily, and Matt doubted he would have spent all this time looking in the wrong direction. The last few weeks had gone too smoothly, reminding Matt of the way a cat played with a mouse, waiting for the right moment to finally pounce.

"Holm is not going to give up until he's captured his prey. It's better that both Kristopher and Ken stay away until we are sure it is safe here." Michel offered Matt a cigarette, but Matt shook his head.

"Kristopher is the one Holm is after," he said cautiously.

"Officially, yes." Michel lit his cigarette, inhaled the smoke slowly, then blew it out. He wasn't usually very forthcoming with information, and this was the first time he'd implied he knew about Ken's history with Holm.

At least to Matt.

"What has Ken told you?" Until they'd met up again in Freiburg, Matt had only met Michel briefly in Berlin. He knew Kristopher better, as he was not as reticent. Matt had gotten the impression Michel didn't have much time for social niceties. He was pleasant enough, though, and it was obvious as hell he cared a great deal for Kristopher.

"We spoke briefly in Stuttgart." Michel shrugged. "Holm is a dangerous man, and once he has made up his mind to achieve something, he doesn't let anyone or anything get in his way. Don't be fooled by his manner. He's the type who would shake your hand while putting a knife in your back."

"I'm well aware of Holm's less than charming nature, thanks all the same." Matt wouldn't forget his meeting with

Holm in a hurry, if ever. Nor would he forgive him for killing Elise. "He's a cold-blooded murderer."

"That's a polite way of putting it." Michel narrowed his eyes and swore under his breath.

Although Matt's French wasn't that good, he knew enough to appreciate the sentiment.

"I believe Ken was foolish enough to promise not to harm him," Michel continued in German. "I take it you have no problem in doing whatever needs to be done?"

"No problem at all," Matt said grimly.

"Good." Michel lapsed into silence again.

Matt sighed and wondered if it was worth trying to make further conversation. He glanced at his watch. "War brings people together who normally wouldn't meet."

To hell with it.

He didn't want to spend the next half hour staring at the wall, thinking about memories better forgotten.

"That's not always a bad thing."

"Once this war is over, we'll go our separate ways and never see each other again."

"That's the plan, yes." Michel arched an eyebrow. Matt wasn't sure whether he was amused or puzzled. "Haven't we already had this conversation? Or am I missing something?"

"Despite everything we've been through, I don't know that much about you," Matt pointed out. "The next few weeks aren't going to be easy, and I figured if there was anything I *need* to know, this might be a good time to discuss it."

"There isn't." Michel stubbed out his cigarette. He lowered his voice. "There's a reason I haven't shared much information about myself, including my last name. My family is not on another continent like—"

"My family is dead," Matt interrupted. "But yes, I understand your concern, and that wasn't what I was asking. I've lost people I care about in this war. Too many people have."

"I know, and I'm sorry about Elise. She was a good woman and helped a lot of people." Michel inclined his head towards Matt. "I will do what I can to keep everyone safe and get your team home."

"We all have things we don't want to, or can't, talk about. But we need to put those things aside and work together. As I said, once this is over, we can go our separate ways." Matt had this crazy idea of making contact again after the war. Perhaps that was all it was. Crazy.

Their mission was a job that needed doing. Were the friendships he'd thought they were building merely an illusion?

He'd begun to think of them as family. Ken was far more than his second-in-command, although it had taken them both a while to realise their true feelings for each other. Matt also enjoyed spending time with Kristopher—he was easy to talk to and had a keen mind and a good sense of humour. Hell, even Liang was beginning to grow on him.

"Talk to Kristopher," Michel said softly. "He is much better at these kinds of conversations than I am. He enjoys them more too."

Matt couldn't help but laugh at that. "I can see why you and Ken get on so well. That's the kind of thing he'd say."

"Ken is more insightful than he gives himself credit for." Michel ran one hand through his short dark blond hair before continuing. "It was his idea for just the two of us to meet this contact. I know I disagreed with it at first, but it is the right thing to do."

"Yes, it is, although I wasn't happy about the suggestion either."

When Ken was right about something, he could argue his case very well.

Matt picked up his cup but put it down again without taking a drink. One sip of it had been enough. By the time he was thirsty enough to be tempted by it, they'd be long gone.

"Better that than all of us walk into a trap, if this turns out to be one." Michel took another swig of the disgusting coffee.

However, it didn't mean Matt was going to agree with them splitting up once they were across the border. This meeting was a couple of hours' detour, nothing more. Getting to the Channel would take several weeks.

"It's better to keep the civilians out of the line of fire for as long as we can." Matt lifted the corner of the curtain and peered out the window. If this contact didn't show in another five minutes, they were leaving. "And if we're captured and we don't know where they are, we can't give them away, can we?"

"This will not be a repeat of what happened last time," Michel said firmly. He leaned back in his chair, seemingly relaxed, but Matt wasn't fooled. Michel was keeping a close eye on both doors, the same way Matt was. "I trust Ken to look after Kit and Liang. I wouldn't have left him—them otherwise."

"I'd trust him with my life," Matt agreed, although he suspected it wasn't so much Ken's argument that had persuaded Michel to go along with it. That had been whatever Kristopher had said to Michel after taking him to one side.

"Although I doubt he'd ever do anything to put you at risk, it's not *your* life I'm trusting him with, and it's safer for —" Michel frowned. "Did you hear that?"

Matt drew his gun and headed for the door leading into the narrow corridor separating the room they were in from the Kaffeehaus. "Come out," he called. "We know you're there."

"The snow melts, but the flood does not come." The woman raised her hands above her head.

"I have yet to see a dove," Matt answered with the second part of the code phrase and lowered his gun. He ushered her inside.

Michel gave her a curt nod. "You're late."

"I got stopped by a Feldgendarme and had to take a different route so I wasn't followed." She was slightly built, with light brown hair and green eyes. "I'm Sigi. I have instructions for you from Frej."

"Matthäus." Matt gave the name on his identification papers. "This is—"

"Gabriel," Michel had obviously decided to keep using his Resistance codename rather than what was on his papers. "Are there any problems we should know about?"

"He will take you across tonight. I will meet with you again in Ottersdorf and lead you to him."

Matt nodded. Ottersdorf was closer to the Rhine, and it made sense not to meet in the same place twice.

"Once you reach Haguenau, someone will make contact." Sigi gave Michel a tight smile. "I was told you might be here, Gabriel. Your contact in Haguenau sends her regards. Apparently it is someone you know."

Michel didn't seem surprised by the information, but then he had said he'd gotten word to his old Resistance cell. "I suspected it would be."

Kristopher wished he could say something to reassure Ken that Matt would be all right crossing the Rhine, but Ken wasn't one to appreciate false sentiment. Although they hadn't spoken again about Matt's reaction in the tunnel when they'd escaped from the cottage in Freiburg months ago, they'd all seen enough to know his issues with the dark could be a problem. Despite Matt's nightmares not plaguing him as often, Kristopher had heard them as he'd lain awake trying to avoid his own demons.

"How safe is this boat?" Liang jammed his hat further forward on his head, the brim hiding his face as they left St. Giles Church.

"Nothing about this is safe," Ken reminded him. He and Matt had exchanged a few words in private after they'd reached Ottersdorf, and neither of them had said much since. Ken had offered to go with Michel to meet with Sigi, but in the end, they'd decided it was better he stay behind. She'd already met Matt, so there was no point putting the rest of them at risk until necessary.

"I haven't felt safe in months." Being in Michel's arms at night had helped Kristopher to forget the danger they were in, but they were living on borrowed time.

If he and Michel managed to go through with their plans to disappear, was this the life they had to look forward to? Looking over their shoulders, hoping no one found them?

It wasn't much of a life, although better than the alternative.

"I'm never going to complain about my office at Cambridge again," Liang muttered.

"I've never heard you complain about it," Ken said.

"It was a lifetime ago, or it felt like it. The only thing I dislike more than boats is jumping out of aeroplanes." Liang shuddered. "I still have nightmares about my parachute not opening, and I swear that experience is the cause of all my grey hairs."

"You don't have any grey hairs." Ken rolled his eyes but had enough sense not to look at Liang when he did it. "And no, I don't want to look for them. Thanks for the offer anyway."

"I wasn't going to offer." Liang snorted.

Kristopher hid his grin. He often wondered if Liang began these conversations to try to put them all at ease, or if he truly did enjoy complaining about everything. As they reached the outskirts of the village, a familiar figure approached them. "Michel's here."

"Matt must be with our contact." Ken peered past Michel, not quite disguising his concerned expression, although there was no sign of it in his voice.

"He is," Michel said. As it was past curfew, they were all careful to stay in the shadows and keep their voices down. "The boat isn't far from here." He glanced around. "You weren't followed?"

"No," Ken told him. "No sign of anyone else who shouldn't be out tonight."

"Good." Michel's gaze lingered on Kristopher for a moment, but he didn't say anything else. Instead he turned to go, expecting them to follow rather than waiting for them.

With the blackout, it wasn't as easy to see the further away they got from the village, but they didn't dare use a torch. It might draw attention they couldn't risk. The moon gave enough illumination to walk without tripping yet made it difficult to see too far away. Although they hadn't seen any soldiers or Feldgendarme, it didn't mean they weren't there. Crossing the Rhine near one of the main bridges would be too dangerous. They'd originally planned to make landfall in France at Seltz, but Sigi had suggested a few kilometres further south in Roquette. Frej knew of a small place that should be safe, as most boats kept to the more frequently used beaches.

They'd stay in Beinheim until morning before heading on to Haguenau.

After travelling in silence for what seemed forever, Kristopher picked up his pace so he was walking next to

Michel. "If we don't—" he started to say, making sure to keep his voice low.

"We will." Michel brushed one hand against Kristopher's very briefly.

Kristopher smiled, although he wished they could hold hands. Would there ever be a day when they could even hint how they felt about each other in public? He hadn't felt happy about Michel going ahead with Matt, but Ken was right. It was the sensible thing to do.

He wanted to ask Michel about the contact they'd be meeting in Haguenau too. Was she a member of his old Resistance cell, and if so, how much did she know about Michel and this mission?

As much as he wanted to ask, he'd have to wait and hope they had an opportunity to speak privately. They'd known when they left Hügelsheim that it might be their last night together. But after months of being able to touch each other and not have to pretend, at least when they were alone, weeks of having to act as though they were just friends was going to be very difficult.

"Let's survive this crossing first," Michel whispered. "You need to stop thinking so much."

"I wasn't," Kristopher began to protest, then stopped. What was the point? Michel knew him a little too well. "I'm sorry."

"Don't ever apologise for being yourself, but this will be easier if you don't think it through too much." Michel stopped suddenly and yanked Kristopher down into a crouch behind some nearby shrubbery.

Behind them Ken and Liang followed Michel's lead.

Kristopher saw a glint of metal. Ken and Michel had drawn their weapons. He glanced around but couldn't see anyone else apart from their group close by.

"Gabriel?" A woman's voice sounded a short distance

ahead. "The dove is not far." She spoke the code phrase to let them know it was safe to proceed.

"It's Sigi. Follow me." Michel led them a few metres to their left, towards the sound of her voice.

A woman wearing a headscarf and a long coat stood waiting for them. "We don't have much time," she said. "I've just received word that an SS officer and his men arrived in Wintersdorf this evening. He is hunting something or someone."

"I'm sure he is," Liang said.

Although it might not be Holm in Wintersdorf, it wasn't a good idea to find out. Kristopher had no intention of meeting any of Holm's men either. Reiniger held grudges. He wouldn't have forgotten their last encounter in Berlin, and there was no guarantee he'd been killed in the explosion at Freiburg.

"Thank you," Kristopher said, "for helping us. I'm—"

"It's better I don't know." Sigi spoke before he could give her his codename.

He wasn't stupid enough to tell her who he really was, and doubted he'd ever use his real name in public again. "Good idea." Kristopher wondered if Sigi was a codename. If it was, it was an interesting choice, considering it meant victory.

"We're almost there," she said. "Stay close."

"Are you crossing the river with us?" Liang asked.

Sigi shook her head. "No. Frej will take you across and return when it is safe. I will wait for him." She eyed them up and down. "He is taking a risk with so many passengers, but better to do one crossing if the SS have been informed you are in the area."

"Do you think it's a coincidence, or someone told them?" Ken asked.

"Difficult to tell. I trust those I work with, but it is often those we trust the most who betray us. Be careful, and only tell your contacts what they need to know."

"How do we know we can trust you?" Kristopher asked.

"You don't." Sigi gave him an approving look. "But then, you don't have much choice, do you?"

CHAPTER FOUR

Matt looked up as they approached. He was waiting a short distance from the river, and there was no sign of a boat or Frej. "Frej is waiting," he explained. "I figured I'd come meet you, rather than staying with the boat. It's a couple of minutes from here, but better to wait a moment before we go any farther."

"In case we were followed?" Michel asked, although it wasn't really a question as he already knew the answer. "Don't worry. We weren't."

"The Feldgendarme will be investigating a report of an intruder a few kilometres from here," Sigi said. "It is a false alarm of course, but it will delay them long enough so you will be gone by the time they resume their regular patrol."

"Thank you," Kit said.

She inclined her head towards them. "Good crossing. I leave you here and will wait for Frej's return." Sigi turned and walked back the way they'd come.

"She is a brave woman." Liang watched her leave.

"Come on. We can't keep Frej waiting, or we'll waste the

time the Resistance has bought us." Matt seemed uncharacteristically nervous.

Ken moved to the front of their group, walking alongside Matt. He leaned in and said something in a low voice to Matt that Michel couldn't hear. Matt nodded but didn't reply.

As they approached the river, a man called out, "Wind is the loving wooer of water."

Kit smiled and nodded. He obviously knew the quote, although Michel hadn't heard it before. He'd have to ask Kit about it later.

Matt answered with the counter phrase. "The water understands civilization well."

"You're on time." Frej took a step closer. "Good."

"I will help you row," Matt offered, although he hadn't been asked.

"Thank you." Frej nodded towards his boat, which was anchored about a metre out from the rocky shoreline. Despite being a little bigger than Michel expected, the boat wasn't large. There was room for all of them, but it would be cramped. A couple of wooden bench seats ran almost half the length of it on either side, with one across the width at midpoint for the oarsman.

"It's very exposed," Liang said.

"If we're caught, a cabin would not save us," Michel pointed out. "Anything suspicious and the boat will be searched. I'd prefer to be in the open where I at least have the chance to dive overboard."

"That is a last resort. You'd have more chance of survival if you surrender. The current is strong, the water is freezing, and in some places the water is not that deep." Frej waded out into the shallow water to the boat. He favoured one leg, yet it didn't slow him down, although it was most likely the reason he hadn't been conscripted to serve his country.

Michel guessed Frej to be at least in his sixties, but as the war progressed, both the young and old were no longer exempt.

Liang hesitated at the edge of the water. "I can't swim."

"You don't need to." Kit strode out into the water ahead of Liang. "It's shallow, and the strong current is much further out. The boat is only moored here because of the rocky beach. We'll probably need to do the same thing on the other side."

"If you say so." Liang followed him hesitantly, his shoulders hunched.

"My father promised to bring us here once, so I read everything I could about the Rhine and this area." From what Kit had said about his father, Paul Lehrer had probably not kept that promise.

"So I can look forward to getting wet again before I've dried out. Wonderful." Liang followed Kit out to the boat, Michel, Matt, and Ken bringing up the rear.

As he reached the boat, Kit turned to look back at the shoreline. Michel caught up with him and brushed his hand against Kit's shoulder briefly.

"It could be au revoir rather than adieu," Michel whispered.

Kit shook his head. "No, I won't be seeing my home again. That life is gone." He climbed into the boat and sat on the far side.

Michel quickly took a seat next to him. He didn't try to reply. It wasn't a conversation for now, and although he'd tried to be reassuring, Kit was probably right.

"I can take the other oar," Ken said to Frej. "I've rowed before, and it will save your strength for making the return journey, as you will be doing it alone."

"Thank you. Many of the people who make this crossing are so focused on escaping they forget all else." Frej moved to let Ken take his place next to Matt. "I have crossed this river at least twice a day for the past forty-five years. I miss the days before the war. I was a bargeman then, and life was a lot simpler. I'll keep lookout while you row. Remember that it is important to let the current guide you rather than make a straight crossing. No talking from now on, unless it is important, and speak in a low voice, or it will carry on the water."

Matt nodded, his lips moving although he did not speak. He was counting as they pulled away from shore, and using the rhythm of his movement to distract himself from the darkness.

The moon's light highlighted the waves lapping around the boat—the water seemed to reach toward them before diving back again. Ken and Matt quickly settled into a unified motion, both focused on what they were doing, although Ken glanced at Matt a couple of times.

Frej signalled for Matt and Ken to change direction slightly and rest the oars for a few moments, letting the boat drift with the current. If Michel squinted, he could see the outline of the bridge in the distance and several shapes moving at either end of it. The guards on duty would hopefully stay focused on the bridge itself and not notice a small rowboat sneaking over the border. Although well guarded, the area had been secured for quite some time, so they would not be expecting trouble.

On the other side of the boat, Liang quickly turned and leaned over the side. As soon as he started to make a gagging noise he shoved his hand over his mouth to silence it. If his seasickness got any worse, it would be difficult to mask the noise of him vomiting over the side of the boat. He was doing his best to silence his dry heaving, but his hunched posture suggested he felt miserable and unwell.

Frej leaned towards Ken and gestured. Ken nodded, rested the oars again, and then he and Matt changed direction. Matt continued to count under his breath, and he gripped the oar tightly.

"Who's there?" The shouted question shattered the silence.

Kit glanced around, an expression of panic on his face.

Michel put a hand on his arm to calm him, but didn't dare whisper the reassurance he wanted to. He turned and strained his eyes, trying to find the source of the disruption. Matt and Ken stopped rowing, the boat drifting back the way they'd come, caught by the current.

He heard boots against wood in the distance—the unmistakable sound of men running, probably over the bridge crossing the Rhine south of their position. "No further or I'll shoot," one of them yelled.

Frej got down on the floor of the boat. Michel and Kit followed, then Liang. Matt kept hold of his oar, trying to keep it as still as he could. He and Ken leaned down into a crouch.

Gunfire sounded from the bridge—a couple of shots in succession before stopping. Michel heard an engine, a vehicle approaching. A door slammed, and then everything went quiet again. The bridge was a good few kilometres away, but Frej was right about noise carrying on the water. If felt too close for comfort.

Frej waited a few minutes. "Row," he whispered urgently. "While they are distracted."

Whoever had attempted to cross the bridge at Seltz hadn't made it. Perhaps their identity papers had not passed scrutiny, or they'd forgotten to add the order that would allow them to be out after curfew.

Michel offered up a silent prayer for whoever had been caught, together with the plea that it didn't make the guards on duty look further afield.

After what seemed forever, Frej signalled it was safe for them to retake their seats.

"Was that a planned distraction?" Liang asked as they approached the opposite shoreline. With their river crossing almost over, it was finally safe to talk.

"No," Frej replied grimly. "That was most likely someone who should know better than to try to illegally cross the border using the bridge at Seltz. I hope they have not put our operation at risk."

"Do you need help to hide your boat?" Matt asked. "Perhaps a longer stay in Beinheim wouldn't be a bad idea? Make the return journey in a couple of days."

"I have friends in the Alsace further up the river." Frej's expression lightened. "I will take the boat up there and return home another way. If I am gone too long, I may be missed and questions will be asked."

Although they'd only met Frej and Sigi, it was doubtful they were the only members of the Resistance in the area. One person compromised could lead to many others losing their lives.

"We appreciate the risks you have taken for us," Kit said.

"Not all Germans agree with what Herr Hitler and his Nazis are doing," Frej said, "but many do not act because they are scared of the repercussions for their families."

"It is easier to risk yourself than those you care about." Kit turned his attention back to the river, but Michel guessed from the way he sat, shoulders slumped, that his thoughts were with his family and everything he'd left behind.

"Hopefully a day will come soon when sacrifices will no longer need to be made," Michel said, "although I suspect that time is a long way off."

"Is that the shore up ahead?" Liang asked. He sounded better than before, although his voice lacked its usual timbre.

"Yes," Frej confirmed. "I'll change places with Matthäus

and bring her closer." Ken got up to move, but Frej shook his head. "I'll guide you. No need to rock the boat any more than we have to, especially with your friend's weak stomach."

"That's a polite way of putting it," Liang muttered. He moved over so Matt could sit next to him. "How are you faring?"

"There is more light than I expected," Matt said, "but I'll be happier once we are on land again."

"I'll be happy if I never set foot in a boat again." Liang groaned. "Part of me is looking forward to finally going home; the other part knows I'll have to cross a large body of water to do it. Tell me why I volunteered for this mission again?"

"You didn't volunteer," Ken reminded him. "You were conscripted."

"Oh yes. That's right." Liang made a rude noise and muttered something under his breath. "Very thoughtful of them to pick me. Oh wait. They didn't have much of a choice, did they?"

Frej shook his head. He seemed amused by the conversation. "Right here, then a few more strokes in this direction." Ken followed his instructions quickly, and Frej nodded his approval. "You are a natural," he told Ken.

"We visited family once who lived close to a river. I spent most of that summer on it. I guess I remember more of it than I thought, as it was a long time ago." Ken passed his oar over to Frej, stood, and stretched the upper part of his body. "I don't remember aching quite this much, though."

"You're out of practice, and age catches up with all of us," Frej said, "although I wish you and your companions many years ahead of you."

"And you. Thank you again. Gabriel, lead the way." Matt gave Michel a nod. "Oskar and I will bring up the rear."

This would be the last time Matt referred to them by

their German identities. As soon as they were safely in France, they'd bury those identity papers and use the French ones the Resistance had provided for them. Michel had discarded his original papers when he'd joined the Resistance, as he could not take the chance they might connect him with his family. On this side of the border, he'd continue to use Gabriel as his codename, but his last name had changed yet again.

"That water's still cold," Liang complained as he waded to shore. "I never thought I'd say this, but I prefer being wet to the other option."

"Being dry?" Kit asked.

"Remind me to be sympathetic if you're ever seasick." Liang stood on the rocky beach and looked around. "The ground isn't moving, is it?"

"No, it's not moving. You'll be fine in a few moments." Michel waited until Ken and Matt joined them. "Bienvenue en France."

They were far from safe, but Michel was finally home.

Karl Holm looked up in annoyance at the knock on his office door. "Enter."

"Good evening, Standartenführer." Obersturmführer Reiniger clicked his heels together, saluted, and stood to attention. He was a tall slim man with light blond hair. Despite having lost weight since his unfortunate accident, the cold gaze from his remaining blue eye still commanded authority, and unsettled those who served under him.

"What is it, Obersturmführer? I sincerely hope you're here to tell me that you finally have the fugitives in custody."

Reiniger hesitated before replying. Never a good sign. "Unfortunately not, sir." The skin around his eye patch twitched. "The informant was mistaken. They were not at Wintersdorf. Although we did arrest someone else crossing the border illegally at the bridge at Seltz."

Karl sighed. "I'm sure the Feldgendarmerie can manage to do their job without your help. I had rather hoped you were managing to do yours a little better than you have been."

Since the incident in Freiburg, the fugitives had vanished. Apart from a couple of sightings—*supposed* sightings—any attempts to find Lowe and his team had been... disappointing. Karl was fully aware his orders were to find Doktor Kristopher Lehrer, and that the fate of the men who helped him escape and evade capture was not important.

However, Karl was not about to let a serendipitous discovery go wasted. He wanted to speak with Lowe further, and Lowe's team was working with Lehrer. Find one man, and the other would be close by. If not, Karl would persuade whomever he caught to divulge the location of the other.

"The initial information given to us by one of their own should have been correct, sir." Reiniger placed his hands behind his back but did not relax his stance.

"At ease, Reiniger." Watching Reiniger stand at attention did nothing to increase Karl's confidence in the man. Nevertheless, he had a point. "Perhaps Doktor Zhou was not trusted by his team as much as he thought he was." He considered the idea as he voiced it. Considering the presence of both Zhou and Lowe on the same team, that was more than likely. After all, Zhou had seemed shocked by the revelation that Lowe was part Japanese. If Lowe did not trust his colleague enough to share that information, what else had he kept hidden?

"Or they realised they had been compromised and changed their plans... sir."

"That is possible." Karl clasped his hands and tapped his

forefingers together. "So… if they are not in Switzerland, what is the other logical place they'd head for?"

Reiniger took a few minutes to work out that the question hadn't been rhetorical. "They'd head for the Channel, sir."

"Exactly." Karl glanced at the papers he'd been reading. "New orders have come through this morning. I am needed in France."

The statement wasn't a lie, but Karl was not about to expand on the content of the letter he'd received. Headquarters was not impressed by his lack of results. As he'd been unable to track down the elusive Doktor Lehrer, he was being reassigned. However, if his assumption was correct and Lowe and his team—along with Lehrer—had foolishly decided to attempt a Channel crossing, perhaps all was not entirely lost.

"We will miss you here in Germany, Standartenführer."

Karl met Reiniger's gaze and smiled. "I have been told to pick my staff, Obersturmführer, and I can think of no better man as my second-in-command. Although you have failed me in your attempts to locate the traitor, Lehrer, and his associates, I am certain you will do better in tracking down and eliminating Resistance cells in the Caen area."

Reiniger was a good soldier, one who enjoyed certain aspects of his work a little too much at times. But that could be used. After all, if Lowe was in France, he'd need help, and enlisting the cooperation of the local Maquis would be a good place to start.

"Yes, sir. I am honoured by your faith in me." Reiniger seemed pleased by Karl's comment. His need to track down this team was personal, and he particularly held a grudge against Lehrer and the man who had called himself Schmitz while he had infiltrated the institute. They had not only undermined Reiniger's authority, but worked with the Allied pilot who had caused the loss of his eye.

"Do not let me down, Reiniger."

"I won't, sir. You can count on me." Reiniger saluted and left the room.

Normally Karl would have reprimanded him for the minute smirk, but in this instance, he thought it suited his purpose better not to.

Let Reiniger think his posting was an honour if it gave him further motivation to get the job done. Reiniger had already proven he would do what it took to get results. Given the delicacy of the situation, he was exactly who Karl needed, and he could be depended upon to pass on whatever information he discovered without it going any further.

After all, Karl's superiors were only interested in apprehending Lehrer. They had made it clear that the survival of those with him was not important. Karl had smiled when he'd read those orders. Surely it meant that as long as Lehrer was delivered in a fit enough state to pass on the formulae he carried, Karl could decide the fate of Lehrer's colleagues. Only Lowe interested him. The last time they'd spoken, the American had clung to the foolish notion that his father was innocent, that he hadn't murdered Heinz Holm—Karl's father—in cold blood. It didn't matter what Patrick Lowe's son thought. He would suffer for what his father had done.

Another knock at the door interrupted his thoughts. This time, however, his visitor did not wait to be told to enter.

Margarete Huber settled herself into one of the chairs in front of Karl's desk, acting as though it was her office rather than his. "Good morning, Standartenführer Holm," she said politely.

"What can I do for you today, Fräulein?" Karl asked. She was there because she wanted something, so he got straight to the point.

"I thought it was about time I asked you about your progress concerning our mutual acquaintance Herr Doktor Lehrer." Margarete smiled, but her eyes were cold. Their dark blue colour had often reminded him of an icy lake hiding its true nature beneath the surface.

"I'm surprised you aren't aware of that already. Or have your contacts disappointed you?"

Margarete laughed and tucked a strand of long blonde hair behind her ear. "It is so much easier working with someone with whom one shares an understanding, don't you think?"

"We are not working together, Fräulein." Karl was wasting his time reminding her of something he considered a fact, but perhaps she could be useful.

"I'm wounded." Margarete looked more thoughtful than hurt. "I do have some contacts in France, Herr Holm. I have waited a long time for you to honour my request, so I've decided to offer my services."

"I have not forgotten your request." Her repeated reminder of it grated on him. Frankly he did not care whether she was present or not when Kristopher Lehrer was interrogated as long as she did not interfere. She had known Lehrer for quite some time, and their families had moved in the same social circles. Although the information she'd given them about Lehrer's musical background had already proved useful, he'd still managed to slip through their fingers.

"Oh good." Margarete tapped one perfectly manicured fingernail against the armrest of her chair. "I will make enquiries. It will be lovely to get out of Germany for a while. It's been so long since I've done any travelling, and I hear France is quite beautiful this time of year."

Karl gave her a terse nod. With anyone else, it would have been enough to dismiss them, but Margarete only followed social cues when it suited her to do so. The thought had crossed his mind that her grandfather, Herr Bauer, found her useful in passing along information he was not privy to, which was why he had placed her at the institute in the first place. However, Karl had never found any proof. Nevertheless, he kept his suspicions in mind when he spoke to her, taking care in what he said. After all, it would not pay to make an enemy of a powerful man with both scientific and monetary ties to the project he had originally been assigned to.

Karl's inability to apprehend an escaped scientist threatened to blot his otherwise perfect service record. He knew Lehrer better than anyone else who might be assigned the task of finding him, and he'd also made the acquaintance of the men travelling with him. The specifics of his assignment might have changed, but his priorities had not.

"Hopefully neither of us will have to wait much longer before this matter is resolved." Karl had hoped his new post in France meant he would no longer have to deal with Margarete, but that would not be the case.

Margarete smiled. "My thought exactly. I'm sure you and Herr Lowe still have much to discuss, and I am eager to renew my acquaintance with Kristopher Lehrer. The project has really not been the same without him."

"I'm sure it hasn't, Fräulein. I look forward to your contribution in ensuring that we will soon be welcoming him back to the fold."

"So do I."

CHAPTER FIVE

"Can we stop a moment? I have something in my boot." Liang leaned against the nearest tree and began unlacing one boot.

"We're at the meeting place, so we can all stop." Michel glanced at his watch. "Our contact should be here soon. We've made good time, and we're early."

They'd walked most of the morning, except for a couple of stops to rest. With all the exercise of the past few months, Kristopher felt fitter than he had for many years. He followed Liang's lead and leaned against a nearby tree while he sipped water from his canteen. Luckily the weather had looked upon them favourably, and the threatened rain had stayed away. The temperature remained chilly but was bearable thanks to the combination of a warm jacket and the decent walking pace.

"There are better ways to see France," Michel said quietly. "Perhaps next time we can see Haguenau properly, instead of keeping to its outskirts and hiding in the forest north of the town."

Kristopher looked up in surprise. He hadn't seen Michel

walk over to stand next to him. "One day we'll be able to stop long enough to enjoy our surroundings." He kept his voice low but couldn't resist glancing at their companions to make sure they were distracted enough to lessen the risk of being overheard. "I've read about a few of Haguenau's historic buildings—I'd love to see some of them one day."

His father had promised Kristopher and Clara several holidays, yet none of them had ever eventuated. Once Kristopher had reached the age of ten, he'd realised his father's words were empty promises, but that hadn't stopped him from reading about the destinations he'd once thought they might visit.

By his late teens, he'd already begun to put aside his foolish childhood hopes and focus on the path he wanted to take in life. Fleeing through Germany, and now France, had reminded him of his youth and the reading he'd done about those places. He hadn't thought about it in years.

Liang had re-laced his boot and was now sitting and sipping from his canteen. Matt and Ken moved to the perimeter of the thicket of trees and were also talking in low voices. Matt waved one hand to get a point across, but Ken shook his head.

Michel smiled. "You're still as optimistic as ever."

"Not really," Kristopher admitted, "but if we don't cling to some kind of hope for the future, we've already lost this fight, haven't we?"

"I don't intend to lose *this* fight," Michel said grimly, "but in saying that, I am far too aware it might still happen."

Although he'd emphasised the word *this*, Michel wasn't referring to the war. He was scared of losing what they had, of them losing each other. Kristopher tried not to dwell on it, but his voiced optimism didn't reflect his inner fear.

He reached for Michel's cheek, to caress it, to offer

comfort, but stopped in time and withdrew his hand quickly. "Sorry," he murmured.

"So am I. Don't lose your optimism, Kit. I need you to keep it alive for both of us."

"There's someone coming," Ken said urgently. He and Matt drew their weapons.

"I don't know how meeting in the middle of a forest is going to work," Liang said. "One tree looks much like another."

"We're not in the middle of it, just on the outskirts, and they will have a compass as we do." Michel stepped in front of Kristopher, his gun already in his hand.

"I hope these are your friends," Kristopher said. If not, they'd have to scatter and go deeper into the forest.

"So do I." Michel whistled the first few bars of a folk song he'd taught Kristopher while they'd been hiding at St Gertrud's.

After a moment's silence, Kristopher heard the answering phrase—the final few bars of the song. A woman stepped into the clearing. She was about Michel's age and had striking blue eyes. Wisps of brunette hair had come free from her headscarf, framing her face. When she saw Michel, her face lit up with an enormous smile and she lowered her weapon, tucked it into the waistband of her skirt, and ran over to them.

"Michel!" she exclaimed, and then spoke animatedly to him in French.

"German, please. My friends do not speak our language well." Michel smiled at her. "It is very good to see you again too, mon amie."

They embraced, and Michel kissed her lightly on both cheeks. Although it was a typical greeting, Kristopher felt a pang of jealousy that he couldn't show his feelings for Michel in public. He started to take a step closer, then stopped. What could he say? He and Michel could only claim friendship, and besides, that was all this woman was to Michel. An old friend.

"Arlette, this is Benoit." Michel gestured for Kristopher to come forward but referred to him by the name on his identity papers. Although he'd told Kristopher he trusted Arlette with his life, they'd decided it was safer not only for them but her too, if she remained unaware of their true identities.

"Pleased to meet you." Kristopher kept his tone polite, then shook her hand. "Michel speaks highly of you."

"Does he now?" Arlette murmured, barely loud enough to be heard. She cleared her throat. "Welcome to France, Benoit. We'll do our best to keep you safe before you take your leave of us."

Matt cleared his throat. "I'm Julien." He shook her hand, then gave Ken a pointed look. "This is Marcel, who is still learning about French customs."

Ken shook Arlette's hand. "Pleased to meet you."

"It is a pleasure to make your acquaintance, and we appreciate the risk you are taking in helping us." Liang held out his hand. "Bonjour, Mademoiselle, je m'appelle Alexandre."

Arlette gave him a huge smile as she shook it. "I thought you said your colleagues didn't speak French, Michel."

"I speak French, German, English, and Mandarin," Liang said in German, "although it has been a while since I've spoken your language, so please excuse any mistakes when I use it."

"Are you going to introduce your colleague, Arlette?" Michel nodded toward the thicket of trees behind Arlette.

"As observant as ever, I see." Arlette tucked the errant lock of hair back inside her scarf.

"It's kept me alive," Michel said. "I suspected it was you

who would be meeting us here, but I'm surprised to see you so far from home. The last I heard you were still in Paris."

"Arlette and I have been tasked with ensuring your safe passage to Normandy." The man who joined them was dark-haired and a couple of centimetres shorter than Michel, although he was more heavily built. "It is good to finally meet you, Michel. My name is Sébastien." He and Michel shook hands. "Arlette speaks very highly of you." Sébastien grinned. "She speaks of you often too."

"Michel and I grew up together." Arlette elbowed Sébastien in the ribs. "We're old friends, and I haven't seen him since he left for Germany." Her tone grew wistful. "It's important to hold on to our friends, don't you think? Especially as we've lost so many of them to this war."

"I hate to interrupt your reunion," Matt said, "but can we go somewhere a little less in the open before we discuss things further?"

"We have a safe house a couple of kilometres from here," Sébastien said. "Once we're there, we will go over the routes we will take to get to our destination. I'm sure you'll want to eat and get some sleep too. We head out tomorrow."

"Routes, plural?" Kristopher had suspected they'd have to split up, as avoiding detection would be difficult in a large group, especially if they were adding two to their number. Whatever happened, he and Michel would travel together. He would insist on it, and Michel would too. They'd have to find a way to justify it without admitting to the real reason.

"Our group needs to split up." Ken glanced at Matt. Kristopher had heard them arguing about it, but he'd thought Matt had finally reluctantly agreed Ken was right. He suspected they'd want to travel together too. "We're too much of a target if we stay together."

Matt sighed. "Sébastien, please lead the way to your safe

house. The sooner we work out the details of what happens next, the happier I'll be."

~

Sébastien traced the route on the map with one finger. "All going well, both groups will meet in Bayeux, and from there we'll travel to Cyrville-sur-Mer." He pointed to another place on the map, this time a small village northwest of Bayeux. "London has organised extraction for you there."

"By boat?" Liang suspected it would be, but he couldn't help but ask anyway. After all, a chap could hope, right?

Arlette looked at him as though he was crazy. "Yes, by boat. Otherwise why would we go to all this trouble to get you to the coast?"

"Alexandre gets seasick," Kristopher said quickly. "He had a rotten time of it crossing the Rhine."

"Better seasick than dead." Arlette didn't seem the sympathetic type, and although she'd been pleasant enough, she kept glancing at Michel when he wasn't looking. Something was going on there, but Liang doubted Michel had a clue.

Since their initial greeting, Michel had treated her the same way he did everyone else, despite her attempts to start conversations with him. Kristopher was the only person Michel spoke to at length, and then it was only when they thought they were alone. Liang had almost walked in on them a couple of times and had retreated quickly and quietly. If they wanted privacy, that was their business, not his.

"I have no intention of dying," Liang said dryly. He nodded his thanks to Kristopher, who nodded back but didn't say anything further on the subject.

"Neither does anyone fighting this war." Arlette moved around the table to stand next to Michel, brushing against him as she did so.

Kristopher glanced at her and tensed. "There have been many losses on both sides. The sooner this war is over, the better."

"Who have you brought us exactly, Michel?" Arlette asked.

"Good men who are doing what they can to make this world a better place," Michel said calmly. "This is neither the time nor place to air personal issues. As Benoit said, there have been losses on both sides. Many of those were good people."

Arlette snorted. "If you say so. You've been away from France for too long. Have you forgotten your brother already?"

"I *am* German, but I do not agree with what Herr Hitler is doing. That is the reason I left my home and family. If you have a problem with that, I'm sorry, but Michel is right. I've seen good people die, people who should have had a long life ahead of them. War doesn't discriminate, and bombs drop on the innocent as well as the guilty. Some of my countrymen have done terrible things, but please do not judge our whole country. The only reason we were able to escape Germany was because of the brave Germans who aided us." Kristopher took a deep breath. "Corin was a brave man, and you do better to honour his memory by not insulting his brother."

Liang raised an eyebrow. He'd hadn't known Michel had lost a brother to this war, and given Matt's reaction, neither had he. Even Ken, who was usually not easy to read, looked startled.

"I'm sorry." Matt laid a hand on Michel's shoulder very briefly. "I had no idea."

"Thank you, but it is not something I wish to talk about." Michel's expression didn't change. "Sébastien's plan is sound, but we need to discuss how we are going to split our group and which route we will take."

"I think it would be better if Marcel and I play the part of German soldiers." Matt spoke as though the decision had already been made. "I speak good German and Marcel's is passable, especially if I take the higher rank and do most of the talking."

"I will travel by train to Paris," Arlette said. "Michel has experience in passing himself off as a German soldier, and he speaks both French and German fluently, so I think he should take the part of the German travelling alone on the train to rejoin his unit. That leaves the decision of who will pretend to be my brother."

"I'm not going to pass as French, although I speak the language." Liang already suspected what role he'd end up with. "I will be one of the prisoners Julien and Marcel are transporting to Caen."

"And I will be the other," Sébastien said. "Arlette and I need to split between the two groups as we know the area and who to contact."

"That leaves me with the role of Arlette's brother." At least Kristopher and Arlette could pass off their animosity towards each other as that of siblings. Nevertheless, it was not an ideal situation to have them working together closely, but when Sébastien had first laid out the plan, Liang knew which way their group would be split. After what had happened a few months ago, none of his friends would be taking any chances of losing track of the person they cared about.

"You're not going to successfully pass yourself off as a German soldier." Matt shook his head. "You've tried that before, and I saw through it in about two minutes."

"I knew you weren't who you said you were either," Kristopher countered.

They'd first met in the Black Forest while using assumed

identities, and worked together for days before trusting each other enough to reveal who they really were.

Matt chuckled. "Touché."

"Is your French good enough?" Arlette asked.

"It's passable." Michel spoke quickly before Kristopher could answer. "If he is playing the part of an injured man, there is no reason why that injury could not hinder his ability to speak clearly. He will still need to keep his head down and not draw attention to himself. Benoit understands more than he speaks and has picked up our language quickly."

"Besides, it is the only role left," Kristopher said.

Matt glanced between Kristopher and Arlette. "If this mission is to succeed we need to put any personal problems with each other to one side. Are you going to be able to work together?"

"I have no problem working with Arlette. I will be travelling with her and Michel to Paris." Kristopher's tone suggested the subject was not up for debate.

"I apologise if I seemed rude earlier." Arlette grimaced. "I have lost too many good friends to this war, and I allowed my emotions to cloud my judgement."

"Apology accepted." Kristopher nodded briefly. "This mission is important, and its success takes priority over all else."

"I agree," Michel said.

"Well, now that's settled, I'm going to have some more of that delicious stew." Matt turned to Sébastien. "Do you need some help in making the final alterations to our identity papers after we've eaten? We have a long road ahead of us, and we all need to get some sleep."

"Thank you. I'd appreciate that, but first could we discuss a few details over a plate of stew?" Sébastien led Matt into the kitchen, Ken following close behind.

"I owe you an apology too, Michel," Arlette said. "I shouldn't have brought Corin into the conversation. From your friends' reactions, I suspect you hadn't told them, and it wasn't my place to."

"No, it wasn't." Michel folded the map, tucked it under his arm, and started to walk away.

Arlette ran after him. "Michel." She linked her arm through his. "We still have a lot to talk about. So much has changed since you left."

Kristopher shook his head, picked up his cold cup of coffee from the table, took one sip, and pulled a face. "I should make some more, but I don't want to disturb anyone."

"We need to talk." Although Liang had originally decided not to say anything, now Kristopher and Michel were going to be travelling with Arlette he couldn't remain silent.

"What about?" Kristopher frowned. "Do you have a problem with this plan? It's me Holm is looking for—"

"Officially, but we both know he also has an interest in Ken, and that he is not a man who gives up easily. I want some fresh air. Join me?" Although Liang intended to speak English for the rest of their conversation, he did not want to risk being overheard. Michel might not speak good English, but Arlette and Sébastien could be proficient in the language.

Liang headed outside, with Kristopher following him. The crisp air was chilly, but not overly so.

"All right." Kristopher folded his arms and leaned against the back wall of the house. "You're worried about something. What is it?"

"Not that obviously, I hope." Liang wondered how best to broach the subject. In the end, he decided to get right to it. "You and Michel need to be more careful," he said in English.

"Careful?" Kristopher sounded puzzled, but he switched languages without questioning why. "I don't understand. We're not about to reveal who we are to anyone. Michel won't tell Arlette who the rest of us really are, although he does trust her. They've known each other for years, even before this war."

Oh dear. Liang had hoped he wouldn't have to be so direct. He lowered his voice and closed the distance between them to ensure no one else would overhear. "I know you and Michel are involved."

Kristopher glanced at him with a shocked expression, which he covered quickly. "I don't know what you're talking about. We're good friends. You're mistaken."

"No." Liang placed a hand on Kristopher's arm. "I'm not." He sighed. "I figure with this war, if you've got a chance for a bit of happiness with someone you love, you should follow it. I'm not going to report it or tell anyone else."

Kristopher relaxed, but he still looked nervous. He shook Liang's hand off his arm. "How long have you known?"

"I've had my suspicions for a while, given the way Michel spoke of you, but the first time I saw the two of you together, I knew." Liang shook his head. "You're not as careful as you think you are. I've seen the way you look at each other, and Michel isn't as closed off around you." He coloured. "I, umm, almost walked in on you one time." He hadn't seen anything, but he'd recognised the way they were leaning into each other well enough, and what it might lead to.

"Verdammt," Kristopher muttered. "No one else has figured it out?"

"I have no idea, but don't worry. I suspect your secret is safe with Matt and Ken, if that's what you are worried about." If Liang was correct, Matt and Ken had their own secrets to keep. "It's easier to recognise the signs of someone in love when you're in love yourself."

"Juliane," Kristopher said softly. "You're not good at hiding your feelings either."

"I don't need to," Liang reminded him, "although it would

not do for her brother to find out." If Holm suspected Liang and Juliane were involved, it would put Juliane in danger too.

"I won't tell anyone." Kristopher hesitated before continuing. "Michel already knows."

"Of course he does," Liang said dryly, "even if he has not figured out that Arlette is flirting with him."

"Excuse me?" Kristopher narrowed his eyes. "She's wasting her time. He's not interested."

"Yes, well, we know that, but he can hardly tell her the reason why, can he?" Liang sighed. For a brilliant man, Kristopher was not coming to the conclusions he needed to. "Can I be blunt?"

"Of course. You have so far. Why stop now?"

Liang winced. He hadn't meant to upset Kristopher, but anything less than directness was not going to be helpful. "Arlette obviously has feelings for him. Not only that, but they know each other well. How long will it be before she works out the truth? The three of you are going to be spending time together. The last thing you need is for her unrequited feelings for Michel to jeopardise everything."

"You're worried about the mission."

"I'm worried about you. Holm won't need an excuse to arrest you if he finds out about your feelings for Michel."

"I won't let Holm harm Michel to get to me," Kristopher said stiffly. He bit his lip. "The possibility is one I've thought of a long time ago. Ending up in a camp because of what I am pales in comparison. I'll do whatever it takes to keep Michel safe."

"That's what I'm worried about. That and a woman scorned. You know what they say about that. I've had women angry at me before. It's something you want to avoid, trust me. Michel needs to stop her flirting with him. Any excuse will do but the truth, and you both need to hide your feelings for each other better. Stop the glances and the brushing against each other when there is anyone else around."

"We haven't been doing that." Kristopher frowned. He sounded genuinely surprised.

Liang snorted. "Yes, you have. And your reaction to Arlette earlier when she kept brushing against Michel? I know jealously when I see it. If someone was flirting with Juliane the way Arlette was with Michel, I'd be reacting the same way. I'm sorry. I wish you could tell her the truth, but you can't."

"This isn't fair." Kristopher closed his eyes. "We're never going to be able to be honest about how we feel. Even if we survive this war, we'll have to pretend to be something we're not. I can't believe our relationship is wrong." He clenched one fist and opened his eyes again before he lowered his gaze, but not before Liang saw a glimpse of frustration and pain reflected in them.

"Not when it feels so right when you're together?" Liang said softly. "I'm so sorry. I wish things were different too, but they're not, and I've lost too many friends to risk losing more. Be careful, my friend. Please."

"I'll talk to Michel. Thank you."

"I'll leave you to think."

Kristopher caught his arm as he went to walk away. "No. Stay." He smiled shakily. "You don't know how much I've wanted to be able to talk to someone about this. It's a relief not to have to keep it a complete secret."

Liang knew about keeping secrets. "Whatever we talk about, it will go no further," he promised.

CHAPTER SIX

Although Michel had spent a good amount of his train journey looking out the window, he found it difficult to focus on the scenery. He felt relieved to be finally back on French soil. However, he could have done without the complication of seeing Arlette again, and the risk of her discovering his true feelings for Kit. He turned to scan the interior of the train before returning his attention to the view outside, or at least pretending to so he didn't draw attention to himself. Although his false identity papers should be enough to satisfy a routine check, their pursuers had his description and had most likely circulated it. If their identities were questioned, they would be trapped. Even if they managed to escape the carriage, they had nowhere to go, and the train was moving too fast to attempt to jump from it.

On the other side of the carriage, Kit also seemed to be watching the scenery, although the slight hunching of his shoulders gave away his uneasiness. His anxiety wouldn't be obvious to someone who didn't know him, but Michel recognised it immediately. Kit gripped his cane with one hand, the front of his beret barely covering his face, or his blond hair.

Arlette sat next to Kit, reading. Occasionally she'd turn to him and make conversation about something inane like the weather or how their parents would be so pleased to see him home again after his accident. He nodded in the right places but didn't reply, except for something whispered at one point, too low to be overheard.

They were both playing their parts well.

Liang had sought out Arlette the night before, on the pretext of wanting advice, to give Kit the opportunity to speak with Michel alone. He'd told Michel what Liang had said, his voice shaking as both of them realised how lucky they were Liang was the one to notice and not someone else. Although Liang had made the comment he'd suspected they were more than friends because of his feelings for Juliane, Michel wasn't so sure it was the only reason. Liang was right. They needed to be more careful. The longer he and Kit were together, the more difficult it became for Michel to hide how he truly felt about him. Being undercover and taking on a false identity before they'd met had been much easier.

How could he have mistaken Arlette's attention towards him for mere friendship? Michel remembered a conversation several years ago, something else he'd dismissed and shouldn't have. A birthday celebration that now seemed a lifetime ago. François had jokingly told Michel he was a lucky man—having not one, but two people falling for him.

"Arlette thinks the two of you should settle down. She's told me you'd make a good husband and father to her children."

"Arlette?" Michel frowned. "We're friends, nothing more." He'd never done anything to encourage her. His mind back-tracked to François's earlier comment. "Two people? You're mistaken about Arlette, mon ami, but who could possibly be the other?"

François smiled shyly and place one finger against Michel's lips. "I've seen the way you look at me, mon ami. If I'm not mistaken, I think you are the same as me."

"What?" Michel protested at first, then found himself kissing François's finger. One thing led to another and…

He still remembered the expression on François's face when, months later, Michel had told him that he didn't love him. Or rather that he wasn't *in* love with him. Michel loved François, but as a friend. Being with François felt good, and he enjoyed the time they spent together, yet Michel had never felt more than friendship for him.

François had been in love with him, and Michel had vowed he'd never again sleep with someone he didn't love. The hurt he'd caused François was something he would always regret and feel guilty about.

Since Michel had found love with Kit, he knew without a doubt what he'd felt for François hadn't been that. He would give up his life to save Kit's, if he had to. He hated seeing Kit upset, and he still had nightmares about when Kit was shot.

Was that really how Arlette felt about him? Or were her feelings for him simply an infatuation? He couldn't tell Arlette the truth. He would be risking not only his own life, but Kit's. François had noticed Arlette's feelings for Michel. What if she'd seen him and François together and figured out the true nature of their friendship? Michel had told Kit he trusted Arlette, but if she already knew his secret, would she continue to keep it if she perceived Kit to be the threat François hadn't been? Her reaction would be a combination of jealously and fear of what might happen if the men who hunted them discovered his and Kit's relationship. Michel pulled his train ticket from his pocket and read the destination again. He'd had no idea what Arlette had planned until she'd given it to him. It made more sense for their team to disembark at Gare de Melun rather than at Gare du Nord. Paris was swarming with German soldiers, and it was safer to avoid the city centre and keep to the farmland around its outskirts.

It hadn't escaped him that the station she'd suggested wasn't far from his parents' farm. Michel had been tempted to go see them one last time, in case it was truly adieu. He'd hated lying to his parents and giving his mother a noncommittal shrug each time she asked when he was going to settle down with a nice girl. His mother would love grandchildren, but would never have them. His brother, Corin, was dead, and even if Michel survived this war, he…

Mon Dieu. He still dreamed of a future with Kit, of the chance to live their lives side by side even if they could never be married or live openly as a couple.

"You should go see your parents." Kit's agreement with Arlette had taken Michel by surprise. "I never got the chance to say goodbye to my father, so there will always be unfinished business between us. Arlette has promised us it is safe, and it will not put them in danger."

Michel glanced over at Kit and Arlette again. Although Kit had not spoken, Michel could still hear his words from that morning repeating in his mind. He'd told both Kit and Arlette he'd think about it.

The door between their carriage and the adjoining one opened. Two armed German soldiers walked through.

"Please produce your identity and travel papers for examination." The soldier was at least a couple of years younger than Michel, and he smiled at the child who snuggled further into her mother's embrace as he walked past.

The older soldier with him didn't waste time trying to put the passengers at ease. He scanned the carriage, and his expression hardened. While the younger soldier might be fooled, this man would notice anything wrong immediately.

Michel retrieved his documents from his coat pocket and waited his turn. So far nothing seemed to be amiss. He glanced at one end of the carriage, then the other, not surprised to see a soldier standing at each exit. Until something happened to confirm otherwise, he would act as though this was a routine check.

"I hope you don't have too long a wait in Melun," the younger soldier said to Michel conversationally.

"Hopefully not." Michel kept his tone noncommittal. According to his papers, he was meeting with two men from his unit there, and they would travel together the rest of the way to Gare d'Évreux-Normandie.

"They're having trouble with the Resistance in Évreux," the soldier continued.

"So I've heard." Michel wished the man would get on with the task at hand. The longer this conversation continued, the more chance he might be recognized.

"Gefreiter, is there a problem with his papers?" The older soldier glanced in his companion's direction. He frowned. "Do I need to check them myself?"

Michel tensed but said nothing. Better to let the Gefreiter get into trouble than for Michel to draw even more attention to himself.

"No, sir. Everything is fine." The Gefreiter gave Michel a nod and returned his papers. "Sorry to trouble you, Obergefreiter."

"Heil Hitler," Michel said. "Keep up the good work."

"Heil Hitler!" To his relief the Gefreiter turned away. "Papers please, Madame," he asked the woman in the next seat.

"What brings you and your sister to Melun?" The Oberleutnant had worked his way a good distance down the other side of the carriage, and up to now hadn't bothered to make conversation. He peered at Kit's papers and glanced at him again, but didn't return them.

"My brother's throat was damaged by a serious illness years ago, so he finds it painful to speak." Arlette answered the question in German. She sighed and dabbed at her eyes with a handkerchief. "Nevertheless he presented himself for national service and worked for the Germans, as my husband still does." She glanced down at the wedding band she wore, and her voice steadied. "We are on our way home to our family, who live in Melun."

Although many single women had hurriedly found husbands to avoid the Service du Travail Obligatoire that had been passed in February the year before, Arlette hadn't. However, she always wore a ring when she was undercover and had made up an elaborate story of a husband who had done his duty, instead of avoiding the STO like Michel and many of his friends who were now part of France's Resistance—the Maquis.

"Why are you not working for the Fatherland now?" The Oberleutnant asked Kit the question, although Arlette had answered for him. "According to your papers you are thirty years old, still far too young to be excused."

Kit spoke in little more than a hoarse whisper and pointed to the cane he held. Michel couldn't make out the words, and they were followed by a coughing fit.

The Oberleutnant frowned. "Stand up. I've seen your sort. It's an offense to fake an injury to avoid doing your duty."

Arlette stood instead. "This is outrageous," she exclaimed. "My poor brother was injured during an explosion and was lucky he didn't lose his leg altogether. He will never walk properly again. How dare you question our loyalty to the Third Reich? We have done our part to ensure Germany wins this war, and this is how you say thank you?"

The Oberleutnant raised an eyebrow. Despite her anger, it would take more than mere words to convince him that she spoke the truth.

Kit started to stand, his grip tightening on his cane. He let out a convincing gasp of pain and grabbed Arlette's arm with his free hand. "Désolé. Ma jambe—" He spoke the words Michel had taught him, coughed again, and then sounded as though he was struggling to clear his throat.

"My apologies, Mademoiselle." The Oberleutnant handed Kristopher back his papers. "Monsieur."

"Merci." Kit sat down again. "Heil Hitler," he murmured.

"Heil Hitler." The Oberleutnant turned his back on them and continued his way down the carriage, checking everyone's papers.

As soon as the soldiers left the carriage, Michel risked a glance in Kit's direction. The woman in the seat directly behind Arlette got out of her seat and moved to an empty one further forward in the carriage. As she passed Arlette, she spat at her and muttered, "Traître!"

"Do you want me to take a turn at driving?" Ken poked his head through the square gap between the back of the truck and the cabin.

"Maybe in about another twenty minutes," Matt replied. Once they'd reached Woippy, he and Ken had switched positions, but Matt had been driving for nearly two hours, so it was time to change again. "I'll keep driving until we get to Bétheny, and then you can take over."

Ken nodded. "If you need to stretch before that, let me know and we can swap earlier."

So far their journey had been without incident, and Ken had to admit he'd enjoyed the drive from Haguenau. The scenery was beautiful, and he'd felt as though they were miles from anywhere, which made sense, considering they were deliberately staying clear of the bigger towns so they had less chance of being pulled over and asked for their papers.

They'd decided to split the driving between them, given they'd be travelling most of the day. Sébastien had shown them places on the map where they wouldn't be noticed and could stretch their legs. Unfortunately, in order for their cover to look realistic, Sébastien and Liang were handcuffed. Matt had considered having the handcuffs on hand in case, but if they were suddenly stopped and their important prisoners were discovered in the back of the truck unrestrained and with only one guard, it would look suspicious.

Liang leaned against the canvas side of the truck, his eyes closed, but Ken doubted he was asleep. He'd muttered a few rude comments when they'd hit a rough patch of road but hadn't complained or said much since they'd left Haguenau.

Sébastien too, had dozed on and off, but he was wide awake now and watching Ken. "I'm trying to figure out what your story is."

"Story?" Ken asked. Unfortunately, Sébastien didn't speak English, and Ken found he was struggling to understand some of his companion's German. While Sébastien spoke the language well enough, his accent wasn't what Ken was used to, so he'd had to ask him to repeat some of what he'd said.

"You're definitely not German or French, and neither is Julien." Sébastien frowned, as though considering his next words. "I heard you speak English last night. American, if I'm not mistaken?"

"I didn't think you spoke English."

"I don't, but I recognise it, and I know you're not British. The accent is wrong." Sébastien gestured towards Liang. "So… my guess is that you're working for the OSS and trying to get him out of France. He's obviously well-educated and I suspect has the important information we're supposed to help you get to the Allies. Benoit admitted he is German, so I figure he's Jewish and getting out of the country while he can. At least that's Arlette's theory, although I wouldn't be surprised if she changes it later. She said Michel could never turn his back on someone in need."

"I thought the less you knew, the better," Ken said cautiously. He was hardly about to reveal the mission to someone he didn't know, especially as Sébastien appeared to have no clue that Kristopher—Benoit—was the Nazi's real target. Or did he? "How much *do* you know?"

Sébastien shrugged. "Next to nothing. Merely that your unit needs safe passage to Normandy and you're carrying important information."

"That's all you need to know." As Sébastien was in a talkative mood, it seemed a good time for Ken to ask a few questions of his own. "How did you get involved in the Resistance?"

"I prefer to fight for my country than help *their* war effort." Sébastien screwed up his face as though he'd tasted something nasty when he said the word *their*. "Many of us fled to the hills once the Service du Travail Obligatoire came into force. That merdeux Pétain, pretending he's working for the French people when he has turned against us."

Ken wasn't sure what *merdeux* meant, but was certain it wasn't polite. He nodded his agreement. "We're all trying to do what we can to end this war."

"At least you get to go home when your mission is finished." Sébastien rolled his shoulders. "I cannot wait for the day they are defeated and we take back France for ourselves. I am tired of all this pretence."

"It is wearing, constantly pretending to be what you are not." Ken knew about that all too well. He hated having to hide not only his feelings for Matt, but his true identity. Some days he doubted he'd ever be able to use the name Tsukino again. Matt seemed to think he would, but Matt tended to have more faith in human nature than Ken did.

Or at least he had before that asshole Holm had tortured him. Matt's experiences at the hands of the SS had changed him, not obviously but in subtle ways. Ken wondered if Matt would ever get over his issues with the dark. Matt had hidden his fears well when they'd crossed the Rhine, but it had cost him. He was more on edge, and his sleep the night before had been plagued with nightmares. Ken had wanted badly to take Matt into his arms and soothe him, but they weren't alone, so he couldn't.

God, he hated this. What kind of a world did they live in where being seen giving comfort to the person he loved was dangerous?

The same kind of world where people were hunted and thrown into camps simply because of their heritage.

"There's a checkpoint up ahead." Matt turned his head and called out a warning. "Move into position, and be prepared."

"I guess that's the end of our conversation, then," Sébastien said. "Wake up, Alexandre. We're about to have company."

"Wonderful," Liang said, "but I wasn't asleep. Too uncomfortable, and I'm really looking forward to sleeping in a bed tonight."

"Your friend has quite the sense of humour." Sébastien wiped all expression from his face as the truck slowed down.

"So I've been led to believe," Ken said dryly. He stood by the exit, his weapon drawn, giving the appearance of being ready to shoot his captives if they took the opportunity to make a run for it. In reality, he was getting into a defensive position in case the men who stopped them didn't believe their cover story.

"Papers, please," someone asked Matt in German. "And please exit the vehicle."

Ken forced himself to stay where he was. A trickle of moisture ran down the back of his neck. If the soldiers didn't believe Matt's story, he was out there on his own, and the rest of them were trapped like rats awaiting capture.

"Your papers seem to be in order, sir," the soldier told Matt. "We will need to check the back of your truck before you can continue your journey."

"Of course," Matt said. "Unteroffizier Raske is guarding the prisoners and has their papers as well as his own."

"Good idea. After all, they wouldn't get far without papers even if they did manage to escape."

The canvas flap at the back of the truck was pulled back, and Ken blinked against the sudden light. He snapped to attention and saluted the Oberscharführer as the SS officer climbed into the truck, followed closely by Matt.

"Heil Hitler," Ken said.

"Heil Hitler," the Oberscharführer replied. The presence of an SS officer was both concerning and suspicious. Did Holm know they were in the area, and if so, had he circulated their descriptions?

The Oberscharführer studied Sébastien closely and then shifted his attention to Liang. "You're taking these prisoners to Caen?"

"Yes," Matt confirmed. "They have important information, and the officer in charge at Caen wishes to interrogate them personally."

They had no plans to pass through Caen, but had decided it made more sense for their cover to pretend they were.

"What a coincidence. I'm heading there myself." The Oberscharführer put out his hand for the papers Ken carried.

While Matt—who had kept the German equivalent of his rank of captain—outranked him, they didn't want to give the SS officer any reason to be suspicious, so going along with his wishes was the best way to deal with the situation. "I'm looking forward to working with Standartenführer Holm. His reputation precedes him. I'm sure he'll deal with these pesky Resistance cells swiftly. Are you going to be stationed there once you deliver the prisoners?"

Ken sucked in a sharp breath but managed to keep his composure. He handed over the papers and said nothing. Better to let Matt do most of the talking.

"Unfortunately we are continuing on to Bayeux," Matt said. "I've heard of Standartenführer Holm. It's a shame our meeting will be a brief one."

Outside the truck, two soldiers kept guard. Despite his making casual conversation while he checked their papers, the Oberscharführer was not taking any chances.

The Oberscharführer glanced at the papers, then at Liang, and frowned. "Hmm, that is a shame." He took a step closer to Liang. "You."

"Yes, sir?" Liang kept his tone polite and deferential.

"You look Chinese and yet your papers are for someone with a French name, Monsieur Berger."

"Berger is my father's name, and therefore mine," Liang said calmly. They'd already decided on a cover story in case he was questioned. "I am only half Chinese. My father is French and met my mother while she was living in Paris. Her family immigrated here before the last war and decided to stay rather than return to China." The story he told was not too far from the truth except for the fact that his family had settled in England, and it was his mother who was English and his father Chinese.

"Perhaps you should have returned to your homeland when you had the chance, instead of staying here and causing trouble." The Oberscharführer handed the papers back to Ken. "Everything here seems in order, Hauptmann," he told Matt.

Matt gave him a curt nod. "I shall make sure I tell Standartenführer Holm that you were extremely efficient, Oberscharführer." He started to climb out of the truck.

"Enjoy your journey." The Oberscharführer followed Matt. "If you get the opportunity to stay a few hours in Caen, I have heard that some of the old churches are quite remarkable. I studied architecture at Dessau before the war, and I'm looking forward to seeing them."

"This war has taken many of us away from our passions, has it not?" Matt continued the conversation as though they were taking a walk in a park somewhere rather than being soldiers fighting a war.

As soon as they were out of earshot, Liang let out a sigh. He looked shaken. "Bloody hell. I swear that man is everywhere we go. Do you think—"

Ken shot him a look. He didn't want Sébastien to know they had a high-ranking SS officer hunting them. "I'd rather not," he told Liang in a low voice. "We'll talk about it later."

"Is there a problem?" Sébastien asked. "Do you know this Holm?"

The truck engine turned over, and they started on their way again. Matt didn't attempt to make conversation over the noise of the engine but instead focused on driving. It was a sensible decision as they'd have to wait until later to discuss their options.

"We're not going to Caen," Ken said firmly. "Holm is well known in Berlin. Most of the Resistance there has heard of him. He is someone best avoided."

Surely it couldn't be a coincidence that Holm was now stationed in Normandy. Did he know they were in the area? This had felt like a routine checkpoint. If the Oberscharführer had any clue they were not who they claimed to be, he would have detained them.

While Ken didn't feel safe continuing with their original plan, he wasn't sure they had a choice. Their papers had said they would be passing through Rouen, and any deviation might look suspicious.

Sébastien interrupted his thoughts. "If you're worried we've been compromised, we can leave the truck at Corneville-sur-Risle and walk the rest of the way. It will only add a couple of hours to our journey, and that way if it's found, it won't lead anyone directly to us."

"Thank you," Ken said. "I'll talk to Matt when we stop and see what he wants to do." Matt was still their commanding officer, and any change of plan had to be his decision.

One thing was for certain, though. Ken had been right about Sébastien. He was an intelligent man and did not miss much. Ken would talk to Matt about him too and warn him to be careful. Although Sébastien was supposed to be on their side, Ken still did not trust him enough to risk him finding out the true purpose of their mission.

CHAPTER SEVEN

"I still remember the first time I saw you out of your uniform." Although Michel had been undercover as a German soldier the first time they'd met, Kristopher preferred him dressed more casually as he was now. The buttoned shirt, loose trousers, and faded jacket suited him.

"Elise's Kaffeehaus?" Michel asked. Kristopher had come out of the bathroom and seen him clad only in his underwear. "I remember thinking your reaction was strange at the time, but I never figured out why until much later."

"If you'd looked closer, you would have figured it out." Kristopher had dashed back into the bathroom in an attempt to rid himself of his erection. "I much prefer you dressed like this. This is who you are. The other is a disguise."

After they'd disembarked the train at Melun, they'd met their contact and changed identities and clothing. Michel seemed more at ease than Kristopher had seen him for several weeks. He'd taken his beret from Arlette and smiled before putting it on.

"I am happy to be home, although it is not the same and I still need to be cautious. I haven't been near the area in nearly a year." Michel took a deep breath and let it out. "Even the air smells different, or it seems to."

"We've been in farmland before, but this…" Kristopher fought to keep the wistfulness from his voice. He needed to get used to living here and put any longing for Germany behind him. He'd known that before they crossed the Rhine but hadn't expected the finality of leaving his country to hit so hard. "France is my home now. Once this is over, I want to build a new life here, with you. I can't go back to being who I was."

"You've changed a lot since we met, but you're still the man I fell in love with. Don't put all of that aside. This is who I am—a French farmer. So much over the past year has been a lie. I'm tired of slipping into identities that are not my own. Whatever happens now, at least I can be French again."

"When we're together, you're very real and honest," Kristopher said softly. "You don't hide from me."

"I don't want to hide from you. You see me for who I am, and I feel safe when I'm with you. I've missed being able to talk like this and not having to worry about being over-heard." Michel reached over and adjusted the beret Kristopher wore. "I know you miss Berlin, and I'm sorry. I wish…"

"Don't be sorry. I'm where I need to be, and who I want to be with." Kristopher wished he could put his arms around Michel and kiss him, but that needed to be kept for somewhere far more private than here. "I know you're trying to make me feel better, but your countrymen will always see me as German, no matter what I wear or what language I speak."

"Don't worry about Arlette. She has lost too many friends to this war, but she doesn't blame you personally, although it sounds like it."

"I don't think she was happy about me coming with you to see your parents." Although Kristopher wanted to meet them, he did not want to impose on what might be the last time Michel saw them. "The only reason she gave in was that the other option was one she wanted to avoid more."

"Arlette has family and friends of her own she wants to see while we are here. She wouldn't want you with her. I told her I was not leaving you alone in a country where you do not speak the language well. It would be foolish."

Finally, after a heated argument with Michel in French that Kristopher had barely understood, Arlette had shrugged and told him she'd drop both of them off about half an hour's walk from the farm, and keep the car as she had further to go. They could meet in the same place an hour before nightfall, which would still give them enough time to reach the safe house. They'd kept off the road and out of sight, but where they were now was fairly isolated, so Michel had thought it safe to walk beside the field until they reached the farm.

"The scenery is as beautiful as you've described it to me." Kristopher shaded his eyes against the afternoon sun. Fields of wheat spread out on both sides of the road, golden in the sunlight. "I've wanted to see this for such a long time." It felt good to stretch his legs again after hours on a train, pretending he couldn't walk properly or stand without the support of a cane.

"I worry about not being here when it's time to harvest. It's only another month away. I'd hoped I'd only miss one harvest and didn't expect to be away this long. Most of the men are either working for the Germans or in hiding with the Maquis."

"We'll be in Normandy by June. All going well, we could be back for at least some of it." Kristopher wished they could disappear together now, but they'd agreed to meet the rest of their team in Bayeux. If Matt and the others didn't report Kristopher's death, the people they worked for would not stop looking for him. Holm had to believe he was dead too.

Michel shook his head. "I think it will be wise for us to lay low for several months before…" He picked up his pace.

Kristopher hurried to catch up. "Michel," he said softly. "Are you sure you want me here when you talk to your parents? I do not wish to make the situation any more awkward than it already is."

"I am not lying to them." Michel stopped when Kristopher put one hand on his arm. "I cannot introduce you as merely a colleague or a friend when you are far more to me than that. I hate having to hide how I feel about you from everyone. I cannot lie about it to them."

"Are you sure it's a good idea?" Kristopher bit his lip. "You need to be able to come home again once this mission is over. I won't be the reason you can't. I can wait a distance away, and then you won't need to explain who I am."

"If they do not accept you, we will find somewhere else to live once this war is over."

"Family is important," Kristopher insisted. "You can't give up yours for me. Your parents have already lost one son. They—"

"Don't you think I know that?" Michel turned to face him directly. "I've given this a lot of thought. Even if they won't accept you, I want them to at least meet the man I love." He sighed. "Besides, do you really think lying would be a good idea? My mother will take one look at us and figure it out."

"We've been careful since we left Haguenau."

"It's easier to pretend when you're already being dishonest about who you are. Let me do this, mon cher. Please. I need to do this."

"Your parents won't betray you." Kristopher had heard enough about them from Michel to know that for certain. "They will not turn you over to the authorities."

"I wouldn't be here if I thought they would." Michel's expression hardened. "They knew Corin and I were Maquis and never said anything. I took my last mission without having the chance to say goodbye. I owe them at least that."

"This doesn't have to be goodbye," Kristopher said. "I can leave…"

"No." Michel gave him a frustrated look. "I love you, Kit, but you don't always see sense, and we often have different ways of approaching a situation. We remind me of my parents in that. They argue, but they always end up compromising and making up." He smiled. "It's usually Papa who backs down. Maman gives him a look, and he ends up agreeing with her."

"Like the look you're giving me now?" Kristopher asked.

"I am not giving you a look." Michel rolled his eyes. "You're the one who gives me that look."

Kristopher couldn't help but laugh. "If you insist, mon cher."

"You've never called me that before in French." Michel seemed taken aback. "The few times you do, you always say it in German—mein Schatz."

The words might not translate from German to the French *mon cher*, but the sentiment was the same. Michel was very precious to him, and Kristopher loved him with everything he was.

"We're in France now. I need to start speaking your… our… language instead of German. I'm never going to get any better at if I don't."

Michel shook his head. "You can't call me that unless we are alone, so keep saying those words in German." He lowered his voice to a whisper. "When you call me mein Schatz, I feel warm inside, the same way as when you say je t'aime. Don't lose who you are. Please, Kit."

"As long as you promise to always say ich liebe dich. I want to keep hearing those words in German until we're old and grey." Kristopher wiped at his eyes. "Come on. We're almost there. Your parents will take one look at both of us and we won't have to explain anything. It won't be just your mother who figures it out."

"Ich liebe dich, Kit Lehrer," Michel whispered. "For as long as I take breath, I am yours."

Kit lapsed into silence as they walked together the rest of the way. Michel glanced at him a couple of times and was rewarded with a smile.

Michel's heart was thumping, and he shoved his hands into his pockets. He hated this. Having to pretend when they were with people he considered friends was bad enough, but he wanted so much to hold Kit's hand as they approached the farm. His mother had always asked him when he would be bringing a girl home. He was about to introduce her to the person he loved. Except, not only was Kit a man, he was German.

Michel wasn't sure which of those his father would be angrier about.

"Having second thoughts?" Kit asked.

The house looked exactly as Michel remembered it, although his mother's small garden in front had finally been weeded. Michel and Corin would offer to tend it for her, but she would shrug and tell them they had more important things to do. Their father wasn't getting any younger and had a farm to run. Their father had spoken to them quietly and told them if they had time to weed their mother's garden for her, they should do it. But before they could, war had broken out, and Michel and Corin had been forced to flee to avoid the STO. They'd both visited their parents since, but only when they were certain no one was around who might report them.

His mother stood in the doorway, watching the chickens run in the yard. One of the dogs hovered by her side. He looked up, barked, and ran towards Michel and Kit.

"Alfred, it's good to see you, boy." Michel got down on one knee and fussed over the dog. Alfred scrutinised Kit and growled low in his throat. "This is a friend. Get down and let him sniff you," Michel told Kit.

Kit crouched down next to Michel, held out his hand, and then carefully patted the dog. Alfred glanced at Michel, then sat down in front of Kit, his tail wagging.

"I've never had a dog, or been too sure how to approach them. They had dogs at the institute, but I wasn't about to go near them."

"Wise decision." Michel smiled at Alfred's acceptance of Kit. Not all the dogs had been vicious, but they had been well trained and were fiercely loyal.

"Michel!" Rosine Faber ran to them.

Kit stood and took a step back as Michel sprinted to meet his mother halfway.

"Maman!" Michel kissed her on both cheeks, then gave her a hug. "I've missed you so much."

Rosine hugged him back tightly, then held him out at arms' length to get a better look at him. "Ma petite crotte, it is you."

Michel's cheeks flamed. "Maman." He waved a hand in Kristopher's direction. Thankfully, Kit wouldn't know the translation for the endearment, but it didn't stop Michel feeling embarrassed by it. "Please. We have company."

"You worried me. I'm allowed to embarrass you." Rosine looked Michel up and down. "You've lost weight. You remember what I said about taking care of yourself and eating properly? Come inside. I have stew cooking. We can talk over a plateful of it." She smiled at Kit when he still didn't move. "You could do with some as well. Come inside, and my son can find his manners and introduce you."

Kit cleared his throat and glanced at Michel as though asking if it was all right to do so.

"I wouldn't try arguing with her," Michel warned him. "Once Maman makes up her mind about something, the only option is to agree with her." He sniffed the air and smiled. "Hmm, boeuf aux carottes. I'd recognize Maman's recipe anywhere. Some days I swear I miss her stew more than I miss her."

Rosine gave him a light whack across his bottom. "Enough of your cheek, mon enfant. Get inside. Your papa will be pleased to see you." She turned back to Kit and held out her hand. "I'm Rosine Faber, Michel's mother. You're a friend?"

"Umm…" Kit hesitated. "Yes, I am. Bonjour, Madame, je m'appelle Kit."

Although he spoke the words clearly enough, his accent was definitely not French. His language skills had improved to the point where he'd probably followed most of what they'd said, including the warning Michel had given him, yet his accent slipped when he was nervous. He was more on edge now than he'd been on the train. His response to the soldier had been impeccable, but then Michel had coached him on different phrases the night before and made him repeat them several times until he got it right.

They'd also discussed what name Michel would use to introduce Kit to his parents. Michel wasn't happy with sharing Kit's real name but didn't want to use a false one. Kit had suggested Kit and had promised he would not reveal his last name.

Rosine raised an eyebrow. "Should I be speaking German to your friend, Michel?"

Michel swallowed. "Kit is German, Maman, but he can be

trusted. I promise. He is… I owe him my life." Better to get the initial introductions out of the way first before adding anything else.

"You've had an interesting time away, I see." Rosine called the dog with a sharp whistle, and he trotted at her heels as she began walking back to the house. "Come along. Eat first, and then I will send someone to fetch your father in from the fields." She gave Kit a nod and continued in German. "Any friend of Michel's is welcome in my home. Please join us. I am looking forward to meeting you properly."

"Merci, Madame. My French is improving, but I understand more than I can speak, and I apologise for my accent," Kit added in German. "Your German is very good."

"My sister-in-law is German, as Michel has probably told you. I learnt her language while she, like you, was struggling with French. It is important to make loved ones feel welcome, don't you think?"

Kit shot Michel a panicked look.

"Yes, it is." Michel forced himself to sound calm, even if he didn't feel it inside. He'd known his mother would figure out that Kit was more than a friend, but how had she done it so quickly?

Rosine chuckled as they followed her inside. "Come now, ma petite crotte, I am your mother. Mothers know such things. I've never seen you at ease with anyone as you are with this man. You keep glancing at him when we're talking, and there is a look in your eyes when you do that I had given up all hope of ever seeing in you. Despite my teasing you to bring a nice girl home, did you really think I did not know what you and François were doing in the barn?"

"Corin—" Michel stopped and shook his head. Corin wouldn't have told their mother. He'd promised to keep it a secret, and he never betrayed a trust.

"Corin didn't need to tell me." Rosine took down two

bowls from the shelf and began ladling stew into them. "Sit and eat."

Michel slid into one of the kitchen chairs obediently, and Kit followed his lead, taking the one next to his. "Does Papa know?" Michel asked.

His mother might accept all of this, but Michel wasn't so sure his father would. Jérôme Faber had, like his wife, learned German, but once France had been invaded by Germany, he refused to speak the language. France was for the French, and the Germans had their own country.

Rosine put two spoons down on the table, then busied herself cutting slices of bread. "Do you love my son?" she asked Kit as she put the breadboard on the table and sat down opposite him.

Kit met her gaze unflinchingly. "With everything I am," he said softly. "I will do everything I can to keep him safe and bring him home to you once this war is over."

"I believe you." Rosine smiled. "You have honest eyes, Kit… Is that your real name or the name you are using?"

"It is my real name. I wouldn't lie to you, although there are questions I can't answer."

"We can't tell you his full name, Maman. I'm sorry. It would be dangerous. We can't stay for long either, but I had to see you in case…" Michel put down his spoon, although he hadn't tasted the stew yet. "I wanted you to meet him, and for him to meet you." Tears welled, and he blinked them back. "I love him, and I hoped we could have a life here together once the war is finished."

"How much trouble are you both in?" Rosine asked.

"As Michel said, we cannot stay, and you have not seen us. I'm sorry." Kit squeezed Michel's hand under the table.

The front door banged shut. Michel let go of Kit's hand quickly.

"In here, Jérôme," Rosine called. "We have company, mon cher."

~

Kristopher would have known the man was Michel's father anywhere. He looked like an older version of Michel—same build and brown eyes flecked with green, although Jérôme Faber's hair was peppered with grey. He was ten years older than his wife, and although it was obvious by the way Michel spoke of him he loved his father dearly, he was clearly nervous about how Jérôme would react when he discovered the truth.

"Michel!" Jérôme strode towards Michel, who stood immediately. The two men kissed each other on the cheek, then hugged. "It is very good to see you, mon enfant." He studied Michel for a moment. "You're in trouble, aren't you?"

"What makes you say that?" Michel asked.

"You're risking a visit, and the war is not over. I heard you had taken an assignment in Berlin, but we haven't heard anything of you since." Jérôme glanced at Kristopher. "Who is this?"

"Papa, this is my—"

Given Rosine's observation of his accent earlier, Kristopher thought it was a good idea not to pretend to be something he wasn't. Michel's mother might appreciate the attempt, but his father wouldn't.

"Je m'appelle Kit." He held out his hand. "It is a pleasure to meet you," Kit continued in German. "Michel speaks of you often."

"Why have you brought a German into our home?" Jérôme ignored Kristopher's hand and spoke angrily to his son in French.

Michel tensed and then his eyes flashed. "It is important

to me that you meet." He faltered a little when his father's eyes widened, and then he glanced at Kristopher. "He… Kit is a good man and has taken many risks to end this war." Michel licked his lips. His mother nodded. "He is my dear friend, and—"

"Did you know about this?" Jérôme turned to his wife. He then said something in French Kristopher didn't understand.

Michel paled but kept standing.

"We do not choose who we love," Rosine said. "Our heart chooses for us. You've said that often enough yourself, mon cher."

"Love?" Jérôme looked at Michel closely, then Kristopher.

Kristopher shifted uncomfortably in his chair. Michel not only stood his ground but placed one hand on Kristopher's shoulder. "Oui," Michel said, "je l'adore, Papa."

"I wasn't talking about him loving a German!" Jérôme shot his wife a glare. "And has it escaped your notice that not only has he brought a German into our home, but he—"

Kristopher pushed back his chair, barely giving Michel time to move out of the way. "I do not want to cause trouble," he mumbled before Jérôme could finish his sentence. Had this been a mistake? "Je suis désolé."

Michel caught his arm and squeezed it. "Don't apologise, and you are not causing trouble, mon cher. Wait outside. My father and I have a few things to discuss. I will not be long."

"If you need me to, I'll stay."

"I won't be long," Michel repeated. "I promise." He turned back to his father and switched languages. Kristopher recognized a couple of swear words before he slipped from the room. Both men's voices were raised, and he'd never heard Michel this angry before.

Alfred nuzzled his head against Kristopher as soon as he sat on the doorstep, and he petted the dog. "He needs to make his peace with his father, not argue with him." Kristopher put his head in his hands, and the dog whined.

The door opened behind him, and he jumped, but it was only Rosine. She sat down beside him, and he moved over to give her more room.

"My husband and son are both protective of those they love. Don't worry about Michel. They will yell for a while, and then they will calm and talk properly. Sometimes I think they are too much alike. Corin was not much better."

"Michel told me about Corin. I'm so sorry for your loss."

"When Corin died, I feared something inside Michel had done so as well. It has been a long time since I have heard him this passionate about someone or something." Rosine brushed his shoulder with her hand. "Do you still have family in Germany?"

Kristopher started to nod but then stopped. With no recent news of Clara, he had no idea whether his sister was still alive. "My father died in the Berlin bombings last year. My sister was arrested… I…"

"And your mother?" Rosine asked softly.

"She died when I was born. I never met her." Kristopher wasn't sure why he was sharing something very personal with someone he barely knew, but Rosine was easy to talk to. She reminded him of Michel in that.

"How much trouble are you in?" Rosine repeated the question they'd avoided earlier.

"A lot," he admitted. "I'm sorry for getting Michel involved in all of this."

Rosine rolled her eyes. "I know my son. He would have become involved anyway. He's a good boy, and he could never refuse anyone in need. He also knows his own mind, so there is no need to apologise." She sighed. "He's come to say goodbye because he thinks there is a good chance he will not come home."

Kristopher started to protest, but she held up her hand to stop him.

"Michel wouldn't risk coming here otherwise, if he is in trouble. I know he wanted us to meet, but there's more to it than that."

"I meant what I said about doing everything I can to keep him safe." Kristopher saw the fear in her eyes and winced. If Michel was caught, Kristopher knew what Holm and his men would do to him. "I can't promise he will survive this, but…"

"We all do what we can in this terrible time." Rosine tilted her head to one side, then stood and gestured for Kristopher to do the same. "They have finished talking. Don't worry. Michel's father loves him and wants what is best for him. As all parents do. He might not like the situation at first, but he will come around. We have already lost one son, and he will soon realise that if he doesn't accept Michel for who he is, there is a good chance he will lose another."

Michel and his father were quiet as they joined Kristopher and Rosine outside. Kristopher met Michel's gaze, and Michel gave him a slight nod.

"Papa and I have talked, and we both think it best if we leave now. We have already risked much in coming here."

"This isn't Michel's—" Kristopher would never forget that the last conversation he'd had with his father had been an argument. He'd do whatever he could to ensure Michel and his father parted on good terms.

"I know, and I am the one who needs to apologise." Jérôme offered his hand to Kristopher, who shook it. "Look after my son," he said in German. "You are his heart. Both of you have a home here when this is over. Make sure you come back to us."

"Thank you," Kristopher replied in French. "I will."

CHAPTER EIGHT

"You should be safe here for a few days," Jacques—the farmer who was their contact in Pont-Audemer—told them. "Take care to stay out of sight. Although the Germans rarely bother us here, one of their officers has taken a fancy to my daughter." He wrinkled his nose in disgust. "She has successfully spurned Leutnant Beutel's advances and has not seen him for several days, but I do not think it is the end of it."

"That doesn't sound very safe to me," Liang said. "Are you sure we shouldn't be finding somewhere else to stay?"

"This is as good a place as any," Jacques said. "Other farms have been forced to billet some of the Hauptmann's men, but those men haven't caused any trouble. Some of them seem to want this war over as quickly as we do."

"That doesn't mean we can trust them," Sébastien pointed out. He looked around the loft but didn't move away from the door.

"Of course not," Jacques said, "but if we keep things civil, they are less likely to suspect we are helping fugitives, oui?"

"Oui." Matt took charge of the conversation before Liang and Sébastien had the opportunity to derail it further. "We appreciate your hospitality and will only stay for as long as we need to. Any trouble and we will leave sooner. The last thing we want is to arouse any suspicions or put you in danger."

Luckily Jacques spoke fluent German, so Matt didn't need either Sébastien or Liang to translate. Shame Jacques hadn't been home when they'd arrived, as Matt's French was not that good, and Jacques's wife didn't speak German or English. He understood more than he spoke but preferred to deal with people directly rather than through a third party.

"If you are discovered, it means we cannot help anyone else." Jacques gave Matt a smile. "Good evening, Monsieur Chastain. I'll have my wife bring up some stew in about half an hour."

"Merci." Matt waited until their host had left the loft and his footsteps had faded away. "Whatever your opinions of the local German occupiers, keep them to yourself or among our group," he told Sébastien. "We have no idea as to Jacques's true feelings or whether he is simply using conversation to find out information he can pass along."

"You do not trust me either." Sébastien nodded approvingly. "I, on the other hand, have Michel's word that I can trust you. Nevertheless, I make my own decisions about such matters. I have been fighting the Germans for as long as he has, and I have seen too many of my own countrymen betray us by collaborating with them."

"So you do not trust Michel either?" Liang raised an eyebrow.

"I have not known him long, and although Arlette speaks highly of him, her opinion is somewhat coloured by emotion." Sébastien dumped his bag on the floor to the left of one of the windows. He peered outside. "This will be the best exit if we need to leave in a hurry. I noticed the pitch of the roof is lower at the other end. We should be able to reach the ground from there."

"I'm hoping it doesn't come to that. I'm also hoping to continue to stay well clear of the Risle and all those canals." Liang hadn't been happy when he'd discovered that their destination was a town with roads crisscrossing the canals, although he'd made appreciative noises about the medieval buildings they passed on their way to the farm.

"We need time to rethink our strategy," Ken said. "Are you sure it's a good idea to stay here?"

He hadn't spoken much since they'd abandoned the truck outside Corneville-sur-Risle. When they'd quickly changed clothes, he'd voiced his concern about Holm being in Caen, but Matt had decided it was a conversation better left for later. They needed to get off the road and reach Pont-Audemer as soon as possible. Once they were settled there, they'd reassess the situation. Apparently, Ken had decided they'd waited long enough.

"Here is as good as any a place." Matt hadn't been pleased to hear about Holm's relocation either, and would be happy if he never saw the man again, unless their meeting came with the opportunity to put a bullet in him.

"What is your connection with this Holm?" Sébastien asked. "Given your reactions, it sounds personal."

"You could say that," Liang said.

"We had the misfortune of meeting him in Berlin," Matt said grimly. He wasn't about to go into details Sébastien didn't need to know. Not only that, but given what Holm had done, he didn't want to reopen old wounds. He and Liang still bore physical scars of their encounter, and Ken hadn't gotten over his meeting with Holm either. The need to discover the truth about his father haunted Ken, and nothing Matt said to try to convince him Holm was lying about Patrick Lowe being a murderer seemed to help.

"Do you think his being in Caen is a coincidence?" Sébastien's eyes narrowed. "If we're working together, I need to know what's going on. I'm not walking blindly into a dangerous situation."

"It's a coincidence," Matt said firmly. It had to be. Months had passed since they'd escaped from Freiberg. "He's a high-ranking SS officer and had been in Berlin a while." With the institute he'd been in charge of destroyed, his superiors wouldn't be happy with his lack of results in failing to find Kristopher.

"Even if it is, he's still dangerous and too close," Ken said. "What if the Oberscharführer mentioned our meeting outside Bétheny?"

"We were using different identities," Matt said, but Ken had a point.

"Soldiers who were supposed to deliver prisoners to him who aren't going to turn up," Ken said. "Even if Holm being in Caen is a coincidence, if he suspects anything, he'll use it as an excuse to resume his hunt for us."

"Mon Dieu," Sébastien swore under his breath. "So you *do* have a high-ranking SS officer hunting you. Wonderful. I had a bad feeling about this assignment, but I let Arlette talk me into joining her."

Liang let out a loud sigh. "It's never a good idea to let a beautiful woman talk you into something. You're not sweet on her, are you?"

Matt hid a smile, amused at how Liang being sweet on a woman had changed his perspective.

"We are at war," Sébastien snapped at him. "This is neither the time nor the place for such things. We could all be dead tomorrow."

Matt noticed he hadn't answered the question. If Liang's suspicions were correct, this complicated matters. "You shouldn't be working together if you are. It changes the way you react. Logic doesn't always work when you have feelings for someone."

Liang snorted and rolled his eyes. Ken gave him a surprised look and then glanced at Matt. Matt chose to ignore both of them. Liang's gesture couldn't be referring to Matt and Ken's relationship—they'd been very careful. Besides, Liang wasn't exactly beyond reproach, considering the goodbye kiss he and Juliane had shared before he'd left Berlin. Matt had almost walked in on them but doubted they'd noticed anything but each other.

"Sometimes you can only make the best of whatever situation you're in," Ken said. "We've all had to do that throughout this mission, and will continue to do so until it's over."

"When you work with someone long enough, it's difficult not to become friends," Sébastien said softly. "I think perhaps we are all guilty of that, oui?"

"I think perhaps we are," Matt agreed, happy to follow that line of reasoning if Sébastien wanted to. "But we are digressing from the matter at hand. I still think this is as safe a place as any to stay the next few days. According to the paperwork the Oberscharführer saw, we are not stopping at Pont-Audemer or even going through it."

"He knows we are continuing on to Bayeux," Ken said. "If we do not report in at Caen, Holm may make enquiries at Bayeux. Michel and the others could be walking into a trap."

"Can we get word to them to go a different route and meet us at Cyrville-sur-Mer instead?" Matt asked Sébastien.

Sébastien nodded. "They have a radio here. I can ask Jacques to give us access to it. Arlette will be checking in with a Resistance cell outside Lisieux. If we can get the message to them in time, they can take an alternative route and avoid Bayeux."

"We should do that now." Ken tilted his head toward Matt, as though asking permission.

"Good idea. Sébastien, take Ken with you," Matt said. "Once you've gotten word through to Arlette's next contact, Ken needs to contact London so they are kept apprised of our situation. It's been too long since we've checked in."

Although Matt doubted they'd have any problems finding a radio transmitter in Cyrville-sur-Mer, Ken had been on edge while they'd been out of direct contact with London. Better to make contact now and at least let them know they'd be in Normandy by mid to late May, as they'd been ordered.

His team would be not given much notice about the specifics of their extraction until it was almost time to leave. Knowing about it now risked the entire operation if one of them were captured. Matt still suspected Kristopher would not be leaving France with them. Matt couldn't delay the conversation he needed to have with Kristopher about it much longer, although there was still time for Kristopher to approach him about the matter first.

Although Ken had suggested it would be easier if Kristopher disappeared, Matt had soon realised it would only complicate matters. Both sides needed to be convinced Kristopher was no longer a threat. London might suspect he'd fallen into the hands of their enemies, as would the Nazis, if they could not produce evidence of his death.

Matt was working on that one. He hoped like hell Kristopher and Michel were too and had a better idea of how to go about it than he did. Evidence of a body aside, Matt and his team would still have to lie about the death of a friend, and he doubted they'd get away with it.

"Welcome to Caen, Oberscharführer Esser." Karl gave the man in front of him a curt nod. "I hope you had a pleasant journey with no incidents."

"An extremely pleasant journey, thank you, Standartenführer." Esser seemed to hesitate for a moment. Karl waited for him to continue. "There were no incidents as such, but I did meet Hauptmann Steube at the checkpoint on the outskirts of Bétheny. A congeniable man. I hope the prisoners he was bringing you for interrogation were helpful."

Karl raised an eyebrow. "Prisoners?" He wasn't expecting any prisoners.

"Yes, sir. His papers confirmed his story. They were prisoners you wished to interrogate personally." Esser paled.

"Interesting." Karl tapped his desk with his pencil, his curiosity piqued. It wouldn't be the first time paperwork had gone astray, but surely if they were prisoners he wished to interrogate personally, he would know something about it. "Could you describe these men, please, Oberscharführer?"

"The prisoners or the men transporting them, sir?"

"Both." A suspicion began niggling at the back of Karl's mind, but he did not dare give in to it yet. Better to get more information first. He smiled. "Don't worry. You are not in any trouble."

Esser nodded but hadn't regained his colour. "Thank you, sir." He was quiet for a moment. A good sign that he was giving the matter some thought. "There were two men accompanying the prisoners, sir. Hauptmann Steube was a couple of inches shorter than I am. He had brown hair and blue eyes. Quite striking eyes, actually. I noticed them immediately."

"Excellent." Karl allowed a slither of hope to surface. Esser's description did match one of the men he was pursuing. If it was Bryant, he had to grudgingly admire the man's nerve in passing himself off as a German officer. "And the one working with him?"

"Unteroffizier Raske, sir. The Hauptmann did most of the talking, although I did notice Raske seemed a little surprised when your name was mentioned. He covered it well, but I figured Steube had not given him all of the specifics of their mission." Esser hesitated again. "It's not unheard of."

"No, it's not," Karl agreed. He opened his desk drawer and pulled out a folder, then opened it and retrieved an old photograph. "Is this Raske?"

"May I examine it closely, sir?" Esser took it from Karl after he nodded and handed it over. "There are some subtle differences, but it is a good likeness." He returned the photograph.

"You have good observation skills." The man would be useful. When Karl had first met Lowe, he'd been struck by how closely he resembled his father—the man in the photograph. It had been only after spending some time with him that he'd noticed the subtle differences between them. "This man is an Allied spy I have been hunting for some time."

Esser lowered his gaze. "My apologies, sir. I should have asked more questions and taken them into custody."

"Yes, you should have, but sometimes fate smiles on us. We know they are in the area, and there are others working with them I need to find as well. This way we can use one group to track the other." Karl smiled. *Yes, this would do nicely.* "Now, can you describe their prisoners?"

"Yes, sir. Both… appeared… to be Frenchmen, although I did question one of them about that."

"Interesting."

"He looked Chinese, sir, but had a French surname. He explained that his mother was Chinese and his father French."

"Very interesting." This man was most likely Herr Doktor

Zhou. That accounted for three of the team, but what of the other two? Karl retrieved a photograph of Lehrer from another folder. "Was this the other man?"

"No, sir." Esser shook his head. "He was dark-haired and much more heavily built than the man in the photograph."

"About your height?" Karl asked, despite doubting it was Schmitz. Although a few centimetres taller, his build was similar to Lehrer's.

"No, sir. Closer to the Hauptmann's… the man masquerading as the Hauptmann, I mean."

Ah, well. That would have been too much to expect. It seemed as though Bryant had split his team, as Karl had first suspected. It was what Karl would have done—the sensible thing to do.

A knock at the door saved Karl the trouble of sending for Reiniger. "Please come in, Obersturmführer. Obersturmführer Reiniger, this is Oberscharführer Esser. He will be working under you while he is assigned here."

"Yes, sir." Reiniger glanced at Esser, as though immediately dismissing him as unimportant. He still needed to learn that it was better to encourage loyalty in the lower ranks by treating them politely, but as long as Reiniger got the job done, Karl would not interfere with his methods.

"Our fugitives have been sighted outside Bétheny. They could well be heading in our direction, but in the meantime, I want you and Esser to travel to where they were last seen and search the area. Take half a dozen men with you. If they are no longer there, widen your search."

"Yes, sir. At once, sir." Reiniger saluted, and a thin smile crossed his face before he turned and left the room.

Esser still stood to attention in front of Karl's desk.

Karl glanced at him. "You're dismissed, Oberscharführer. Unless you have more information I should know about?"

"No, sir. Thank you, sir." Esser saluted. "Heil Hitler. It is a pleasure to serve under you, sir."

Karl doubted Esser would feel that way after a few days taking orders from Reiniger, but that wasn't his concern. He picked up his telephone. "Could you please send Fräulein Huber in? I wish to speak with her."

If Bryant and his team had already reached Bayeux, he wanted to ensure they would go no further. Margarete had claimed to have connections with the Resistance in that area. It was time for her to make discreet enquiries. Between her and Reiniger, Karl doubted it would be long before he was face-to-face with his prey once more.

He smiled and steepled his fingers. He was very much looking forward to it.

"Please, leave me alone." Germaine spoke in a whisper, yet her voice still carried. "My father will be home shortly. It is better that you leave now."

Matt paused on the bottom step of the stairs leading to the first floor. He shouldn't reveal his presence but had no intention of abandoning the girl if she needed help. Jacques and his wife had left for town a short time ago and wouldn't be home for at least another hour.

"Nice girls don't tease." The man spoke in German, his voice slurred as though he were drunk. "And I asked you nicely."

Germaine's voice shook. "I haven't teased you, Leutnant, I swear. I've done nothing to encourage you. Please let me go." Her breath hissed. "Please. You're hurting me."

Matt sighed. He turned and crept over the partially open door to peer through the gap to see what was going on. He'd come inside a few minutes before because he'd heard the sounds of a motorbike approaching. Germaine was a sweet girl, and only sixteen. Her father had warned them about his man.

The German officer had pushed Germaine against the outside wall. Not only that, but he had his mouth next to hers, as though about to steal a kiss. She looked terrified, frozen in place.

"What the hell do you think you're doing?" Matt strode over to the man and pulled him off the girl. The Leutnant lashed out with one hand. Matt ducked out of the way, narrowly avoiding being punched. His opponent fell forward and hit the ground.

Germaine stared at him. She put her hand to her mouth yet didn't move.

"Go inside and lock the door," Matt told her. "Your father will be home soon. Stay inside until he is."

The Leutnant—Jacques had told them his name was Beutel—growled and picked himself up off the ground. He eyed Matt up and down. "You have struck an officer of the Third Reich." His eyes were bloodshot.

"No, I didn't. You fell because you tried to strike me. Not only that, but you're drunk and attempting to have your way with a young French girl. What would your superior think of that?" Matt stood his ground.

Although he didn't know this man, he'd met men like him. There had been a couple of them he'd had to deal with in his unit before he'd shipped out on his first mission. However, he'd been their superior officer in that case, so they'd had to respect his authority. This man was German, and Matt was dressed as a Frenchman, although he was speaking German.

He'd have to think fast.

"It's my word against yours, Frenchman." Beutel spat his

last word, then wiped his mouth. He smiled, looking pleased with himself. "Who do you think will be believed?"

"Let's see." Matt ignored how fast his heart was beating and kept his tone casual. "You're drunk." He leaned in closer as though about to impart a huge secret. "You've jeopardised an undercover operation that is so crucial to the war effort your superior isn't aware of it. I outrank you, soldier. On your feet, and salute me. Now."

Beutel paled. He shuffled to his feet and saluted sharply. "Forgive me, sir. I had no idea."

"Obviously," Matt said dryly. Now to move in for the kill. His mouth was dry, but he didn't dare swallow and risk Beutel figuring out his bluff. "As I said, this operation is crucial. I can't afford to draw attention to the fact I'm here or risk the locals discovering I am not who they think I am. You keep my secret, Leutnant, and this will go no further."

"Yes, sir." Leutnant Beutel saluted again. "Heil Hitler!"

"Heil Hitler." Matt paused until he saw the man's relief start to slip before continuing. "If anything like this happens again, I will be contacting your superior. Do I make myself clear?"

"Yes, sir." Beutel stood still, unmoving. He didn't offer his name or seem to notice Matt hadn't asked for it. That suited Matt fine, as he had no intention of giving his own.

"You're dismissed." Matt waited until he heard the motorbike engine start, then leaned heavily against the wall. "You can come out now."

"You never could walk away from someone in trouble, could you?" Ken said softly from behind him.

"How much did you hear?"

"Enough to wonder if I'd have to step in and do something we would both regret. The man was drunk. I hope he doesn't look back on the situation more clearly once he's sober."

"At least this way we've bought some time." If his ploy hadn't worked, Matt would have had to pull a weapon on him. "Better this than having someone come looking for him."

As much as he regretted letting Beutel go, at least this way they wouldn't have to hide a captive or a dead body.

"As long as they don't come looking for you." Ken leaned one hand briefly against Matt's shoulder. "You're a good man, Matt. Don't ever change, but please don't do that again." He removed his hand. "Not until we get home, anyway."

"You know I can't promise that." Matt also knew if the situation were reversed, Ken wouldn't have stood back and done nothing either.

"I know." Ken sighed. "We'd better warn the others. It looks as though we'll be leaving here sooner than we planned."

CHAPTER NINE

"They're here. I know it." Gernot Reiniger growled low in his throat, ignoring the sideways glance Esser gave him.

"If they are, Hauptmann Gerstle doesn't seem aware of it." Esser snapped to attention when Gernot glared at him.

They'd found the truck Bryant and his men had used outside Corneville-sur-Risle. Gernot had sent men in several directions to cover whatever route his prey might have taken on foot. Freshly dug soil had revealed two buried German uniforms, hidden but not well enough. Tracking dogs had lost the trail near the Risle, and with night falling, Gernot decided to spend the night at Pont-Audemer and continue his search in the morning.

"Did I ask for your opinion, Oberscharführer?" Gernot asked. This new man was eager to help but hadn't yet learnt his place. Gernot sighed and massaged his temples. The scar tissue above his missing eye throbbed, as it tended to do when he was tired.

He missed Müller. He'd had known how to follow orders without question, while Esser seemed to have an opinion about everything. Not only that, but Müller hadn't been afraid to go that extra step to ensure success. Gernot wasn't sure Esser would… yet.

"No, sir. Sorry, sir." Although Esser finally seemed to realise his place, the demure tone suggested he had adjusted his behaviour too far in the other direction.

Gernot took a deep breath. Standartenführer Holm was relying on him, and he wasn't about to let some eager-to-please junior officer jeopardise that. Besides, Esser did not have Gernot's knowledge or experience, especially about this mission and their prey.

"We have been tracking these traitors for some time, Esser. They are desperate men and not above using those who might be sympathetic to their cause. If it was that easy to discover their whereabouts, we wouldn't still be looking for them months after our last encounter, would we?"

Although it had taken far too long to find Bryant and his team, a few extra hours would not hurt now. Gernot smiled and allowed himself to contemplate—only for a moment—how much he would enjoy the interrogation he'd been promised. While Holm was focused on finding Lehrer and Lowe, Gernot knew that the real way to get Lehrer to cooperate was to hurt Schmitz. Lehrer, after all, had been prepared to give himself up to save his friend in Berlin. Schmitz deserved everything he got. Not only had he pretended to be a loyal member of Gernot's unit at the institute, but Gernot held him directly responsible for the loss of his eye.

While one might argue it had been the Allied pilot who had detonated the explosives, Gernot would not have been there if he hadn't been hunting Lehrer—and by extension Schmitz, the man who had helped him to escape. It wasn't that much of a stretch of logic to place the blame squarely on the person who was really responsible.

Gernot was going to very much enjoy reminding Schmitz why he deserved every bit of pain he was about to suffer.

The quiet knock at the door was followed by Hauptmann Gerstle's entrance. Although he outranked Gernot, Gerstle had offered him the use of his office while in Pont-Audemer. "I think I might have a lead for you, Obersturmführer. A man matching one of the descriptions you've given us was seen yesterday on one of the farms on the outskirts of the town."

So they were in the area. Gernot nodded, taking care to hide his true emotions. At last! He'd waited so long to finally renew his acquaintance with at least one of their prey. "That's interesting. Send men out to search the area immediately."

"I've already done that." Gerstle nodded his approval, then gestured towards the still half-open office door. "Beutel, please enter."

Gernot eyed the Leutnant with interest. He was a younger man yet had already begun working his way up the ranks. Whatever he had to say for himself might be the turning point in his career—small incidents had the ability to either make or destroy a man's future, depending on how his decisions were perceived by a superior.

The Leutnant saluted and stood to attention. He stared straight ahead.

Gernot sighed. While he appreciated men who followed the chain of command and knew their place, it did sometimes become tiresome when they had to be prodded to impart information. "You may speak, Leutnant Beutel. Hauptmann Gerstle tells me you might have a lead as to the whereabouts of the men we're seeking."

"Yes, sir." Beutel cleared his throat. "I was making a routine check of the outlying farms in the area when my questioning of one of the locals was interrupted by a man claiming to be an undercover agent."

"I see." Gernot smiled thinly. "So you were questioning a local farmer?"

"No, sir." Beutel paled. "I was questioning his daughter, sir. I thought she might have information that could be beneficial."

"I see," Gernot said again. He studied Beutel more closely. He was not only young, but a man a woman might give a second glance. "One must pursue any useful leads, don't you think?"

"Yes, sir." Beutel frowned and seemed to relax a little. A slight smirk crossed his face, although it disappeared quickly.

Gernot suspected Beutel had done rather more than question this girl. However, if his behaviour led to the apprehension of at least one of the fugitives, Gernot didn't care what the man had done. "Please continue, Leutnant. What did this man look like?"

"About my height, sir. He had blue eyes and brown hair, and he spoke with a Berlin accent." Beutel paused for a moment as though remembering. "He didn't give his name, but he threatened me, sir. Said if I revealed he was in the area, he would make up a ridiculous story and claim I'd attacked the girl."

"Ridiculous." Did this idiot actually believe Gernot hadn't worked out what had happened?

While the description wasn't that helpful, Gernot couldn't afford to dismiss it. After all, Bryant spoke German with a Berlin accent, and the description fitted. However, as there were many Germans who came from Berlin, it didn't necessary mean this was Bryant. It would be like Bryant to risk breaking cover to save a peasant's daughter, though. He'd been very upset about the death of his friend at the Kaffeehaus.

It was a long shot, but one he couldn't afford to ignore. If the man in question was really an undercover agent, a quick conversation would dismiss him as a suspect. If not, he would be persuaded to help with their enquiries. Gernot's orders were not just to bring in Lehrer and those working with him. He was also tasked with tracking down Resistance cells in the area. The only way to discourage foolish Frenchmen from such things was to make an example of those who kept insisting they could free their country.

"Esser," Gernot ordered, "accompany Beutel back to this farm and arrest anyone found on the premises."

"The farmer and his family will be there," Esser reminded him. "It is after curfew."

Gernot struggled not to roll his eyes. "I believe I said anyone, Oberscharführer. That includes them. Obviously they are not undercover German agents as this man claimed to be, but they might have information about him that will be useful."

"Yes, sir." Esser saluted and left the room, Beutel following him.

"Is it a good idea to arrest a local farmer?" Gerstle asked. "We haven't had a lot of trouble here because we leave them alone, for the most part."

"If they've been helping fugitives of the Third Reich, they're already in trouble, Herr Hauptmann." Gernot felt the familiar thud above his eye again. Why did he continuously need to deal with these men who insisted on treating their enemies with respect they did not deserve? "Actually..." Gernot pondered for a moment. "Send men out to knock on doors. I want four arrests. Men, women, or children. I don't care who."

Given the time of day, everyone would be home. If anyone was caught breaking the curfew, Gernot wanted a word with them, anyway.

"Herr Obersturmführer, I don't—"

"I am here as a representative of Standartenführer Holm,

and have been told to use whatever means I think necessary to complete my mission." Gernot reached for the telephone. "However, your protest is noted. I will contact the Standartenführer immediately and confirm his approval of this course of action."

"I'm sure that isn't necessary, Herr Reiniger," Gerstle said hurriedly. He'd backed down on something else earlier with the reminder that Gernot was Holm's representative for this mission. "After all, it is not as though it will come to anything, will it?"

"Of course not." Gernot replaced the telephone receiver on its cradle.

If they found their prey, it wouldn't come to anything at all.

Ken looked up at the sound of footsteps on the stairs. Not just footsteps but someone running. He reached for his gun and edged towards the door. As it opened, he grabbed the man who nearly fell through it and hauled him to his feet.

"Jacques, what's wrong?" Matt stepped forward. Ken let go of Jacques with an apologetic look, hoping he hadn't been too rough on the old man.

"Vous devez partir!" Jacques glanced fearfully through the open door behind him.

"Bloody hell," Liang swore softly. "Now what?" He and Sébastien exchanged a worried look.

"You need to leave," Jacques said, this time in German. He bent over, his hands on his knees. When he spoke again, it was clearer but no less insistent. "Leave. Now. There is no time to waste."

"Marcel, check downstairs." Matt gave Ken an order. "Find out what that noise was."

Jacques shook his head. "That was my family leaving. I've sent Jeannine and Germaine to my brother-in-law's. I've had word that there are German soldiers heading this way. They are under orders to arrest anyone found here. It is better to risk being arrested for breaking curfew than to be here when the soldiers arrive."

Ken stopped, already halfway out the door, but didn't put his gun away.

"If we're leaving, you're coming with us," Matt told Jacques. Ken dived back into the room, grabbed his bag and Matt's, and handed Matt his coat. He gave Matt a quick glance.

Was this because of what Matt had interrupted yesterday? Even if it was, he would not chastise Matt because of it. The soldier's behaviour had been unacceptable. If Matt hadn't stepped in, Ken would have.

"Alexandre, Sébastien, go now. We'll be right behind you," Matt said. They'd already organised a meeting place at a safe distance in case their current location was compromised.

To Ken's surprise, Liang hesitated. "You're not going to do something foolish," he said to Matt. It wasn't a question. "Now isn't the time to play hero."

"Don't worry," Ken said grimly. "I'll make sure he doesn't, but whatever happens, stay out of sight. If we're not there in an hour, head for the next safe house."

"Good luck," Liang said. "See you soon." He and Sébastien disappeared down the stairs.

Matt shouldered his duffle bag. "You're coming with us," he told Jacques. "If your family are at your brother-in-law's, you should join them there."

"No." Jacques shook off Matt's hand. "Hauptmann Gerstle is a reasonable man. I will tell his men no one is here and give you time to get away."

If Gerstle was so reasonable, why had Jacques sent his family away?

"Does he usually send his men out after curfew to arrest people?" Matt put Ken's thoughts into words. Something might have happened for Gerstle to feel the need to authorise this kind of search. From what Jacques had told them of the man, he didn't tend to waste his resources on anything he didn't deem necessary.

Jacques shrugged. A shadow crossed his face but was quickly replaced by a determined look.

"What aren't you telling us?" Ken asked. There had to be something, or Jacques wouldn't have sent his family away.

"I'll be fine. You're wasting the advantage I'm trying to give you. Go join your friends. I am going to make some tea. It is what one does when home alone for the evening, oui?"

"Jacques…" Matt gave Ken a look. *Help.*

"We need to go." Ken grabbed Matt's arm and steered him toward the door. He'd seen Jacques's stubborn look on other men. They wouldn't be able to change his mind. Not only that, but he suspected Jacques would see it as an insult if they tried. "Jacques is right. If he comes with us, there's a good chance we'll all be caught." He lowered his voice. "You'd do the same if you were him."

"Ken…" Matt's voice was dangerously low.

"Thank you," Ken told Jacques. He didn't wait to hear what Matt was going to say next but shoved him out of the room. "Don't play the hero. You saved his daughter. Let him return the favour."

They both froze at the knock at the front door. "Open up," someone yelled in German.

Matt turned around, pushed past Ken, and headed back up the stairs. If there were soldiers at the front door, they'd hardly leave the back unguarded. "The roof," Matt hissed. "It's the only way."

"I'm coming," Jacques called. He placed a brief hand on Matt's shoulder when they passed on the stairs. "Good luck," he said quietly before raising his voice again. "I'm coming!"

Once they were through the door, Ken closed it behind him. Matt strode over to the window and opened it. He adjusted his bag on his shoulder. Luckily they'd split the supplies between them. Leaving their bags for the soldiers to find wasn't an option.

Ken peered out the window. Sébastien had underestimated the distance when he'd said it wasn't far to the lower part of the roof. "It's a good few feet," Ken muttered. He looked down and wished he hadn't. Ken had never been fond of heights, but he usually gritted his teeth and got on with it.

"It's not too high," Matt said quietly. "I'll go first, and you can follow me instead of looking down."

"I'll be fine," Ken insisted, but he stood back to let Matt go first. Better that one of them got away, and he'd prefer it was Matt.

Matt swung his leg out the window and looked one way, then the other before edging out onto the roof. The moon provided some light to guide them. Instead of standing, he stayed in a crouch. "Crawl," he whispered.

Not only would it be easier that way, given the pitch of that part of the roof, but they'd be less likely to be seen. Ken didn't bother to reply but climbed out the window. He swayed and quickly dropped to a crouch. If he followed Matt, he'd be all right.

Only a few feet. Only a few feet and they could get down.

Matt crawled forward slowly but steadily. Ken could hear voices below them. Jacques sounded angry. A loud bang nearly made Ken lose his balance, but he kept shuffling forward. The noise had been a door slamming. The soldiers were searching the house. It wouldn't be long before they found the loft and the open window.

Damn it. Ken wished he'd thought to shut it behind them. "Hurry up," he hissed.

Matt ignored him and held up one hand while he waited for Ken to catch up. "Nearly there," he whispered in Ken's ear. "There's a drainpipe about a foot ahead of us. Follow me and do what I do."

Ken nodded. Matt straightened when he got to the drainpipe and began climbing down. Ken took a deep breath and followed him. The few feet down seemed a lot longer. When he finally felt the ground under him, he was shaking. Matt put his arms around Ken to hold him steady, pulling them both down so they were out of sight. Ken smiled and brushed his lips against Matt's briefly, knowing Matt would understand it meant he was fine.

Voices came closer as the soldiers passed by their hiding place with their prisoner.

"I told you my family is not here," Jacques said. "They are staying with relatives for the night. We do not have anyone else living here."

"Then you will not mind answering a few questions, Monsieur Dubois."

Ken frowned. Matt nodded. He too had recognised the voice of the Oberscharführer who had pulled their truck over outside Bétheny.

"I will cooperate in any way I can, Oberscharführer Esser." Jacques had lost his anger, and there was a strained quality to his voice Ken hadn't heard before. "We do not want any trouble. Hauptmann Gerstle—"

Another man interrupted the conversation. It was the Leutnant Matt had spoken to the day before. "Hauptmann Gerstle is not in charge of this operation. We are reporting to Obersturmführer Reiniger. I'm sure he'll be pleased that you wish to cooperate."

~

Gernot glanced up as the prisoner was dragged into the room. He feigned disinterest and wrote a few more notes on the paper in front of him before putting down his pen. "I hear you're not being cooperative." He checked the name in his notes. "Monsieur Dubois."

"I have told you everything I know." Jacques Dubois lifted his bruised face and met Gernot's gaze directly.

"Of course you have," Gernot murmured. "I know we both want the same thing… Jacques." Holm had told him that if a prisoner was not forthcoming with information, to try another method. Politeness and pretending to care often got results violence did not.

Beutel took a step toward the prisoner, but Gernot shook his head. Beutel had done a good job with his interrogation. One of Jacques's eyes was half-closed, and he winced when he moved one arm. Gernot suspected there were other not so obvious injuries elsewhere on the man's body. It was shame he was so stubborn. He reminded Gernot of another prisoner they'd once had. One he wanted to get his hands on again.

"Beutel, leave us for a moment." Gernot wondered if having Beutel help with the interrogation had been a good decision. After all, the man had been accused of attacking Jacques's daughter.

"Yes, sir." Beutel saluted and left the room. He'd wait outside the door, as previously arranged.

Gernot smiled. "I apologise for the Leutnant's behaviour. It must have also been upsetting for you to hear about his supposed… altercation with your daughter."

"I only found out about it late yesterday. Thank you for your apology. I'm sure he won't—"

"You misunderstand me." Gernot pushed back his chair

but didn't stand. "I was apologising for his behaviour in interrogating you." He waved his hand. "I have no proof he did anything to your daughter, and he claims he only questioned her. Perhaps I should arrange for your daughter to be brought in so she can testify on her own behalf?"

"There's no need for that. I'm sure it is something best forgotten, oui?"

"Oh, no, I insist." Gernot paused for effect. He rather enjoyed seeing the growing panic on Jacques's face. "However," he said thoughtfully, "I do believe there was another witness to the incident. An undercover German officer. If we can find him, we won't have to investigate further, will we?"

Jacques shifted slightly. It appeared he thought the suggestion might have some merit, although not enough for him to answer.

"Oh come, now." Gernot stood and walked around the desk so he was less than a metre from Jacques. "While I am disappointed you do not hold your fellow villagers in high regard, I really thought you might cooperate to save your daughter's reputation."

Jacques's eyes widened. "I don't know what you're talking about."

Gernot tsked tsked. "Didn't Beutel tell you?" He glanced at his watch. "If I don't find this so-called German officer and the men with him before curfew this evening, four people will be executed in their place. I'm looking for four men. If I can't find them, these poor innocents will have to pay the price."

"He didn't tell me." Jacques's voice shook.

"Oh yes. That's right. They would have been arrested around the same time you were." Gernot sighed. "Unfortunately no one has come forward with any information, so it appears these poor people are going to lose their lives in a couple of hours. I feel sorry for them, giving up so much for traitors they don't even know. It's a shame this war has come to this, isn't it?" He walked around Jacques. The man needed to be taught to reply when spoken to. "*Isn't it?*"

"I can't help you. Sir." Jacques held his head high.

Gernot sighed again. He really hated these people and their principles. What was it about their need to protect others? Gernot had never seen the point of it.

Oh well, he'd tried to follow Holm's advice. It wasn't his fault it hadn't worked.

He grabbed Jacques's injured arm and twisted it behind his back. "Oh, I'm sure you can," he hissed in Jacques's ear. "You might not give up these men for your friends, but I'm sure you will for your daughter. After all, someone with her reputation might be considered easy prey for men wanting a good time. If she encouraged one officer, she will encourage others."

"Please. She's only sixteen. She's still a child. You can't."

Gernot twisted his arm further. He heard a satisfying crack. Jacques's breathing sped up, but he didn't cry out. Under different circumstances, Gernot might admire Jacques's stubbornness, but he was the enemy and had information Gernot wanted.

"Standartenführer Holm has placed me in charge of this investigation. Not only that, but he has given me the authority to use whatever means necessary to find these men." Gernot let go of Jacques's arm and took a step back. "I consider this necessary. I'm giving you a final chance to change my mind."

Jacques took a deep breath. Good, he seemed to be considering. He glanced at Gernot and then at the clock on the wall.

Interesting.

"I was the only one who knew about these men being in the area," he said in a hoarse whisper. "Do what you want with me, but leave my daughter alone and let the other prisoners go."

"Please continue." Gernot wasn't about to agree to any such terms. He was in charge here, not Jacques. In fact, Jacques wasn't in a position to demand anything.

"You'll let them go?"

"Please continue," Gernot repeated.

"There were four men. Two who spoke German but not much French, a Frenchman, and a man who looked to be part Chinese."

Reiniger smiled. "There, that wasn't too difficult, was it? One of the men pretending to be German was the man who saved your daughter, wasn't he?"

Jacques nodded. "Yes. He used a French name, but I heard him and two of the others speaking English. They didn't realise I spoke the language."

"Do you have any idea where they were headed?" Gernot allowed his smile to grow wider. This had to be Bryant and the men he was travelling with when Esser encountered them outside Bétheny. Holm would be pleased.

"No… sir." Jacques hung his head. Gernot grabbed him by the hair and pulled his head up so Jacques was looking directly at him. Jacques swallowed and then continued talking. Now he finally loosened his tongue, he was almost babbling. "The man who saved my daughter… he called one of the other men Ken."

"Lowe," Gernot said softly, "which makes his companion Herr Bryant. I thought as much." He let go of Jacques. "Thank you. You've been most helpful. These men are dangerous. Consider yourself lucky you are rid of them."

"Thank you, sir." Jacques seemed subdued, but Gernot wasn't fooled for a moment. He'd seen this kind of deceit before.

Gernot spoke into his telephone. "Esser, please come to

my office. I have a task for you. Tell Beutel to come in as well."

It only took a moment until the door opened and the two men entered. Both stood at attention, although Esser glanced at Jacques and raised an eyebrow.

Gernot decided to ignore Esser's unspoken question. He'd soon learn to stop his incessant questioning. Esser was there to follow Gernot's orders. Nothing more and nothing less.

"Oberscharführer, take this man away." Gernot sat down and began sorting through the rest of his papers. "Oh, and Esser?" he added in a casual tone when Esser had almost reached the door.

"Yes, sir?"

"Kill the hostages. They are no longer useful."

Jacques turned and stared at Gernot, a look of horror and disbelief on his face. "But I told you everything I know. I don't know where these men have gone."

"Yes, and I've thanked you for your information." Gernot smiled. "I *might* even consider ignoring your poor daughter's reputation. It's such a shame it is in shreds." His tone hardened, the smile no longer necessary. "Don't take me for a fool. I know you waited for as long as you could before telling me what you knew. I saw you glance at the clock several times. You were giving the traitors time to get away. Consider yourself fortunate I don't order your execution as well."

"But you promised…"

Gernot gave Beutel a nod. "Find this excuse for a man a cell with a view of the execution, and show him what to expect if he continues to hold back information when I ask for it." He had another job for Esser, one that would teach him the importance of following orders without question.

"Yes, sir." Beutel saluted. He shoved Jacques forward, and they left the room.

Gernot considered for a moment. He hadn't promised Jacques anything, had he? After all, it wouldn't pay to show any weakness. No, he hadn't. It wasn't his fault people continuously heard what they wanted to.

"Esser." Gernot glanced up at him. "I've decided you can organise the firing squad. Make sure the executions are carried out efficiently and quickly. There is no point waiting another hour until curfew. Our prey is long gone, and we don't want any further unpleasantness." He'd found from experience that loved ones tended to cause trouble if their relatives and friends lingered in pain. "Oh, and arrange to get any mess cleaned up. I don't want any sign that this ever took place."

"Yes, sir." Esser saluted. "And the girl, sir? The prisoner's daughter?"

"Bring her in for questioning. He obviously cares for her, which might be useful." Gernot uncapped his pen and began reading through the rest of his papers. He didn't know how Holm found the time for all this paperwork. It was tiring, and he had more important things to do. Bryant and his team were still out there, but not for much longer. After months of no leads, the game was in play again.

He stretched and poured a glass of water, then looked at his watch and tapped it to make sure it hadn't stopped. How long did it take to line up four people and execute them? It appeared Esser was waiting until curfew after all. Gernot felt a trickle of annoyance. He sipped his water and walked over to the window, glass still in his hand.

Gernot stood lost in thought for a while, allowing himself to imagine Lehrer's expression when he found the broken body of the man he'd made the mistake to call friend. Finally he forced himself back to reality. As pleasant as his musings were, he needed to deal with Esser and remind him of his orders. He was about to pick up the telephone when four gunshots sounded in the distance, followed by the pathetic noise of a woman crying.

His stay in Pont-Audemer was almost at an end. Although he'd allowed his prey to slip through his fingers, it would not happen again.

CHAPTER TEN

Arlette had been quiet since they'd left Lisieux. The message she'd received from Matt's team hadn't said much, but given the warning to avoid Bayeux and take another route to Cyrville-sur-Mer, something must have happened.

Although Michel had questioned her further, she didn't appear to know anything more. Instead, she'd asked him whether there was something he wasn't telling her. Was the search of the train simply a random check? He'd turned the conversation back towards her, asking if she was certain the villagers of Cyrville-sur-Mer could be trusted. She'd muttered something about whether he trusted her—glanced at Kit—and then asked whether their friendship was as important to him as it was to her.

Kit, sensibly, had stayed out of the conversation, although Michel could tell he was concerned. If Matt's message was because they'd had a near encounter with Holm or one of his men, Michel and his team could be walking into a trap instead of a safe house.

"She's worried," Kit whispered as they approached one of

the farms at the outskirts of the village. "She also thinks you're lying to her."

"I hope you're not suggesting I tell her everything." Michel raised an eyebrow. Surely the look she'd given Kit didn't mean she'd worked out the real reason he'd gone with Michel to meet his parents? It was more likely she was questioning their mission and Kit's true identity.

Arlette had gone ahead, insisting she make sure the farm hadn't been compromised, so they had a few minutes to speak freely.

"Of course not, but—" Kit stopped midsentence. "Matt's approaching. Perhaps this is a conversation we should continue later, hmm?"

Matt smiled when he saw them, although he didn't look happy. "Our truck was pulled over by one of Holm's officers outside Bétheny, and Reiniger was in Pont-Audemer. He didn't see us, but it was a close call. Did you run into any trouble?"

"Just what was probably a routine check on the train," Michel said. "Arlette is concerned it was more."

"Oh?" Matt raised an eyebrow. "You said 'probably.' So you don't think it was routine either?"

"The soldiers didn't appear to be looking for anyone specifically," Kit said. "If they'd had our descriptions, I doubt we would be here now."

As they approached the cowshed, Michel heard raised voices. A moment later, it grew quiet, also not a good sign. He didn't need to hear the specifics of the conversation to know Arlette was angry.

"Sébastien knows Holm is hunting us. My guess is he's just told Arlette." Matt paused at the bottom step of the stairs leading to the room above the shed. "I can try to talk to her first if you'd like."

Michel shrugged. "I doubt it would make any difference."

Nevertheless, he waited a minute before following Matt up the stairs.

Part of him didn't blame her, although he still thought he'd made the right decision. The less anyone knew about this mission, the better.

Kit caught Michel's arm. "You did what you thought was right," he murmured. "She wouldn't have been happy learning about this if you'd told her."

"I know, but she won't see it that way." Michel steeled himself for what was to come, then sprinted up the stairs to join the rest of the team, Kit following behind.

"You should have told us about Holm!" Arlette turned to face Michel as soon as he entered the room. He flinched from the anger in her voice and instinctively took a step back.

"You were told what you needed to carry out your mission," Ken said calmly. "If London decided you needed to know anything else, they would have passed along the information."

"Marcel is right." Matt stepped into the conversation. "Our mission is classified. The fewer people who know about it, the better."

Arlette kept glaring at Michel as though the whole situation was solely his fault. "I wasn't—I'm not asking for the specifics of your mission," she said evenly, "but I think the fact that you have SS officers hunting you might be pertinent to trying to keep you safe. It's more difficult to go unnoticed when they are circulating photographs and descriptions of you."

"We don't know—" Michel started to say.

"Of course they'll have your descriptions, even if they don't have any photographs." Arlette shook her head. "I would have never suggested taking the train if I'd known about this. What if you'd been recognised! You're risking all of us."

Now Holm had confirmation they were in the area, he'd step up his search. Months of no news would have hampered his ability to do so. Even SS officers had to follow orders from their superiors, and his would be growing weary of his continued failure to find them. The sighting in Port-Audemer was exactly what he'd needed.

"It wasn't Michel's decision." Kit stepped between them. "He is acting under orders, the same way you are."

As much as he appreciated Kit trying to protect him, Michel didn't want him stretching the truth on his behalf. "We hadn't seen Holm or his men in months. We'd hoped we'd lost them."

That wasn't exactly the truth either. While they'd hoped they'd lost Holm, it had always been a matter of *when* rather than *if* he caught up with them again. Holm was not a man who gave up easily, especially when his reputation was at stake.

Sébastien rolled his eyes. "Hoped? How do you expect us to complete our mission when you withhold important information? As Arlette said, we're not asking about the specifics of your mission, but *our* mission is—"

"Your mission was to get us to Normandy safely, and you've done that," Matt reminded him. "I'm sorry you're angry about this, and I can understand it, but nothing has gone the way it was supposed to since we arrived in Germany. We've lost good men and people we care about. If you want to be relieved of your duties and return to your original Resistance cell, I won't stand in your way."

"I'm not leaving. Someone has to stay and make sure this doesn't happen again. You're lucky you weren't caught and killed." Arlette folded her arms, and her expression narrowed. "Who is Holm after exactly? I doubt it's all of you."

"That's… complicated," Michel said. The less she knew about Kit's role in all this, the safer he'd be. "We can't tell you that without compromising the security of the mission. We need to get our team out of France and will do what is needed to ensure that happens."

"Are you going with your friends?" Arlette asked.

Michel shook his head. "No. I'm…" He fought the urge to glance at Kit. "I'm staying in France and continuing our fight to free our country once this is done."

"Good." Arlette's expression softened. "I apologise for my outburst. I knew this mission was dangerous, but I didn't realise it was personal. It is, isn't it?"

What else had Sébastien told her?

"That's one way of putting it," Liang muttered. "Sébastien, are you still with us too?"

"I'll stay and see this through. I didn't sign up for the Resistance without realising the danger involved. I still say it's better to die this way than to spend the war working for *them*." Sébastien glanced at Michel but directed his next comment to Matt. "I still agree with Arlette about needing to know the SS is after you. It's difficult, not to mention dangerous, making decisions when you only have half the information."

"Thank you," Matt said. "We will share any information that we are able to, but I'm not about to disobey orders and risk my team by telling you anything else."

"Fair enough," Sébastien said. "I will keep my opinions to myself as long as you do not place any members of *my* team in unnecessary danger because of the secrets you must keep."

Although Michel didn't know Sébastien that well, Arlette had told him that he was originally from Lisieux and had worked with the Resistance in the Normandy area since joining the Maquis.

"Fair enough," Matt echoed. "Now, the sooner we check

in with London, the sooner we can make plans to leave." He looked at his watch. "It's time we met with the Resistance here. There should be a message for us, and we need to compose an answer to send to London."

"We're supposed to meet at the church," Sébastien said. "Don't worry. We're not spending the whole time we're here in this room above the cowshed. The local priest has made arrangements for a safe house we can use."

"I'm looking forward to a proper bed." Arlette turned to Michel. "Do you remember Nicolas and Théo?"

"Yes." The two boys had grown up in the same village as Michel and Arlette, but they'd moved away just before the war. They'd been good friends and inseparable. Michel had once wondered if they were keen on each other until Théo had been caught kissing a girl behind the church. Shortly after he'd left, she'd discovered she was pregnant, but Michel had no idea whether Théo knew about it or not.

"They're with the Resistance here. We'll be working with them." Arlette chuckled at his expression of disbelief. "They're only five years younger than we are. Hardly the boys you remember. Nicolas's wife, Cécile, is active in the Resistance too."

"Did Théo marry?" Now Michel thought of it, he remembered Théo had family in Normandy. When he'd left the Melun area, Nicolas had followed him.

"No. I don't think he ever got over his broken heart." Arlette seemed to be relishing the chance to update him with the local gossip now she'd recovered her good mood. "Sometimes you only get one chance at true love. I think it's very romantic, but I feel so sorry for him."

Liang said something quietly to Kit, who shrugged. Michel met his gaze, but Kit shrugged again. Kit felt uncomfortable when Arlette insisted on taking over a conversation like this. Michel wished he could tell Arlette the truth, but it was part of what couldn't be said.

"Don't go too far, and don't be long," Matt warned Liang as he and Kit began to walk away. "We'll be back from the church soon, and we need to relocate to the safe house. This place will be safe enough in the meantime, but remember Holm has men in the area. The last thing we need is to have our presence confirmed."

"Because that's so much better than him sending men to hunt us down on the off chance we're here." Liang gave Matt an apologetic look as soon as he'd spoken. "Sorry," he mumbled. "The thought of meeting that man again brings back memories I'd prefer to forget."

"No need to apologise. I feel the same way." Matt had a different way of hiding how he truly felt than Liang, although his cheerfulness often didn't quite ring true. The few times he'd mentioned Elise, he hadn't managed to completely hide his grief over her loss. Wounds like that took a long time to heal.

"Do you want me to come with you?" Michel didn't want to spend too much time in Arlette's company reminiscing about a past he didn't want to focus on.

"Marcel and I can handle this," Matt said. "Michel, if Alexandre and Benoit don't return in a few minutes, tell them to continue their conversation inside." Kit and Liang tended to forget the time once they started talking, but although Matt seemed to think they were discussing science, Michel knew better. Kit had found someone else he could confide in, and Michel had encouraged it. He trusted Liang, and it was good to have another perspective on their situation.

"I'll come with you, Julien, and introduce you," Sébastien said to Matt. "As Arlette knows at least two of these men, it might be a good idea if she did as well. Besides, you will need someone to translate. They speak a little German, but not much."

Arlette gave him an annoyed look. Michel hid a smile and thanked Sébastien silently. "Good idea," he said.

The village of Cyrville-sur-Mer wasn't very big, but it had an active Resistance cell that had made its presence known in the Normandy area. Matt followed Arlette and Sébastien as they led the way to the church. The steeple in the distance towered over the two-story brick-and-mortar houses.

Arlette paused as they entered the square and shook her head in response to something Sébastien said to her. They were speaking French, and Matt couldn't follow their conversation as they spoke quickly. While his understanding of the language was growing the longer they were in France, he was well aware of how much he still didn't know.

"She's still angry with Sébastien for suggesting she come with us," Ken said softly from behind Matt. "I can hear it in her voice. Alexandre thinks she is sweet on Michel."

"He's not interested in her." Matt still suspected Michel and Kristopher were together, although he hadn't said anything to either of them. They glanced at each other and Michel's expression softened when he talked to Kristopher, but they'd gotten more discreet since Arlette and Sébastien had joined their group. If they were together, it complicated the conversation he had to have with Kristopher about staying in France. Matt had wondered whether he should broach that subject with Michel first, but he wasn't the easiest man to talk to.

"You'd think she'd get the hint. He's made it clear enough." Ken fell into step with Matt, walking next to him. He kept his voice low, though, so they wouldn't be overheard, and continued speaking in English. "I hope he's not making a mistake."

"You think he should play along with her?"

"No, but he can't tell her what we suspect is the truth either. If she reacts badly and reports it, they'll be arrested." Ken had sounded surprised when Matt had voiced his suspicions about Michel and Kristopher, but a couple of days later had agreed with him. "It's an impossible situation, and she was angry enough when she found out we hadn't told her about Holm."

"She and Sébastien both," Matt said. "He doesn't show his anger as obviously as she does, but it's there all the same. The tone of his voice changes, and he has a twitch above his left eye."

Arlette and Sébastien began walking again, her shoes echoing against the cobbled street. Sébastien followed a little way behind her, his step more deliberate, and dragging one leg slightly behind him. She kept to the shadows once they'd crossed the square. A couple of villagers gave her a nod, and she replied in kind.

"I hope you're not suggesting we tell them about our mission." Ken slowed his pace to keep a decent distance between them and Arlette and Sébastien. Instead of crossing the square, he and Matt walked around the outskirts and took care not to draw attention to themselves.

"That's not my decision, and even if it were, I don't think it's a good idea. We're working with them because we have no choice, but be careful." Matt hadn't made up his mind yet about either of them. Arlette's feelings for Michel complicated things, and Sébastien asked too many questions.

Sébastien turned left and headed down a narrow street. He didn't check that Matt and Ken were still following. A couple more minutes led them to a house near the church.

Arlette opened the door and went inside, but Sébastien waited outside for them to catch up.

"This house belongs to the church," he explained. "It's often used for meetings." He ushered them inside.

To Matt's surprise, there was no one there save a priest who looked up as they entered.

"Bonjour, je m'appelle Père Aubert." He stood and held out his hand.

Matt shook it. "Bonjour, Père. Je m'appelle Julien."

"Marcel." Ken shook the priest's hand in turn.

Sébastien said something to Père Aubert in French. Aubert nodded and smiled.

"Welcome to our village," he said in halting German. "My apologies. My German is not good." He was an older man, at least in his sixties, with his hair greying at the temples.

"I don't suppose you speak English, Father?" Ken asked hopefully in English.

"A little." Aubert held up his thumb and forefinger, then narrowed the distance between them to about half an inch. "A very little."

Probably as much as Matt spoke French, if that.

"Merci. Can you tell him not to worry about it?" Matt asked Sébastien. "And thank him for his help."

Sébastien nodded and said something to Père Aubert in French.

The priest nodded and smiled. "Merci."

They'd need to rely on Arlette and Sébastien to translate. As soon as he was able, Matt would organise for Michel to meet Père Aubert and confirm the information he'd been given matched what he was supposed to have been told. Liang, too, was fluent in French, and could be helpful in speaking directly to those helping them. Any report reaching Holm that a Chinese man had been sighted might alert him to their presence, but if Liang only spoke to those who knew they were there anyway, it wouldn't be too big a risk and worth it for ease of communication.

Given Holm most likely suspected they were in the area, they'd all need to keep out of sight. Not just because of that, but to prevent questions being asked about how they'd avoided the Service du Travail Obligatoire. They'd chosen Cyrville-sur-Mer as a location in part because there were only a couple of Germans posted nearby. Both of them had gone to Caen for the day, so it was safe for Matt and the others to be out in public. If they were stopped by the local Gendarmerie, they had papers feigning an injury to excuse them from their duty.

"Follow me." Sébastien opened what looked like a cupboard door and knocked on it with a staccato pattern. The rhythm sounded familiar, but Matt couldn't place it. Sébastien then pulled back the shelves, which were full of linen, to reveal another door behind it leading to steps. Matt followed Sébastien down into a room with no windows. Although it was well hidden, it also had the potential to become a trap.

He wondered if the room had once been a basement of sorts. A lone uncovered bulb provided enough light to see by, but it didn't quite reach the corners of the room, leaving shadows skulking there that Matt didn't want to think about. He shivered, dismissing memories that were better left in the past where they belonged.

Two tables at right angles took up the centre, with a collection of mismatched wooden chairs around one of them. The other held a radio set. Ken walked over to it immediately, examined it quickly, and then gave Matt a thumbs-up signal. Once they got the introductions out of the way, he'd want to use it.

Sébastien must have noticed Matt scanning the room. He

smiled. "There is a trapdoor in the corner. Don't worry. We have no intention of being caught like rats down here."

"Good." Matt hoped it wouldn't come to that. Crawling through a tunnel to escape Reiniger once had been enough. He still felt embarrassed about how he'd reacted to the dark, enclosed space, but wasn't sure he'd cope with it any better a second time.

Two men and a woman looked up as they entered. They were all a little younger than Matt and Ken but not by much. Arlette had gone ahead and was talking animatedly with the woman. The conversation died as soon as she saw Sébastien.

What had they been talking about? Matt wasn't sure he wanted to know.

The woman stood and held out her hand. "Bonjour, je m'appelle Cécile." She indicated the men with her. "Nicolas and Théo."

Matt shook hands with her and then with the men. "Bonjour. Je m'appelle Julien." He introduced Ken. "Marcel."

Cécile nodded, then turned to Arlette.

"Cécile is our courier," Arlette explained. "Nicolas, her husband, has expertise with explosives. Théo is our radio operator. They do not speak much German, so it is better if Sébastien and I interpret. There are others in our group, but we do not all meet at the same time. It is safer that way."

"Yes, it is," Matt agreed. "Once Marcel has contacted London, we'd like to work out how we can help you while we're here." They'd not sat idle while making their way across Germany, and this would be no different. He, Ken, and Michel had skills and experience that could be useful to the Resistance. Kristopher wouldn't be happy being left out, but he was too valuable to risk in the field.

Arlette nodded and presumably translated what Matt had said. Nicolas replied in French and smiled. "All help is gratefully accepted," she said. "They've lost a few men and women over the past months."

"Contact your superiors, and then we will go from there." Sébastien said something to Théo, who hesitated, but after Sébastien repeated whatever it was he'd said, he took Ken over to the radio set. "He is protective of it," Sébastien explained, "but I promised him you're experienced and will give it the respect it deserves."

"Merci." Ken examined it for a moment, then smiled. "He built this?" Sébastien nodded. "Tell him I'm impressed."

It was a shame Ken and Théo couldn't speak directly. It had been a while since Ken had had someone to talk to about his passion for radios. Matt followed along as best as he could, but despite his background as a mechanic before the war, his knowledge about the specifics of how to build a radio was limited. Perhaps Liang could translate for Ken so he and Théo could at least have a conversation of sorts.

As soon as Ken began tapping out the coded message, Matt turned away. He wasn't about to hover, and Ken didn't appreciate it. Ken would tell him what was said, and in the meantime, Matt would do his bit to distract their new friends from listening in too closely.

"Is our lack of French going to be a problem?" he asked Sébastien. "We understand more than we speak, but it is limited. Benoit's French is better than ours, though the language is new to him too. Alexandre is fluent, so perhaps he could help to save you and Arlette from having to continuously translate for us. He also doesn't have much in the way of field experience, so doing that would work better too."

"I figured he didn't." Sébastien looked thoughtful.

Liang had already told Matt about the conversation he'd had with Sébastien in the truck. If he wanted to think Liang carried the information they needed to get out of France, that was fine with Matt.

"Does Benoit have any field experience?" Arlette asked. "I'm guessing not, but I'm sure we can find something he can do." She paused. "I wouldn't have thought he was Jewish, but then appearances can be deceiving, and no one is what they seem in this war, are they?"

She was fishing for information, which Matt wasn't prepared to give her. Better to let her think Kristopher was a Jew they'd helped escape from Germany. "Not always," he agreed.

"We're going to be here at least a couple of weeks." Ken got up from the radio and walked over to Matt. "London says we are to wait for further instructions, but it may be a while. Meantime we are to help the local Resistance in any way we can, but…"

Matt guessed what was coming. "We keep the parcel safe and out of sight?"

"Yes, and they will organise extraction. They are sending someone to collect… it, so our mission is almost complete. He or she will be arriving next week with the supply drop." Ken shrugged but didn't comment further, although Matt had a fair idea what he was thinking.

When Ken had contacted London after Matt had been captured by Holm in Berlin, he'd been told that their priority was to get Kristopher and the information he carried to the Allies. Matt, and by extension, the rest of the team were expendable. Liang had already confirmed the validity of the formulae, so he was no longer needed either.

If they survived the next few weeks, they'd be going home. Matt sighed. If London was sending someone to make sure Kristopher left France, their situation had just become even more complicated. He couldn't put off the conversation he needed to have with Kristopher any longer. A decision would have to be made and soon. They were running out of time.

CHAPTER ELEVEN

"Get down!" Michel hissed. He dived behind the shed next to the main station building and crouched low. Beside him, Ken laid a hand on his shoulder, pointed behind them, and shrugged.

Michel cocked his head, silently asking where the hell Sébastien and Nicolas were, but Ken shook his head. The two men had been a couple of metres behind him a moment ago.

This mission from the SOE wasn't going according to plan at all. It was supposed to be straightforward—blow up a section of railway track to delay supplies being shipped to Caen this next evening. They had received the mission specs directly from London, so they knew it was an important one.

The shed they were hiding behind was part of an old railway station the Germans had taken over, so it wasn't used by civilians. The station wasn't always manned, and tonight it was supposed to be deserted. Why were these soldiers here?

"Search the area!" The Oberleutnant in charge barked the

order. "You're looking for explosives and anyone out after curfew." Footsteps pounded the ground near them. At least six men, if Michel had counted correctly. He heaved a sigh of relief as they passed by his hiding place, although it would only be a matter of time before they returned.

Not only were the soldiers here when they weren't supposed to be, but they knew the Resistance had targeted this section of track that night.

Michel heard a noise to their left. He pulled his gun, ready to shoot whoever came around the corner.

"It's only me," Sébastien whispered. He ducked down to a crouch next to Michel and Ken. "Nicolas has gone to check the explosives. I told him not to, but he wouldn't listen."

"He'll either get caught or blown to hell," Ken said grimly. They were lucky the soldiers hadn't found the explosives yet. It was only a matter of time before they did. "Either way, we need to stop him. That, and we need to retreat. We can't risk any of us falling into enemy hands."

"This mission needs to be completed." Sébastien started to argue, but Michel shook his head.

"I agree with Marcel. We've heard enough to know the soldiers are looking for explosives. For now, they only suspect we're still here, and I'd prefer we didn't confirm it."

"I overheard one of them talking," Sébastien said. "They don't merely suspect we're here. They know we are. Either we have a traitor in our cell, or it's a very lucky guess we'd target this spot tonight."

Ken glanced at Michel. "We'll discuss that later. Michel, you and Sébastien get out of here. I'm going to get Nicolas. Whatever happens, keep going."

"I'm not leaving you here," Michel protested.

"Someone has to tell the others we've been compromised," Sébastien said. "Nicolas knew the risks. We all did."

"We're wasting time arguing," Ken said. "We've started this, and I want to see it through. Get out of here. Now."

Michel thought quickly. "You'll need a distraction." He reached into his bag and pulled out a stick of plastic explosive. Nicolas had figured they probably wouldn't need all the explosives they carried, and he'd been right. No point in wasting what could be put to good use next time, he'd said.

"That might work," Ken said. "What are you planning to blow up?"

"What about this shed?" Sébastien suggested. "Nicolas has set his charges further down the line, and it's not as though we're planning to stay here with those soldiers coming back."

"Good idea." Michel nodded. "Sébastien, you head back to the church now so you can pass the information on to the rest of the cell, and I'll wait long enough to give Marcel time to get to Nicolas."

"And for the soldiers to come back around this way," Ken pointed out the flaw in the plan.

"It's going to take them at least ten minutes to secure the area. If we do this now, I have at least five before they return, and a couple to get clear." Michel didn't miss the dubious look on Ken's face. "Don't worry. I'll set the charge with a long enough delay so I'm nowhere near it when it blows."

"All right," Ken said. "Be careful. Don't wait for me or Nicolas. We'll meet both of you at the church."

Sébastien nodded and slipped away into the darkness. Michel caught Ken's shoulder before he could leave. "If I'm captured, tell Kit I'm sorry, and make sure he leaves the area immediately."

"I will." Ken gave Michel a curt nod. "See you soon."

❧

Kristopher looked up in surprise when Matt placed a steaming cup of tea in front of him and then sat down on the chair opposite. "Thank you." He'd wondered why Matt hadn't volunteered for this mission when he seemed keen to be out in the field. It appeared he was about to find out. "What do you want to talk about?"

"That obvious, huh?" Matt's voice was light but strained. Whatever it was he wanted to discuss wasn't good.

"A little." Kristopher took a sip of his tea, if it could be called that. Still, it was better than what was masquerading as coffee.

Michel, Ken, and Sébastien had left with Nicolas a couple of hours ago. Liang had gone with Arlette to the church. He'd said he wanted to learn more about the area, but Kristopher had overheard Matt asking him to speak to the members of the Resistance cell directly, as he didn't need a translator. While Michel trusted Arlette, Kristopher didn't, but suspected his feelings towards her were coloured by her flirting with Michel.

"Have you thought about what you're going to do when it's time to leave?" Matt asked.

"Yes." Kristopher put his cup down. "You've thought about it too, haven't you?"

Had Matt come to the same conclusion Kristopher and Michel had? Kristopher laced his fingers together, his knuckles white, and waited for Matt's reply.

"If this weapon is as dangerous as you say it is…" Matt sounded cautious as though he wasn't sure how Kristopher was going to react.

"It is."

"Benoit…" Matt cleared his throat.

"We're speaking English," Kristopher said softly, "and we're alone. If we're going to talk about what I think we are,

I'd prefer not to use assumed names. This conversation will be difficult enough without that."

"Although we're alone, I'd prefer not to take any chances. If Holm found out you were here…"

"That's true." Kristopher thought for a moment. "Why don't you call me, Kit, hmm? It is still my name, after all." He needed to get used to others besides Michel and Clara calling him that if it was the name he was going to adopt after this was over. He'd also introduced himself to Michel's parents as Kit.

"Thank you." Matt seemed surprised by the offer.

"I'd like to think we're friends after everything we've been through together. I'd even go as far as to say close friends." Kristopher would miss Matt and the others. Michel would too, although he'd probably not admit it so readily.

"I'd like to think that too." Matt sighed. "There's no easy way to say this, and I know you well enough to suspect you've probably thought about it already."

Kristopher could see Matt's struggle to say what needed to be said. "I'm not crossing the Channel with you. This weapon is dangerous and shouldn't be in the hands of either side. I need to disappear, and it would be better if there was some kind of proof that I'm dead."

"I've thought it through a lot, and so has Ken, but we're struggling to come up with a way to provide the proof." Matt shrugged. "I'm guessing you and Michel have talked it over too?"

"Yes." He wasn't surprised Matt had talked to Ken, or that Matt figured Michel knew Kristopher wasn't planning to leave France. "We…" Kristopher caught himself in time. Even if Matt suspected the true nature of Kristopher and Michel's relationship, it was safer not to voice it aloud. "Michel has contacts. It would be easy to disappear." He took a deep breath. It had to be done and although they weren't talking about his actual death, it still unnerved him a little to talk about it. "We're not sure how to fake my death. We'd need a body, and neither of us is prepared to kill someone to get it."

Matt held up his hands. "We're not prepared to do that either. The good thing is that I don't think anyone on our side has your description. Hell, I thought we were looking for a much older guy, although I worked out quickly who you were after we met in the Black Forest."

Kristopher wasn't sure whether to be insulted by that comment or not. "I'd like to think it at least took you a couple of days."

Matt laughed. "It's difficult to hide when you're living with someone in close quarters for a few days."

"I guessed who you were too, but I couldn't risk saying something only to find I'd made a mistake." Kristopher lowered his voice although they were alone. "It's not always wise to put thoughts into words."

"No, it's not." Matt nodded slowly. Hopefully he understood what Kristopher was saying. "Especially when it's something you really want to tell someone or talk about."

"I won't need my identification papers." Kristopher moved the conversation back to safer ground. "What if I leave them with you, and you plant them on someone who is already dead?"

"You have new ones?" Matt asked the obvious. "You won't get far without them."

"Yes. Michel's arranging it. As I said, he has contacts." Kristopher drained the rest of his tea and grimaced at the taste. It was definitely better hot. "The less you know, the less you have to lie to your superiors about."

"There are ways of lying while still telling the truth. Don't worry about that. And this stays between us."

"I will be telling Michel about our conversation, as you will be telling Ken." Kristopher hesitated. "Liang needs to know too. He's an intelligent man and a good friend." He felt as though a weight had been lifted off him. "I thought we'd be doing this alone, and I felt bad about deceiving you, about letting you think…" He trailed off, not wanting to add the words.

"This mission is going to fail," Matt said firmly, "at least from the perspective of our superiors. But I think we've taken the only course we can. There's one problem, though." A frown creased his brow. "I know we're at war, but I don't see any convenient dead bodies lying around, do you?"

"I'm nearly done." Nicolas turned around long enough to give Ken a quick glance before focusing on the explosives in front of him. He'd known more German than Arlette had claimed, which made this mission a lot easier.

"Leave it," Ken ordered. "Mission's been compromised. The place is crawling with Germans. We need to get out of here."

"I *said*, I'm nearly done." Nicolas retrieved another detonator from his bag and crushed the end of it under the heel of his boot. "Good thing I came back. Not sure why it didn't go off, but I hate going to all this effort for nothing."

"I don't want to be the one to explain how you got blown to pieces." Ken knelt in the dirt next to Nicolas. Perhaps if he got down to Nicolas's level, it would help to get the message across. "Especially to your wife."

"You don't have to." Nicolas inserted the detonator into the explosive, threw his tools in a bag, and stood. "I'm done." He shook his head. "You need to have more faith, mon ami."

"How long is the timer?" Ken asked.

"Long enough." Nicolas spoke as though he was

imparting casual information about a timetable. He turned suddenly and frowned. "Oh, that's why… Merde! Run!"

Ken didn't need to be told twice. He turned and ran, Nicolas behind him. They'd barely gotten clear before an explosion behind him lifted him into the air, and he hit the ground with a loud thud. He stood and wiped mud off his clothes. "What the hell?"

"The detonator I thought hadn't worked, decided to work after all." Nicolas grinned as he sat up next to Ken. He ran a muddy hand through his hair, then replaced his beret. "Good thing there was something soft to cushion our fall, hmm? We should go. I'm sure that's attracted attention."

"I'm sure it—" Ken automatically ducked at the sound of another loud explosion further down the track. Michel had detonated his explosive and blown up the shed. Hopefully the soldiers would head there first as it was closer. "That's our distraction. Come on."

Luckily Nicolas followed Ken without arguing. "The Germans won't know which way to go first."

"That's the idea, so we're going completely in the opposite direction, and the long way back through the woods. Michel was going to give himself plenty of time, rather than cutting it short like we—you—did."

Matt would be worried, especially after Sébastien told him what had happened, but better late back than not at all.

"Sometimes these things have a mind of their own. That's one of the challenges of—" Nicolas froze. "Did you hear that?"

Ken grabbed Nicolas and ducked behind some shrubbery. He drew his gun and motioned for Nicolas to say silent. A few moments later, two soldiers ran past their position. Fortunately they were heading in the opposite direction towards the railway line.

Oh hell. Not good. Not only were there soldiers by the original target, but patrolling the woods nearby.

"They knew we were coming," Nicolas whispered. It wasn't a question.

"Yes," Ken said grimly. They'd have to sit there and wait until they were sure it was clear.

"They'll be here." Matt paced across the hidden room in an attempt to stay calm. When Liang had come to the safe house to tell them Ken and Nicolas hadn't returned from the mission, Matt and Kit had headed for the church immediately. Liang remained behind in case Ken and Nicolas returned to the safe house instead of the church.

Matt turned to Michel. "You're sure the Germans were expecting you?"

Théo looked up from his beloved radio set when Matt spoke to Michel in German, but didn't comment.

"Yes, I'm sure." Michel winced as Arlette cleaned his grazed arm. "It's fine," he told her. "It doesn't need any more attention, and I can look after myself. It's only a scrape, and I've had worse. Better to hit the ground hard than be caught in the explosion itself."

"Fine." She took the cloth and water away.

Matt saw Kit frown. So apparently did Michel.

"Merci," he said to Arlette. "I'm sorry. It's been a long night." He wound a crepe bandage over the graze, tucked the end of it in to hold it in place, and then pulled his sweater down over it.

"Yes, it has." Arlette placed a reassuring hand on Cécile's shoulder. "Your husband will be back soon. If the area is crawling with Germans as Michel said—"

"I already told you it was," Sébastien interrupted. "I'm going upstairs to keep watch."

As he started up the stairs, Matt heard a creaking noise above their heads. "Someone's there," he hissed. He drew his gun and aimed it at the top of the staircase. Sébastien, who was halfway up the stairs, pressed himself against the wall, his gun in his hand.

Arlette silently extinguished the light, and the room plunged into darkness.

Someone knocked at the door and then repeated the rhythm.

"Offenbach," Kit said softly. "It's them."

So that was why the rhythm seemed familiar. Offenbach's *Orpheus in the Underworld*. Elise had loved that operetta.

The door swung open. Sébastien blinked in the sudden light. "You're late." He wrinkled his nose. "And you stink. What happened?"

Arlette turned the light back on. Ken and Nicolas slowly walked down the stairs. Both were covered in mud. Ken looked around the room and smiled when he found Matt. "Sorry we're late. There were soldiers everywhere, and it was safer to wait."

"I was worried." Cécile pulled Nicolas into a hug and kissed him soundly. "Don't do that again!"

"I'm sorry too, ma chérie." Nicolas stroked her hair, leaving muddy streaks through it. He spoke to her quickly in French, no doubt telling her what had happened. Her expression grew dark, and she shook her head.

Matt gave Ken a nod. "*We* were worried." Matt was unable to stop the hoarseness of his voice. God, he wanted to hug Ken and hold him tightly. He glanced at Nicolas and Cécile, wishing he and Ken had the freedom to express how they felt about each other when other people were around.

"I know," Ken said quietly. "I'm sorry."

Once they were alone, Matt intended to show Ken how worried he'd been, and help him get all that mud off too. "They knew you were coming."

"It seemed that way," Ken said.

"I trust everyone in this cell." Arlette hadn't said she trusted everyone in the room.

"Perhaps there's another explanation," Kit said quickly. "I've given this some thought."

Arlette scowled and opened her mouth to argue, but Michel narrowed his eyes.

"Let him speak. If K—Benoit says he has an idea, it's usually worth listening to it. Please continue, mon… ami."

"Merci." Kit took a moment before continuing. "Your cell was operating for some time before Holm took charge of the area. The first thing he would have done is work out whether there are patterns in your attacks. He would have figured out what sabotage would do the most damage and rank those targets in order of importance."

"Maybe you're the traitor." Arlette took a step closer, but Michel stepped between them.

"No," he said firmly. "I trust him with my life. He is no traitor. Listen to what he is saying. It makes sense."

"It's simple strategy, and one he often used when he played chess," Kit explained. "He's a keen chess player and often uses the game to size up potential… allies. Or opponents. We've… umm…" He glanced at Michel as though unsure whether to continue. Michel shook his head, but Matt guessed what Kit had been about to say.

Kit and Holm had played chess together. Probably more than once. It made sense. Holm had been in charge of the institute where Kit worked.

"What do you suggest we do?" Matt asked before Arlette could interrupt again.

"Chess is not merely about wiping your opponent off the

board. There's more finesse to the game than that." Kit avoided looking at Arlette. Probably a good thing as she was glaring at him. "Tonight's mission succeeded in part because you split your attack and took out a target that wasn't essential. I suggest that's what we try next time. We target something not so important first and use that as a distraction while we hit the real one."

CHAPTER TWELVE

"Yes, sir. Very good, sir." Karl waited until the person on the other end of the phone hung up, then shook his head before replacing the receiver on its cradle. Relocating to Pas-de-Calais wouldn't do at all. Luckily his superior had listened to reason in this instance, but Karl's time in Normandy was running out.

He'd bought himself a few days, maybe a week, but no more.

Karl poured some cognac and took a couple of measured sips. How could Lowe and his group disappear so completely? After the sighting in Pont-Audemer, his hopes had risen, only to be dashed again. He'd sent Reiniger and his men to search the Bayeux area but hadn't expected them to find anything. Although Bryant's papers said that was his destination, he wasn't foolish enough to leave such an obvious trail of breadcrumbs.

A knock on the door disturbed his musings. He looked up, then ignored the sound. He was not to be disturbed. This situation required some thought, and he didn't appreciate the distraction.

Whoever it was knocked again, this time louder.

"Herein."

Whoever and whatever this was, it had better be important.

Margarete Huber walked in, holding a pile of papers. "Good morning, Herr Holm," she said cheerfully. She smiled, and for a moment, it almost felt genuine.

"Good morning."

Either she had news, or she was planning something. Or both. Although tempted to send her on her way, he was running out of options. If she had information that might give some clue to the whereabouts of his prey, he'd grit his teeth, return the smile, and feign politeness. Otherwise, the annoying woman was just as likely to mount her own hunt and take credit for the outcome.

Hmm, maybe not. Margarete preferred to work behind the scenes, pulling strings like a puppeteer. Easier that way to keep her hands clean and blame others if it all went wrong. Still, there was the risk she might take the information to someone else if he didn't show some interest.

Karl didn't care about taking credit for Lehrer's arrest, although it would be an added bonus. As long as Lehrer was found, arrested, and paid the price for betraying his country, that would be sufficient. Karl's superiors were not impressed Lehrer's escape from the institute had happened while he was in charge of security. It reflected badly on his career, and worse than that, made him look a fool. Add to that the fact Lehrer was now working with Lowe…

"Do you have something?" Karl asked. Margarete hadn't furthered the conversation, so it was up to him to do it. He hated these games she played. They were not helpful and had cost him valuable time on several occasions. He'd enjoyed her absence while she'd been in Bayeux, although he'd known his peace and quiet wouldn't last once she returned to Caen.

"Why, Herr Holm, here I was thinking you were pleased to see me. Surely you haven't tired of me already? I've been back less than twenty-four hours." Margarete placed the pile of papers she carried on his desk and then sat on the chair opposite him. A piece of paper poked out between two files, and she leaned over to retrieve it.

Karl reached for it. "Allow me, Fräulein." Whatever information it contained was most likely classified. Although she'd probably read whatever she wanted in the files she'd brought him, he had less chance of being implicated if he acted as though he had no knowledge of it.

"Of course, Herr Holm." Margarete lowered her head demurely. "Some things don't stay where they are meant to, do they?"

"That can—" Karl's attention was caught by something familiar, a coincidence he couldn't afford to ignore. "Why was this not brought to my attention before?"

He scanned the rest of the page quickly, turning it over when he'd finished, hoping for some clue to its author. This wasn't a part of the files Margarete had brought in. The note was handwritten by someone whose German wasn't very good, judging by the spelling mistakes and incorrect syntax. However, the mistakes could have been deliberate and intended to direct blame away from its perpetrator.

"Why, we've only just found it." Margarete seemed genuinely curious. "Or rather you've just found it. Would you mind enlightening me as to what seems to have captured your attention so intently?"

"I think you know exactly what this is." For all he knew, she'd put it there for him to find in the first place. Whoever had written the note claimed to have intimate knowledge of a local Resistance cell that had recently gained new members. "But if you want to play your games, so be it."

Her eyes widened. "I never play games, Herr Holm." Margarete managed to sound indignant. "I assure you everything I do has a purpose, and I am as committed to this cause as you are."

That he could believe.

Now wasn't the time to argue with her if he wanted her continued cooperation. Margarete Huber was not a woman he wanted to make an enemy of, and Karl wasn't foolish enough to think he'd come out of any war with her unscathed.

"My apologies, Fräulein," he said hurriedly and handed her the note. "While I am unsure as to whether this information will lead us to Lehrer, it would still be unwise to ignore it."

Margarete read the note and then looked up at him. "The author of this note speaks of a Resistance cell working out of the village of Cyrville-sur-Mer. Isn't that close to an area where the Resistance has been quite active of late? I remember hearing something about disruptions to travel west of Bayeux very recently."

"A station along the Mantes-la-Jolie to Cherbourg railway line was targeted several nights ago," Karl confirmed. He had reprimanded the officer in charge for his negligence. The man had been told that portion of the railway line was a potential target. He had shirked his duty and would not do so again. It had not been that difficult to figure out where the Resistance might strike next and increase security in those locations. Nevertheless his men still managed to let their enemies escape.

Margarete read a part of the note aloud. "One of the men claims to be German yet speaks English with an impeccable British accent. He is referred to as 'Kit' by others in the group when they think they are alone…" She grew silent as she finished reading the note, then handed it to Holm. "How interesting. An English spy pretending to be German and working with the French Resistance. Why, it sounds like fiction." She looked thoughtful. "Hmm… although. There's something familiar about the code name he's using. I'm certain I've heard it before."

Karl glanced at the note again. "I'm not aware of any English spy who uses the name Kit." Perhaps this was yet another false tip? He'd had a few, but none of them had led to the men he sought. Although he'd made several arrests, these Frenchmen and women were annoyingly stubborn when it came to persuading them to share information.

"Oh!" Margarete exclaimed. "That's it. Of course."

"Of course?" Karl asked. Did she expect him to drag every bit of information from her?

Margarete looked smug, as though she'd only now worked out whatever it was. "Kit is an English nickname for Kristopher."

"Kristopher Lehrer?" Lehrer spoke English, but to be mistaken for an Englishman? It was ridiculous. His mother had been English but died before Lehrer was born. The man had been raised a German and had never set foot outside the country until now. "It could be a coincidence."

"Perhaps, but I think not. I've heard Clara Lehrer call her brother by that name, although not often. You know how it is… one forgets oneself at family gatherings." Margarete smiled. "Of course, it's been several years since our families met socially, which is why I didn't remember it immediately."

"It would make sense that Bryant's team would make contact with a local Resistance cell, and lies work better if there is some truth to them. Not Bayeux, then, but still in that area." A familiar hope built inside Karl. "I'll send someone to investigate immediately." The village wasn't large, so it didn't have many places to hide.

"I'd suggest waiting a day or so. If we move too quickly, they may scatter again, and we'll lose them. Whoever wrote this note can probably be persuaded to share more information. I think he or she is focused on whoever 'Kit' is. The other new additions to their cell are only mentioned in passing, as though they are unimportant." Margarete paused as though reconsidering what she'd said. "Or maybe they are important to him or her, and this Englishman is perceived as a threat and we are a means to an end. It's interesting what motivates someone to betray those they work with, isn't it?"

"It is." Karl hadn't missed the way she'd said "we" rather than "you."

"It will be more efficient if we have a precise location so they are not given the opportunity to run like last time," Margarete continued. "Think of how good it would be to catch not only Lehrer, but the members of the cell who have been causing so much disruption in the area."

"Cast the net wider and catch more fish," Karl said slowly. The idea had merit, although he would discretely keep a closer eye on Cyrville-sur-Mer. No point in being greedy and losing everything because of it. Sometimes in order to win, sacrifices had to be made, and pawns were often not the important piece they thought themselves to be. Whoever had written the note was foolish to think Karl would simply allow them to deliver his prey and walk away.

He had no time for traitors.

Matt glanced at his watch. Two more minutes and Michel's team would be ready with their diversion. So far, so good.

"Sébastien's keeping watch." Ken crouched beside Matt.

"There are a couple of guards on duty and two more inside having supper. If Arlette's information is correct, this will be all over by the time the shift change happens."

"I would have expected more men posted here." Matt shouldn't question their good luck, but he didn't like it. He mentally crossed his fingers and hoped they weren't going to be caught by twice the number of soldiers they expected.

"It's not the only place in the area where this kind of sabotage would be effective." Ken looked up at the telegraph pole a few feet away and swallowed. "As soon as we get the signal, I'll head for the pole."

"That's what we agreed, yes. Or rather what you insisted on."

"You don't agree?" Ken had that edge to his voice that usually came before an argument. He wasn't a man who raised his voice, but Matt hated it when he sounded calm and matter-of-fact about something that was anything but.

"That pole is very high. You're going to have people shooting at you. It makes more sense for me to do it." Matt didn't want to pull rank, but he would if Ken refused to back down. He held out his hand, and Ken handed over the wire cutters.

"Thank you, but we'll talk about this later."

Light lit the sky in the distance and then again about a mile west of the first explosion.

Men's voices raised as the soldiers on duty tried to figure out what was going on. Matt heard running as the guards inside joined in. Better to have all four men in view, rather than be surprised by one being where he wasn't expected.

Nicolas had set timers on several explosives. There should be one more, and then it would be time for Matt's team to move.

Right on schedule, the third explosive blew. They'd decided to hit more than one target that night rather than use the explosions as just a distraction. The Germans would presume one act of sabotage was a distraction for the other, yet both would achieve as much damage. Cutting overhead wires cost the enemy precious time without communication so they didn't find out about Allied bombing raids until it was too late.

"Cover me," Matt hissed. He ran for the pole and began to climb quickly. It wouldn't take long before the soldiers realised the real target.

Crap, how high was this thing? Matt gritted his teeth and continued to climb.

Gunshots sounded below him, an exchange of fire between his team and the soldiers.

One foot missed a foothold. A bullet whizzed past, and he bent his body out, then in again, barely avoiding it. He looked up. Only a few more feet and he'd be there.

Ken and Sébastien could hold their own down there. Four men against two, but they'd fought against worse odds.

The gentle breeze increased in force the higher he climbed. His imagination and fear gave it more power as it buffeted against him and tugged at his hair.

One foot, then the other secure, Matt balanced carefully and pulled out his cutters. He used one gloved hand to hold on to one of the climbing brackets and cut the wires quickly.

Someone yelled out in German below. Shots rang out again.

"Damn it," he muttered after another bullet came way too close. He ducked, then scrabbled to find a hold as he fell. He grabbed one of the metal brackets with both hands, hung there for a moment until he felt something solid under one foot, then the other.

Someone screamed in pain. He peered beneath him and edged down as far as he dared. Too high and he wouldn't survive the fall. Another couple of feet. Almost there. He tensed and leaped, then hit the ground with a dull thump.

"Down," Sébastien yelled.

Matt dived as a shot went over his head from behind him. Fuck. Were the soldiers behind him? The longer he stayed here, the more of a target he was.

Shots hailed around him as soon as he started running. Some from behind, others from the side. Someone—either Ken or Sébastien—covered him as he sprinted across the road to the nearby fence, vaulted over it, and hit the dirt on the other side.

He heard the sound of boots against gravel and a couple more shots. Then suddenly nothing, sounds he expected swallowed up by silence. Matt kept his head down, not daring to look up to check whether it was clear. Give it a few more seconds. Then he'd take the chance. The soldiers could be biding their time and waiting for him to make a mistake. The fence wasn't very high, and if they opened fire, it wouldn't give him much protection.

Matt raised his head a fraction, but couldn't see anything. The front of his shirt felt wet, and something stank. He stifled a cough, his stomach heaving in protest at the horrible smell.

Oh great. He'd dived into a cowpat.

Ken slid in next to him, lying flat in the dirt. "Keep down," he hissed. He raised his gun and shot at someone over the fence.

Matt heard another exchange of bullets from the other side of the fence, then silence. He counted to twenty, sat up, and looked in the direction Ken had fired. A German soldier lay still, face down on the side of the road.

"It won't be long before this area is swarming with soldiers." Ken stood and pulled Matt to his feet. "It's not only the gunfire, but their telephone lines have gone dead. They'll send someone to investigate when the men on duty don't report in, and I doubt they'll wait until the shift change to do it."

Sébastien poked his head over the fence. "I've secured the other guards. Two are wounded, but they'll recover. The other is unconscious. I didn't check his injuries. Come, we need to leave." As Matt and Ken walked over, Sébastien screwed up his nose. "I'm driving. You can both ride in the back. Try and stay downwind until we get back, oui? That smell is disgusting."

Ken handed Matt the soap. "That's twice in one night. I swear, at this rate, I'll be grey before my time."

"Twice what?" Matt rubbed the soap over the wet cloth he was using to clean himself, shivering when the cold water splattered across his skin. He'd already washed his hair, glad he'd trimmed it back to a short military style before they'd left Haguenau, although it still felt damp after he'd dried it.

Sébastien had left them outside by the back door to clean up. They'd moved to this safe house after the mission at the train station. Despite Kit's theory that Holm might have used logic to figure out their target, they'd decided to move to a disused workers cottage on a farm on the outskirts of the village.

Matt had only seen the farmer a couple of times when he'd brought them supplies. The old Frenchman usually only spoke with either Arlette or Sébastien, although he'd had one conversation with Michel about his crops and the work they'd offered to help with. Sébastien was careful to continue to drag his left leg whenever he ventured out so no one would question that his injury prevented him being conscripted yet enabled him to still work on the farm with the help of his wife. Arlette played her role well, and if Matt hadn't known, he would have sworn she was what she pretended to be. He suspected the farmer was a part of the Resistance, but the less either of them knew about the other, the safer it was for everyone.

For the most part, their team kept to the farm, only venturing out for missions and to meet at night with the Resistance cell based at the church.

The village had been well chosen as a safe place to hide, and they were careful to select targets that would not lead back to them. Théo had picked up a few transmissions that confirmed the Germans knew there was an active Resistance cell in the area, but they hadn't figured out their location yet.

"No sign of Sébastien with our clean clothes." Ken took the cloth from Matt and soaked it in the pail of water. "He's either debriefing the others, or he's waiting until it's safe to come near us again."

"Who knew he had such a sensitive nose?" Matt would have laughed at Sébastien's response but didn't know him well enough to know how he would react.

"Turn around. I'll wash your back, and then you can wash mine." They'd taken off their shirts to wash once Sébastien had left, but Matt had kept watch on the door and his back to the fence. "Don't worry, no one can see. I'll make sure of it."

"Thanks." Matt closed his eyes, his breath hissing as Ken gently ran the cloth over the scars on his back. They no longer hurt, but he still tended to flinch whenever someone touched them, even Ken. He preferred that no one saw them, as he didn't want to answer the questions that would follow. While their team knew what had happened to him, Arlette and her cell didn't, and he wanted it to stay that way. "You didn't answer my question. Twice what?"

"It should have been me up that pole."

"You don't like heights. It made more sense for me to do

it." Matt had known how dangerous it would be, and the chance he'd be shot at while he was up there. "There was enough to think about, along with trying not to fall while getting shot at, without diverting your focus. I know how much it takes to ignore the fact you're in the middle of somewhere that scares you shitless."

"You could have been killed." Ken stilled the cloth. "I saw you trying to hang on. I thought you were going to fall." He lowered his voice to a whisper. "I wanted to run to you, but there was nothing I could have done. For one horrible moment, I thought I'd lost you. I… kept seeing you fall, and then when that soldier was shooting at you when you leaped the fence… I thought I saw you go down."

Matt turned so he could see Ken. Ken's face was shadowed, fear reflected in his eyes, and his breathing was ragged with emotion. Even now, the memory of what could have happened clearly terrified him. God, Matt hadn't thought. Ken's fear, and then thinking Matt was going to fall…

"I have nightmares about losing you in the dark," Matt said softly. "You always tell me you'd find me, and I know you'd walk through darkness for me. The same way I climbed that pole today for you." Not only for Ken, as they'd needed to cut those wires and someone had to do it. Matt would never ask someone to do something he wouldn't. But of late, that principle he'd always lived by had become complicated. It wasn't that he wouldn't venture into the dark… He *couldn't*. One thought of it, and he froze and couldn't convince himself he needed to move. He'd only gotten through that tunnel in Freiburg by focusing on Ken's voice, and even then, he'd come too close to breaking down when they'd reached the end only to find there wasn't an exit. Losing Ken scared him more than being lost in the dark.

Thank God it had still been light when he'd climbed the pole. Matt knew he'd never have been able to do it otherwise.

They'd debated waiting until dusk, then decided it was too dangerous at night. The area was deserted, apart from the soldiers on guard who would have been alerted to the presence of saboteurs no matter what time it was, and in the daytime, their truck wouldn't be pulled over because they were breaking curfew.

"No matter what, I'm not leaving you behind." Ken calmly dunked the cloth in the water again.

Matt watched the fragments of mud spread through the bucket. "We'll get through this together." He took the cloth from Ken, squeezed it out, then lathered it again. "Your chest is still dirty. You missed a spot." He worked quickly, rubbing it against Ken's skin, watching the rivulets of water lazily drip down towards his navel. Matt leaned in, stopping the errant drops with his palm. "I'd go through darkness and fire to save you, Ken Tsukino, the same way I know you'd brave heights to reach me if I needed you."

Even as he spoke the words, he shivered. He'd have to find the strength somewhere, but those nights he found himself back in his nightmares, he wasn't so sure he could, even to save the person he loved.

"I'm sorry. I shouldn't—"

"Let's not make promises neither one of us is sure we can keep. The intention is there, that is what matters, right? I know you'd do whatever you could, and that's enough." Ken placed his hand over Matt's, turning as he did, so their joined hands could not be seen. "Please don't scare me like that again too soon."

"I'll wait a few days first, hmm?" Matt kept his tone light and could see by the way Ken's lips curved at the sides that he'd taken it for the joke it was meant to be. Damn it, he wished he could take Ken into his arms and kiss him, that they could hold each other and give in to the illusion that being together was all that mattered in the world.

But it wasn't, and they had a mission to complete.

"Stop thinking," Ken said softly. "It doesn't pay to, with everything going on. Not about this or about us. There will be time for that later."

"Will there?"

"I don't want to think about it until I have to." Ken spoke the words in a matter-of-fact tone, almost devoid of emotion. He did that when he didn't want to talk about something, even if it needed to be said.

"I don't either." Usually Matt would have cracked another joke to try to lighten the mood and move the conversation along, but he couldn't bring himself to do it, and doubted Ken would appreciate it.

Once Matt had finished washing Ken's chest, Ken turned around so Matt could wash his back. Matt could hear Ken's breathing, slow and steady, and he focused on it and the job at hand. After all the crap they'd been through, the last thing they needed was for everything to fall apart now.

"I think that's as clean as it's going to get," Ken said finally. "You've done enough. If there's any smell left, Sébastien is going to have to learn to put up with it."

"We can't stay out here forever." Matt picked up the towel, finished drying himself, then handed it to Ken. There was nowhere to completely hide in this damn place. Only a few stolen moments here and there that could be the final memories either of them had of each other.

"Do you want to?" Ken's question took Matt by surprise.

"Sometimes," Matt admitted, "but it's not a luxury that bears thinking about."

Ken knew what he meant, that they both wished they could ignore the war and live their lives, or what was left of them.

"There are a few of those." Ken folded the towel into quarters once he'd finished with it, picked up the bucket of dirty water, and poured it onto the garden by the side of the fence. He retrieved their filthy shirts and put them in the bucket, then placed the towel on top.

"Everything in its place." Matt had noticed that about Ken very soon after they'd met in basic training.

"Not everything." Ken gave him a smile. "Come on, let's go inside."

Liang met them on the doorstep. "I was coming to find you. We finally have news from London."

"They've been in contact?" Matt frowned. Had he been that distracted he hadn't noticed Cécile arriving? She usually brought any information Théo received that needed to be passed along.

"You could say that." Liang's voice shook as though he was trying not to sound too emotional. Whatever this was, it was big. "Kristopher and I were listening to the BBC. They broadcast the code phrase."

"The first three lines of the Verlaine poem?" Ken raised an eyebrow, disbelief spreading across his face. "Are you sure it was that?"

"Of course I'm sure," Liang said irritably. "Kristopher recognised it immediately, and Michel confirmed it."

"The Allied invasion is imminent." Matt placed one hand on Ken's shoulder and squeezed it. "That's what they meant by sending someone with a supply drop."

"I thought they were referring to our mission," Ken said slowly. "But they weren't. This could be the beginning of the end of this war."

CHAPTER THIRTEEN

"Michel?" Kristopher reached out for Michel, but instead of the warm body of the man he loved, he felt the coldness of a bed that had never been slept in.

He sat up with a jolt and glanced around the room.

What the hell? What was he doing in his bedroom back in Berlin? He'd left that life behind him months ago.

Kristopher reached for his robe, only to find he was already dressed. The room felt chilly, and he could smell blood. He crept quietly down the stairs. He'd been here before. Not just in this house, but…

"No," he whispered. "Not again. I don't want to see this again. I know what I need to do. Isn't that enough?"

"Too late." Clara's whisper echoed around him, impossible to ignore.

"Too late." A new voice joined Clara's. Kristopher recognised it immediately.

"Leo?" This couldn't be real. Leo was dead. He'd died months ago, sacrificing himself to save a group of men he'd barely known.

"Kit!" Michel cried out. "Kit! Help me. Please."

Kristopher didn't think, he reacted. Throwing caution aside, he ran to the dining room and threw open the door.

And found himself in Holm's office.

"How nice of you to finally join us, Herr Doktor Lehrer." Holm smiled. His expression sent a shiver down Kristopher's spine.

To Holm's left, Reiniger stood holding a gun. Michel knelt in front of Reiniger, his hands bound behind him.

"Why did you come? We agreed you wouldn't." Michel looked up at Kristopher. Blood ran down his face from a deep wound across the length of one cheek. "You're supposed to leave me to die." He turned away. "One more thing you've promised to do and can't. Being with you is a death sentence. This is your fault."

Kristopher flinched at Michel's accusing tone. "I… I can't watch you die." He bit his lip, but he couldn't feel any pain. Couldn't feel anything.

"You chose to protect your work. You can't save him." Holm laughed. "People like you don't get happy endings. It's already too late for that." He gave Reiniger a nod.

Reiniger drew a knife, yanked back Michel's hair to expose his neck, and then dragged the blade against his skin, the steel drawing a thin line of blood that trickled down to join the stain already spreading over his shirt.

Kristopher rushed forward, but strong arms held him back.

"No, you can't," Michel hissed into his ear. "Don't give in. You can't let them have this weapon whatever the cost."

Kristopher pulled free, turned, hope rushing through him. But no one was there. He'd only heard another whisper of someone he couldn't save. "Stop it. Stop it. Stop it," he screamed. "I'll give you anything. I'll help you destroy the world if you let him go!"

"Too late." Clara spoke again although he couldn't see her.

Michel fell forward and lay still. He hadn't screamed. His death was silent like the ruined, abandoned city from an earlier nightmare that had haunted Kristopher for so long. Reiniger stepped over the body and handed Kristopher the knife. "You've killed the man you love. Why save the rest of the world?"

"Kit? Kit!"

He heard his name yet couldn't move. The man who called him was gone, his voice joining the choir of those who already haunted him.

"No!" Kristopher stared at the knife. Blood covered his hands, dripping onto the floor, colouring the grey world around him. He dropped the knife and ran to Michel. Kristopher turned him over, frantically looking for any sign of life. The ugly line that ran across Michel's throat confirmed that the man Kristopher hadn't loved enough had been ripped away from him. They'd wanted a future together. Was it really too much to hope for? "This isn't real. It's not too late. It's not—"

"Kit! Wake up."

Kristopher opened his eyes. Michel leaned over him. Kristopher backed away. "You're..." He couldn't bring himself to say the words.

"Shh, mon cher," Michel whispered. He pulled Kristopher close. "I've got you now, and I'm not leaving you. It was a nightmare. It's not real. We're both safe. We're together."

Kristopher saw the unspoken words reflected in Michel's eyes. He nodded, acknowledging them, although he didn't want to say them aloud.

For now.

~

Liang pushed the chessboard to one side. "You're distracted," he told Kristopher. "Why don't we continue the game later, hmm? It's not much of a challenge when you keep making foolish mistakes."

"It is that obvious?" Although Kristopher had figured a game of chess would help to shift his focus elsewhere, he had to admit it wasn't working. Not only had he lost a knight, but he'd followed that not so brilliant move by placing his queen in peril.

"A little." Liang took another sip of tea, leaned back in his chair, and closed his eyes for a moment. Frown lines creased his forehead, and when Kristopher's chair scraped against the floor, he jumped.

If he'd heard Kristopher's nightmare, he hadn't said anything. No one but Michel had spoken of it. Yet Kristopher couldn't rid himself of it or the words that still haunted him.

It's too late. It's too late.

"I'm not the only one who is distracted," Kristopher pointed out, shoving the memory aside. He couldn't afford to dwell on it. "It took you two moves longer than it should have to take my knight," he said calmly, "and I'm not entirely sure you've noticed my last move, or you would have made yours before pausing the game."

"What?" Liang peered at the board. "Oh, of course." He moved a pawn and knocked Kristopher's queen over. "There, that's better. Now we're ready to pick up where we left off."

Nicolas had found a chessboard tucked away at the back of a cupboard at his home. He and Cécile had played the game in the evenings before joining the Resistance. He'd passed it along to Kristopher with the comment it might make the waiting easier.

"You're a good player and usually more of a challenge than this. Do you want to talk about it?"

"Do you?" Liang asked. "About what is troubling you, not

what is troubling me, I mean." He sighed and rolled his eyes. "All right, that didn't come out right. And before you say anything, yes, I know I just admitted there's something."

"It appears we are both avoiding conversations we need to have." Kristopher didn't waste time disagreeing with Liang's earlier observation. Some of his distraction was because he had to talk about what was on his mind but wasn't sure how to bring it up.

"Why don't you go first? I'll even make more tea before we start. I can only stomach this brew if it's nice and… forget I said nice." Liang got up and put the kettle on the stove to boil, then retrieved their cups and rinsed them. "It's hot, and if we drink tea, we can pretend we're being civilised. I'd prefer that than reality at the moment."

"Given that we're hiding in a safe house while our friends are out there risking their lives?" Kristopher didn't like staying behind, but it would be foolish to take part in the mission and risk capture. While he had left the cottage for a few brief walks and travelled between there and the church, he'd taken care to ensure it was a time when not many people were around and no soldiers were in sight. "I keep reminding myself that they've had several successful missions since we've started sending out two teams instead of one. But…"

"I know it's not easy, and it must be worse for you with Michel out there." Liang didn't attempt false optimism. If he was unhappy about something, he didn't keep it to himself, which was why it was strange he hadn't already talked about what was bothering him now. "I'm clinging to the fact this will soon all be over. I don't like staying here any more than you do, but I know my limitations. Besides, someone has to stay here and make sure you don't wander off."

"It's a good thing I know your sense of humour can be sadly lacking at times, my friend." Truth be told, Kristopher enjoyed Liang's company, and it did make the waiting more bearable.

Liang chuckled. "I'm surprised you recognised the code phrase so quickly, given what it was." He refilled the teapot and waited for the tea to brew.

"Verlaine's 'Chant d'automne' is a favourite of one of Michel's cousins. She plays the violin as I do, and given it speaks of the long laments of violins in autumn, Michel figured I might enjoy learning it and practice my French pronunciation at the same time." Kristopher smiled, remembering Michel's patience. "I'm afraid I mangled his language when he first started teaching me. Les sanglots long les violins de l'automne."

"Blessent mon cœur d'une langueur montone." Liang finished the stanza while he poured the tea. When those words were broadcast, it would signal that the Allied offensive would begin within forty-eight hours. "I think your French has improved a lot since we came to France."

"I still have an accent that definitely isn't French." Kristopher was certain that as soon as he opened his mouth, any Frenchman would know he was German. Either that, or English. "My English is much better as I learnt it as a child."

"Your English is impeccable." Liang handed Kristopher his tea, then sat opposite him. "I'd swear you were English when you speak it." He started to pick up his cup, then placed it back on the table. "We are both procrastinating, aren't we? How bad is this thing that you wish to talk to me about?"

"It's… let's say… hypothetical."

"Right." Liang nodded. "After all, if we don't speak specifics, I won't be lying if I say I know nothing when I'm questioned about it."

"Exactly." Kristopher wouldn't have to waste time explaining the reasons he'd chosen to discuss it in this way. During the months they'd known each other, they'd learned to respect each other's ways of approaching a situation. Kristopher would miss Liang after this was all over. He was a good friend, as were Matt and Ken.

Kristopher took a sip of tea, using the motion to gather his thoughts and figure out how he was going to tell Liang what he needed to know. Michel had agreed with Kristopher's decision to tell Liang of the code they'd decided to use, and it would be safer to send the message to him after the war. He wasn't in the military like Matt and Ken and had said several times he planned to return to his quiet life at the university once this mission was over.

"I was thinking… that not everyone is likely to survive this war. Sometimes someone is reported dead when they're still alive. Hypothetically, if that were the case, it might be a good idea to work out a way to get a message to that person's friends so they know he's not dead."

"Hypothetically," Liang said slowly, "I think that's a good idea. After all, those friends would like to know if he survived the war."

Kristopher nodded. "It might not be wise for him to reveal he's still alive." He took a deep breath. "Perhaps he has information that could be used to do a lot of damage and shouldn't be allowed to fall into the wrong hands, whether there's a war on or not."

"The last war was supposed to be the one to end all wars, and not even two decades later we're fighting another one." Liang grew quiet for a moment. "Are you certain this is the right thing to do?"

"I can't see another way. I thought perhaps only until the end of the war, but Michel…" Kristopher shook his head and took a long sip of tea.

"Michel is right." Liang reached over the table and squeezed Kristopher's hand, a gesture that not only was unexpected but appreciated. "You shouldn't trust anyone." He hesitated. "Very few people are whom they seem to be."

"I wish I could forget what I know and everything I've seen, but I can't." Kristopher hated his eidetic memory. At least he was still alive to remember. So many weren't, and there would be more deaths before this was over. "I considered not faking my death, but I couldn't do that to Michel." The look of horror and pain on Michel's face when he'd thought that was what Kristopher intended still haunted him. They'd found some privacy that night, their lovemaking desperate as they'd held on to each other as though they could be ripped apart at any time.

"He has lost enough." Liang cleared his throat and let go of Kristopher's hand. "This is all hypothetical of course, because if you were planning anything, I wouldn't know about it. I couldn't know about it." He bit his lip and flinched. "We already know I'm not good at keeping secrets."

"No one is good at keeping secrets under torture." Kristopher kept his tone even. "Unfortunately, even when there are no secrets to tell, that doesn't stop anyone asking about them."

If his friends were captured, they'd be tortured for information about his whereabouts whether they knew the truth or not. Holm wouldn't stop until he got the answers he wanted, so Kristopher wasn't about to share his and Michel's plans for their future. They'd all done enough things they'd never forgive themselves for without carrying guilt for something they didn't need to.

"As much as I want to believe we will all have a good life after this, I don't need to know the details. Knowing you survive is enough." Liang shrugged. "Although, of course, we're not talking about us, just some blokes we haven't met and aren't likely to."

"Of course." Kristopher could hear the shake in Liang's

voice. Despite his nonchalant tone, he obviously wouldn't be happy about parting ways forever either. "Sometimes I wonder if the cost of all of this is too high already."

"Yes, it is, but we don't have a choice. Tell me about this code of yours, and then we'll change the subject. I don't really want to think about any of it until I have to. It doesn't sit well with what is already on my mind."

"I'm nearly done," Kristopher said. They should have talked about what was troubling Liang first. "I'm sorry, Liang. This isn't easy."

"Kristopher," Liang started to say, but Kristopher shook his head.

"Kit," he said softly. "Call me Kit. You're more than a good friend, Liang. This team is the closest I have to family now." Kit blinked rapidly to clear his eyes of the tears that threatened to form. Why did he feel as though he was saying goodbye already?

"The code… Kit." Liang's voice was hoarse. "Then we'll take a walk, and I'll tell you what you need to know. I'm hoping like hell you can help me come to terms with it, because I'm struggling."

"We could—"

"No." Liang spoke firmly. "Finish this, and then we move on and never speak of it again."

"All right." Kristopher drained his tea. After this he'd be happy to join Liang for some fresh air. His head was beginning to throb. He'd dreaded this conversation, and with good reason. "This person who can't survive…" Oh to hell with this. They both knew who they were talking about, although Liang would deny it afterwards. "If Michel and I survive this war, we'll send a playing card to your office at the university. Four of hearts means we are both alive and well. You can find a way to let Matt and Ken know. I'm going to talk to Matt about meeting in Paris a year after the war ends. Michel has spoken of a café we could use, but if it no longer exists, we'll find another. You should have somewhere to meet, even if we can't join you. I… I'll find a way so… I need to know what happened to my sister. If it's possible…"

"I'll do what I can." Liang nodded. "Four of hearts if you both survive. What if—"

"There is no what if." Michel was his strength, and although Kristopher did not want to carry his secret through a long life alone, he might not have a choice. If it came to that… he'd find somewhere else to disappear to, where no one would know who he was or what he'd done. "I'm sorry, but I won't be contacting you if I'm alone. Michel…"

Michel had already lost too much. If he was alone, Kristopher doubted Liang and the others would ever hear from him again. For an instant, he almost felt Michel's fingers brush his cheek as he remembered Michel telling him about Corin and François, and how scared he was that Kristopher might join them.

Kristopher pushed back his chair and grabbed his coat, then shoved it on and crossed his arms. Although it wasn't chilly outside, he wasn't sure he'd rid himself of the cold he felt inside.

"I'd say it's all right, but it's not." Liang briefly put an arm around Kristopher, who hadn't noticed him get up from the table. "I'm sorry."

"I know. So am I." Kristopher managed a smile. It wasn't like Liang to be so demonstrative. He'd squeezed Kristopher's hand, and now this. If talking about it hurt the people they cared about so much, what was it going to be like when he had to go through with the reality of it? Kristopher hoped he could find the strength to do what needed to be done.

"Walk with me. We can be back before the others return so they won't know we were gone. I don't know about you, but I need some fresh air."

"You wanted to talk to me about something." Kristopher waited for Liang to put on his jacket.

Liang studied Kristopher for a moment before shoving his hands into his coat pockets. He lowered his gaze. "When Holm and I had tea, just before…" Liang shuddered and visibly pulled himself together. "He told me he couldn't understand why I would be working with Ken."

Kristopher frowned, yet knew he needed to wait until Liang had finished.

"I didn't believe what he told me next. I couldn't believe it. Ken and I might argue at times, and he can be insufferable, but then so can I. I wanted to think we were friends, so when he and Michel rescued me, I decided Holm was wrong. Then…"

"What did Holm say to you?" Kristopher prompted.

"He told me Ken was half Japanese." Liang looked up suddenly, accusation in his eyes. "Did you know?"

"No, I didn't." Even if Kristopher had, he wouldn't have told Liang. That decision wasn't his to make—it was Ken's. "He's not an easy man to get to know, and Matt never said—"

"Matt knows. I overheard them last night. Matt called Ken by another name—Tsukino." Liang strode to the door. Kristopher had to run to catch up with him. "That's the thing," Liang said. "A couple of months ago, I couldn't have comprehended a Japanese man working for the Allies. I thought all Japanese were… I lost family in Nanking. I know what they did to us."

"You can't judge one man by what others have done." Kristopher caught Liang's arm. If Liang truly thought that, what must he think of Kristopher—a German fighting a war started by Herr Hitler, a man who claimed to be fighting on behalf of the Fatherland.

"I know that now." Liang shook off Kristopher's hand. "A couple of months ago, I would have reacted badly and confronted him. It wouldn't have gone well. But now… as you said, Kit, we're friends, and yet you're German. You've shown me that I can't judge a good man because of what others have done. And Juliane…" Liang's voice softened when he mentioned her name. "Juliane's risked so much, especially considering who her brother is."

Kristopher hadn't been surprised to learn Juliane was part of the Resistance, although she'd hidden it well. She and Clara had been friends for several years. He'd renewed his acquaintance with her when he started work at the institute, and they'd chatted a few times over coffee. He'd always been struck by her intelligence and wit. It was a shame Liang hadn't met her under different circumstances, as they'd be well suited. Whenever Liang spoke of her, it was obvious he was smitten.

"Ken's a good man, as are you. I've known Juliane for years, and she has very high standards. She wouldn't fall for just anyone. We're all keeping secrets because it's too dangerous not to. I've heard a little of what is going on, not only in America but England too. People thrown into camps who have done nothing wrong. Hell, Hitler is hunting Jews for the same reason. Surely we're better than that? I know you are."

"Thanks for your confidence. I know my reaction is foolish, yet a part of me replays the stories my grandmother told me. I'm struggling to reconcile the men in those stories with the man I consider my friend."

"Will you tell him you know?" Kristopher wasn't sure it would be a good idea, but if it was affecting Liang in this way, it might be better to clear the air.

"I don't know." Liang opened the door and breathed in the fresh air. "Walk with me a while? I think we both have far too much to think about, don't you?"

Another few minutes and this mission would be done. Ken rolled and shrugged his shoulders, trying to get rid of the kink across his neck. This time he, Michel, and Arlette were providing the distraction, while Matt and Sébastien unbolted a piece of railway track further up the line. While Matt's mission should be safer, as it wasn't drawing attention to his position by blowing it up, nothing about these missions was safe.

Ken would be glad when they were finally on the way home, although he'd miss the adrenaline rush that came with these acts of sabotage. They hadn't received the final coded message from London yet, but the weather hadn't been great, and it made sense to delay the invasion until it cleared. Hopefully that evening they'd get the go-ahead and only have forty-eight hours to wait until the Allied troops arrived.

A noise sounded behind him. He spun, yet couldn't see anything. Where were Michel and Arlette? They should have set the explosive by now and be on their way back. Nicolas had been annoyed he hadn't been able to come with them, although he had a bad cold and kept sneezing. In the end, he'd left his precious explosives in Michel's care, but refused to listen to Cécile's orders to go to bed. Ken smiled at the memory of the banter between Nicolas and his wife. It was very obvious they cared for each other deeply. He envied them being able to show that affection in public.

"What kept you? Any problems?" he asked when, a few minutes later, Michel finally slipped out of the shadows and walked over to where Ken was hiding. He kept his voice low. "Where's Arlette?"

"I'm here." Arlette ducked down next to Michel. "We ran into a patrol as we were about to set the explosives. Luckily they didn't see us, but we had to wait until they'd gone to complete our task."

"Better to be safe." Ken nodded his agreement. Matt would wait until the explosion created the diversion he needed as there was a good chance it might be delayed. "Any other problems?"

"No, but something about this worries me." Michel kept glancing behind them. "The patrol walked right past us, and I would have expected them to stop and search the area for the guard who should have been there."

"I hope you're not suggesting we shouldn't have restrained him?" Arlette muttered something in French that Ken thankfully couldn't understand.

Michel raised an eyebrow, then shook his head. "No, of course not, although you did hit him harder than was necessary."

"German pig deserved what he got." Arlette glared at Michel. "We've done our job well this evening. Let's head back." She shoved her gun into the waistband of her skirt, then stood and walked away without waiting for either Ken or Michel to follow her.

"She's angry. She'll get over it. Arlette rarely backs down from an argument." Michel shrugged. "It's difficult to do that if you're always right."

"She can be as angry as she likes as long as her behaviour doesn't give away our position." Ken had learned to trust Michel's instincts. If he thought something was off about the patrol, there probably was. "Arlette is right about one thing. We should head back."

He wanted to be clear of the area before the explosives went off. Although they were creating a diversion away from the real target, he had no intention of being caught.

"Yes." Michel glanced at his watch. "We delayed it longer

than we discussed because of the patrol, but we're still running out of time."

"Matt will figure that out and wait as long as he needs to." Ken holstered his gun. Although he wanted to be prepared if there was still a patrol in the area, it wasn't a good idea to advertise the fact he was carrying one.

Michel nodded but said nothing. He led the way silently, and Ken waited a few minutes before speeding up his pace so they were walking together. With the long walk ahead of them, Ken didn't want to waste any time with small talk. One reason he enjoyed Michel's company was that he didn't insist on conversation. It suited Ken—he wasn't one for talking much either, except when he was with Matt, but then Matt had a way of bringing Ken out of himself that no one had done before.

A loud explosion was quickly followed by another. Ken didn't bother looking behind him. He knew what it was, and it wouldn't be long before the Germans were alerted to it as well. No sign of Arlette yet, but she'd gotten a good head start. She'd probably reach the safe house first and report the success of their mission.

Scratch that.

Kristopher and Liang were at the safe house, and Ken doubted she'd want to talk to them. Arlette seemed to get along with Liang all right, but she and Kristopher only exchanged words when they had to.

In the distance, a flock of birds suddenly took flight. Michel grabbed Ken's arm and ducked behind a tree.

"Someone's up ahead," he hissed.

"The birds?" Ken mouthed, not surprised when Michel nodded. Given his expression, he didn't think it was Arlette, although she would have probably reached that point. Hopefully she hadn't run into trouble because she'd allowed her anger to distract her.

Another few moments and it grew quiet again. Perhaps an animal had spooked them, but Ken didn't think so. They hadn't seen anyone since they'd started walking, and he would have at least expected them to have to dodge a patrol by now. They were half an hour's walk from Cyrville-sur-Mer, and this was an area patrolled by the Germans, as it was close to the railway line. It was still before curfew, but that didn't mean anything. Ken had heard of men and women being stopped on a whim rather than because they were suspected of anything.

"Do you think we should get rid of our weapons?" Ken asked Michel. If they were caught with them, they'd be arrested immediately, as civilians were not allowed to carry them.

"I'd thought about it," Michel admitted. He glanced around again. "I don't like this. I'm thinking we should change direction. If we're being followed, I don't want to lead them to the safe house."

"Spend the night in the forest and head back in the morning?"

"Yes." Michel pulled his jacket collar up. "This weather should break very soon, or at least I hope it does." He held out his hand. The overcast sky was turning to rain. "I don't fancy a night in the open if this keeps up."

"You've considered the possibility that Arlette's in trouble?" It would explain their suspicions that someone was up ahead. One person walking silently wouldn't have upset the birds to this degree. A group of people might, especially if there had been a skirmish of some sort.

"Yes, but if she's been arrested, we won't be doing her any favours by ending up in the cell next to hers." Michel turned to walk in the opposite direction, then stopped. "Merde," he muttered. "If she has been arrested, she knows too much. We'll need to warn the others."

"Arlette's smart and she's tough. If she has been caught, mounting a rescue isn't a good idea."

"I'm only suggesting reconnaissance, not a rescue. You know as well as I do that even someone tough will crack under the right torture. We can't ignore this, as much as I'd like to."

"I never thought we should ignore it," Ken said evenly. "Just get close enough to find out what's going on, if anything. It could have been an animal that spooked those birds."

"Perhaps. If you want to head back to the safe house and warn the others, I can investigate this on my own. As you say, it might be nothing."

"You don't really think that, do you?" Ken shook his head. "If we do this, we'll do it together and watch each other's backs. All right?" So much for his telling Matt they'd both be back in time for supper.

"If you insist." Michel didn't seem happy with the suggestion.

"I'm as concerned about warning the rest of our team as you are." Ken wasn't sure why he was wasting time with an explanation. A few months ago, he wouldn't have. There might be something to Matt's theory that their team had grown together in something akin to family.

Maybe.

"I know," Michel said softly. "Thank you. But no more talking. We need to stay quiet, oui?"

Ken noticed Michel had begun slipping the occasional French word into his speech since they'd returned to his country. How long had he gone without speaking his native tongue? Although Ken's German was much better than it used to be, and his French slowly improving, he couldn't imagine it not being safe to speak English to anyone for months at a time.

"Oui."

Michel smiled at the response and gestured for them to move out. They walked in silence for a distance, keeping off the road and taking care to stay silent. As they approached the thicket of trees where they'd seen the birds, Michel stopped and put his fingers to his lips. He pointed to the road and edged out towards it.

The distinctive sound of a truck rumbled a short way off. Not a good sign. Ken drew his gun. Even if Arlette had avoided capture, were they walking into a trap?

The truck could be nothing. After all, the explosion should have alerted the Germans that something was wrong.

"Oh hell." Ken suddenly realised what was niggling at him. The explosion had been at least ten minutes ago. Why wasn't the area crawling with soldiers?

Normally he and Michel would be long gone. The explosives had been set on a timer to give them the chance to get out of the area. They'd stuck around to find out what was going on.

To hell with Arlette. She was probably closer to the safe house than they were, and this was a very dangerous wild goose chase.

Michel sprinted over to him. "We need to leave now," he hissed, obviously having come to the same conclusion.

A woman screamed. The noise was muffled and suddenly cut off.

They both froze.

"Damn it." Ken had hoped they wouldn't find what they were looking for. Michel had been right. What were the chances of it being another woman? It had to be Arlette. "We have to leave her. The others need to get the hell out of the safe house. The whole cell could be compromised if she talks."

Michel pulled his gun and crept forward. "*If* she talks?" he said grimly. "It's more a case of when."

"Going after her now would be suicide." Ken grabbed Michel's arm and yanked him back the way they'd come. They'd have to reach the safe house by another longer route and hope to God they weren't too late.

"That scream was Arlette's. I'm sure of it. Don't worry, I'm not going after her." Michel pushed Ken's arm off him. "She's a friend, but as much as I want to save her from being tortured before she's killed, it's not practical. I also promised someone I wouldn't do anything foolish."

"That's almost a shame." Reiniger walked out in front of them. Where the hell had he come from? Or had he been waiting silently the whole time? "Herr Schmitz. Herr Lowe. Predicable as ever, I see."

Ken didn't turn around. He raised his arms in surrender, as did Michel. Reiniger wouldn't have come alone. Like all bullies, he preferred the safety of a group.

The approaching truck slowed down and stopped at the edge of the road. They'd definitely been expected. But how?

Reiniger snapped his fingers, and a soldier dragged Arlette into view. He had his hand over her mouth, and her arms were handcuffed behind her. The red mark on her cheek was slowly bruising over, and when the soldier removed his hand, Ken saw blood at the side of her mouth.

"I'm sorry," she said. "They were waiting. They knew we were here."

"Enough talking," Reiniger snapped.

Ken's arms were yanked behind him and the cold steel of handcuffs snapped around his wrists. Out of the corner of his eye, he saw Michel being handcuffed too.

Reiniger walked over to Michel and punched him hard in the stomach. Michel gasped in pain but didn't double over. Reiniger leaned in close. "That's for what you and Lehrer did to me in Berlin." He brought his hand up again and slapped Michel across the face. Michel stood still, staring straight ahead, blood running down his mouth. "And that's for my eye. Take them away. Standartenführer Holm is looking forward to renewing his acquaintance with them… and the rest of their so-called team."

CHAPTER FOURTEEN

"I thought this was supposed to be summer." Liang was glad for the beret he wore, although it wasn't much protection from the cold. Still, it was better than the uncomfortable helmet that accompanied a German uniform. He thought back to the fedora he used to wear. That, and lecturing at the university, seemed another lifetime ago. "It feels more like midwinter."

"Do you want to go back?" Kit picked up his pace. Although he had said several times that he didn't like the cold, it didn't seem to be deterring him now. Or was his mind elsewhere? Talking about his decision to fake his death hadn't been an easy thing to do, and Liang admired his courage. He wasn't sure he'd be able to go through with something like that.

"Not yet." Liang was as distracted as Kit. Speaking to someone about what had been going around in his head had helped, although he still hadn't worked out whether telling Ken what he knew was a good idea. If his suspicions were correct, Ken already had another secret he wasn't prepared to share. Would one less to hide make it easier or not?

Liang also couldn't figure out how to bring it up. Admitting he'd heard Matt calling Ken by what was obviously his real name would only make them both panic that their other secret had been revealed too. Liang had watched an intimate moment between them—well, as intimate as they were able to be—and should have walked away. It wasn't often he saw that more open side of Ken, and he had to admit he was curious about the relationship.

He also wasn't in a hurry to upset Matt. For the most part, Matt was very easygoing, but Liang had no wish to experience his anger firsthand. Besides, Matt had enough issues with his nightmares and fear of the dark without adding something else to the mix.

"Did you hear that?" Kit had stopped walking and stood a short distance behind Liang.

"Hear what?" Liang turned and retraced his steps to stand beside Kit. "I can't—" As he started to speak, the unmistakable noise of tires against gravel was followed by men's voices. "Oh hell." He grabbed Kit's arm, and they both sprinted for the small barn nearby. They'd barely dived inside when two military vehicles drove past.

"This road leads to the safe house," Kit whispered. "There's nothing else out here."

Liang peered out the window. "There's a third vehicle following behind." Although he wished he could see more clearly, it wouldn't change the fact their safe house was now anything but. "I can see the men are in uniform, but that's about it."

"The safe house has been compromised. Either we have a traitor, or..." Kit swallowed. "One or both of our teams have been captured."

"Not necessarily." Liang turned to look at Kit. God knew what he must be imagining. Probably the same thing Liang was. He couldn't get caught again. The thought of going through… He couldn't… Liang turned back to the window.

"You don't really believe that, do you?" Kit sounded hoarse. "We can't stay here. If they start searching the area, there's nowhere to hide."

The barn was almost empty, as the livestock were outside, and the closest building apart from the safe house was the farmhouse. They needed to get as far away from both of them as they could, and quickly.

"I'm open to suggestions. How are we supposed to get somewhere else without being seen?" Liang tapped his fingers on the windowsill. If they'd stayed at the safe house like they were supposed to, they'd probably be in custody by now.

"We need to get to the church and hope that's still safe." Kit sounded a little too calm.

"Michel will be all right," Liang said softly. "He's always very careful, and Ken is there to watch his back. Those two work well together. After all, they did break me out of Gestapo custody in Stuttgart."

"Matt thought we might have been compromised. What if he was right?" Kit balled one fist, then unfurled it. "What if Holm's been waiting for the right moment to strike? If we hadn't taken a walk…" He bit his lip. "If Reiniger has Michel, has any of them, they will be far from all right. You don't—"

Liang placed his hands on Kit's shoulders. "Yes, I do. I bloody well know exactly what those bastards are capable of. Don't ever presume I don't."

"I didn't… I'm sorry." Kit lowered his gaze. "Verdammt, I'm sorry." He looked up after a few moments. Liang shivered at the lack of emotion in his eyes. It reminded him of something he'd seen before, but he couldn't place it. "We're not staying here until we're found," Kit continued. "We need to assess the situation and get word to the rest of our team. If they haven't been caught, they'll be walking into a trap when they return."

"If you're caught, this is all over," Liang reminded him. It suddenly dawned on him why Kit's expression seemed familiar. "This isn't some formula that needs solving, Kit. Taking yourself and your emotions out of the equation might not be a good idea."

"I can't afford to let them in at present. I need some time to process… I don't want to think about what might be happening…" Kit shook himself free from Liang's grip. "You're right. If we're caught, there is no reason for Holm to keep any of our friends alive." He reached into his pocket and drew a gun Liang hadn't realised he was carrying. "I've let my emotions dictate my actions before, and it didn't work. I have to at least try this. Better to take action than sit here and wait to be arrested. We'll talk once we're away from here and I know for certain what we're dealing with."

"All right." Liang answered the unspoken question at the end of Kit's sentence, but it didn't mean he agreed with it. All he could do was make sure he was there to support Kit later if their suspicions about their friends were correct or if this all went horribly wrong. "As I said before, I'm open to suggestions."

Kit nodded slowly. "It won't take long before the soldiers realise the house is empty. That gives us a limited window of opportunity. There's a thicket of trees halfway between here and the dense bush a distance away."

"That's closer to the house than we are now, but there's a good chance they'll see us. There's no cover between here and those trees." Liang could see Kit's point even if it felt a bit too much like jumping from the frying pan into the fire.

"It's that or attempt to run across several metres of open farmland in the other direction. At least this way, there's the fence between us and the house, and there's a good chance the soldiers won't be looking this way. The trees will provide us with cover once we get there. Unless you'd prefer to stay here?"

"I'd prefer to not have to deal with any of this, but that's not going to happen, is it?" Liang opened the door and took a quick glimpse outside. The soldiers' focus did seem to be the house for the moment. "As this is your plan, you go first, and I'll be right behind you." He hoped Kit knew what he was doing. At least this way, they had a chance, although it wouldn't be an option for much longer.

Kit nodded instead of replying. The sun was finally setting, so if they made it as far as their next hiding place, they would be able to stay there until they could move under the cover of darkness. He shoved his gun into the waistband of his trousers and took several deep breaths, then sprinted towards the thicket of trees.

"Better this than stay here." Liang muttered the words under his breath. *I hope. Focus on following him. Nothing else. Nothing. Else.* If he let himself think about the soldiers spotting them and opening fire, he'd be done for.

Run. Run.

Shit, there's movement at the house. Liang picked up his pace, his heart pounding. His legs felt like they were burning.

He skidded to a stop behind the bushes. His vision wavered, and he fell to his knees, his breath coming in gasps. With all that had happened over the past seven months, he thought he was fitter than this.

Kit had his hands on his bent knees, catching his breath. He caught Liang's eye, and they shared a minuscule smile. At least Liang wasn't the only one who'd spent too many years behind a desk.

One of the soldiers walked out of the house. The man stood near the front door, lighting a cigarette while he surveyed the area. He took a couple of puffs and then marched around the house so they couldn't see him.

Liang let out the breath he'd held. He began to whisper something, but Kit put his fingers to his lips and shook his head.

The soldier—an Oberscharführer—reappeared, strode towards the back fence, and out of their line of sight. Liang heard the noise of something being dragged. What the hell was the soldier doing? Then suddenly the man peered over the fence, looking around until he noticed the bushes they were hiding behind, and smiled.

No. No. No.

Should they make a run for it? Had he seen them?

Kit paled. He'd obviously seen the soldier too. He tensed, drawing his gun.

"Oberscharführer!" another soldier called out from inside the house.

The Oberscharführer stubbed out his cigarette on a fence post and climbed down, disappearing from view.

Liang sighed in relief, but his hope they were safe was short-lived. He'd recognised the man, and searched his memory for the name Matt had told him. "That's Esser," he whispered to Kit. "We met him on the way to Pont-Audemer. He works for Holm."

"Damn it." Matt muttered as he pressed against the crumbling wall and hoped like hell he hadn't been seen.

Bad enough they'd had to abandon the mission because of the platoon of soldiers already there, but to finally reach the truck they'd parked in a nearby village only to find it was under surveillance? It couldn't be a coincidence. Given these soldiers were trying hard to be inconspicuous, they must be part of a trap. Matt had only figured out they were there because he'd stopped at the far side of the wall while waiting for Sébastien to catch up. Otherwise he would have already been at the truck and most likely in custody.

"Problem?" Sébastien asked, coming up behind Matt.

"You could say that." Matt gestured towards the other side of the wall. "If you look closely, you can see a couple of soldiers by that alcove over there." The soldiers stood at the top of the steps leading to the side door of the building, so they weren't immediately noticeable from the street. "I heard one of them sneeze."

"My guess is they're waiting for someone." Sébastien frowned. "But how did they know about the truck? It's hidden from the road. They would have had to walk at least ten minutes off their usual patrol route to find it."

"That's my thought too. If they're waiting for us, they've probably also gotten our descriptions, so I didn't see the point in risking a confrontation." Matt had no desire to end up in handcuffs anytime soon or being handed over to Holm. Once had been more than enough.

"One hell of a coincidence." Sébastien's tone was noncommittal. "I guess we'd better start walking, then. If we start now, we could be back at the safe house before dark. Trying to get to the truck would be foolish. If they have no clue we were here, it gives us a head start while they wait for us to show."

"We're not going back to the safe house," Matt said grimly. He had a nasty feeling it was already too late for that. Better to be safe than deliver the rest of his team to Holm and his men. "We'll get as close as we dare so we can assess the situation, but I'm hoping like hell Alexandre and Benoit haven't been caught."

"What about Michel's team?" Sébastien asked the question Matt had preferred not to think about.

"You don't think this is a coincidence either, do you?" Matt had no doubt Holm was behind this. They'd been on borrowed time ever since they'd reached Cyrville-sur-Mer, but he'd hoped luck would stay with them until the Allied invasion.

If Holm had Ken… Matt dug his nails into his palm. Fuck. If Holm hurt Ken, Matt would kill the bastard.

"No." Sébastien watched the truck for a few more minutes. Was he having second thoughts about taking it by force?

"I only saw two soldiers. There might be more. I'm not going to start a fight I might not be able to win. If… *if* some of our team have been captured, we'll need to use our resources to rescue them."

It wasn't only Ken he wouldn't leave behind. The rest of their team were more than friends—they were family. Not only that, but he couldn't risk Holm getting his hands on Kit and the information he carried. If that happened, this war could be over, no matter the outcome of London's current operation.

Sébastien raised an eyebrow. "A rescue? If they've been captured, it's only a matter of time before our entire operation is compromised—if it hasn't been already."

After one last glance at the truck, Matt turned away and started walking. He pulled his jacket collar up to partially obscure his face and hoped he'd be far enough away before the soldiers realised no one was coming.

Sébastien caught up with him quickly. They walked in silence for about a mile before Sébastien spoke again. "You think we have a traitor?"

"Don't you? This isn't the first time we've had a mission compromised."

"Someone could have noticed the truck and contacted the

Gendarmerie. I trust *my* team and have worked with them many times. Do you still trust yours?"

"Yes, I do. With my life." Matt doubted this was something simple like a concerned citizen reporting them to either the Gendarmerie or directly to the Gestapo. Perhaps he was being too suspicious and this was a coincidence. Their mission being compromised didn't mean the others were in trouble. It could merely be bad luck all round.

"You're not only trusting them with the lives of your team, but with those of my team as well. And *we* don't have a high-ranking SS official after us. I told you I would keep my opinions to myself as long as my team was not threatened. We've had not one but two missions compromised because someone knew our plans. Perhaps it is time you and your men moved on, oui?"

Michel tried to figure out how long they'd been travelling, but in the end decided to give up. What was the point? Their chances of escape were virtually zero, unless someone decided to attempt a rescue.

This wasn't how it was supposed to end.

He wanted a life with Kit, damn it, both of them growing old together far away from any of this.

Please don't come for me, mon cher. Stay safe and live your life.

He wouldn't be used as bait to get Kit to surrender. He'd rather die first. But that wouldn't guarantee Kit's safety. Michel knew how this kind of situation worked and that Kit would cling to the belief Michel could be saved until he was presented with proof otherwise.

Who the hell had betrayed them? This was the work of a traitor. It had to be. Reiniger knew they'd be there. Was it someone from Arlette's cell? If so, they'd betrayed one of their own too.

He risked a glance at Arlette. She stared straight ahead, dried tears on her cheeks, shoulders stiff. Ken had his eyes closed, his expression completely unreadable.

Matt might be able to stop Kit from giving himself up, but he wouldn't leave Ken behind. *Might.* Michel almost groaned aloud. Kit would stubbornly justify his being a part of a rescue attempt as "necessary" and convince Matt he'd stay "safe." Michel had seen Kit's definitions of those words before, and it still sent chills through him.

Merde. If they had a traitor in their midst, that person would know about any rescue attempt too. It might be only a matter of time before they were all caught if they weren't already. Matt wouldn't leave anyone behind, but if he and Liang were caught too... Michel wasn't sure Sébastien would risk his team to save them.

Michel took several deep breaths and forced himself to calm. Their captors would use any sign of weakness against them. He wouldn't give Kit up to them. Kit was his strength. And his weakness.

He closed his eyes. If he couldn't see his surroundings, he could believe it wasn't real, hide in an illusion, at least for a short time. He'd spent months undercover, and months before that taking part in dangerous missions. But he hadn't had so much to lose then. His brother and his closest friend were already dead, and he'd figured if he'd lost his life helping to free his beloved France, so be it.

Now he had someone to live for, and he was terrified, not for himself but for Kit.

"Thinking about your future?" Reiniger's question jarred Michel back to reality. He'd crouched down next to him in the truck as it had slowed down. "I wouldn't waste my time, Schmitz. Traitors don't have that luxury."

Michel gazed at him unflinchingly. He didn't bother replying. Anything he'd say would only serve to aggravate the man. Michel's stomach still ached from where Reiniger had hit him, and the side of his mouth was sore, but that was nothing compared to what Reiniger was capable of. He'd seen one of Reiniger's interrogations before, and the results of others.

Better not to think of that until he had to.

"Herr Holm has said I can have you when he's finished." Reiniger sneered, his breath hot against Michel's cheek. "You'll pay for what you've done." Reiniger dropped his voice to a whisper. Did he really think no one else would hear him? "It won't take long before you're no longer useful." He smiled.

Michel kept staring straight ahead as though Reiniger wasn't there.

The truck lurched to a stop. Reiniger gestured for them to stand and exit. Each of the prisoners had their own personal guard. Holm definitely wasn't taking any chances. Michel felt the butt of a rifle in his back, and he climbed down carefully, not wanting to go sprawling as his hands were still bound behind him. He'd hang on to whatever dignity he had for as long as he could.

As soon as Ken and Arlette had disembarked, Reiniger led his men into what looked like some kind of bunker. The sun had set, so there wasn't much light, but Michel could hear waves crashing against the shore. They were close to the sea. Could this be a command bunker attached to one of the long-range artillery batteries?

A couple of doors before the end of a long corridor, Michel and the others were led into an office. Holm sat at his desk, writing something in a thick file. He looked up when they entered and smiled. "I've been looking forward to remaking your acquaintance, Herr Lowe, and you too, Herr Schmitz, or whatever your real name is." He inclined his head towards Arlette. "And where are my manners. Good evening, Fräulein. I don't believe we've been formally introduced, despite our correspondence."

Correspondence?

Michel felt cold. "You're the traitor?" It couldn't be true. He'd trusted her. Mon Dieu, they'd grown up together. She was one of his oldest friends. He glanced at her, hoping to see denial and shock on her face. She bit her lip and lowered her gaze.

Holm spoke the truth. Anger rose, the emotions Michel had tried to contain boiling to the surface. He took a step towards her, but the end of a rifle butt across his back sent him sprawling to the floor.

"Why?" Michel struggled to his feet, but only got as far as his knees. "Pourquoi?" he asked her again.

Arlette turned to Holm. "This wasn't our arrangement. You were supposed to leave him out of this. I promised you the rest of his team. I said I'd deliver the English spy."

English spy? Michel stared at her blankly. They didn't have an English spy in their group. Surely she wasn't referring to Liang? He was the only Englishman on their team and had already escaped Holm's custody once. Liang wasn't the target, had never been Holm's target. Why had she promised Holm something that didn't exist and she couldn't deliver?

One of the soldiers dragged him to his feet. He stood, trying to steady himself, physically and emotionally.

Ken didn't say anything. He didn't look surprised, didn't show any emotion at all.

"Oh, come now, Michel." Margarete Huber walked into the room. How long had she been standing at the door, listening? "It's so interesting watching people's reactions, don't you think? You've always struck me as so stoic, and yet now a simple betrayal shows your weakness." She smiled. "But I doubt this woman is really your weakness, is she?"

Holm steepled his fingers. "We don't have time for games, Fräulein Huber. You've proved your point about the usefulness of revealing this woman's betrayal now instead of later. However, she hasn't delivered what you promised me she would. This is hardly the rest of the team, now is it? After all, we still need the man she is convinced is an English spy." He chuckled. "It's interesting what people believe, isn't it? What was that name he was using again? Ah yes. Kit."

Michel swallowed. She'd betrayed them in order to deliver Kit to Holm? Why? And how had she known his real name? They'd been so careful.

Kit had said Liang thought Arlette was sweet on Michel. Was this some kind of misplaced jealously? Could she seriously believe Michel would want anything to do with her after this? Or that Holm would let her go after she'd given him what he wanted?

"I always said if we captured you, we'd soon have dear Kristopher." Margarete walked over to Michel and looked him up and down. "So predictable, although I'm not entirely sure what he sees in you." She ran one manicured finger across his cheek. He struggled not to flinch. His stomach churned. She'd touched Kristopher like this and tried to flirt with him. "To each his or her own, I suppose…" She shrugged.

Holm cleared his throat. "Still playing your games, Fräulein Huber?" He nodded to one of the soldiers, the one guarding Arlette. "Release her. I have a task for her."

"You promised me you wouldn't hurt Michel if I delivered the English spy to you," Arlette said. "Let him go. Please."

Did she really think Holm would agree to her terms?

"He'll kill us all," Michel said calmly. "You're a fool, Arlette. A traitor and a fool."

Holm shook his head. "I am a man who keeps his

promises, Fräulein. *I* haven't hurt him. However, you still need to keep your side of our arrangement. If you don't, I can't guarantee his safety, or your own. It wasn't difficult to find out who you are, and once I had, naturally I sent someone to watch and apprehend you. It made sense that you wouldn't be far from the man you seem so determined to protect, so I told Reiniger to wait until you were together and an easy target. Your *friend,* in turn, will give me the man I seek. We are fighting a war, after all. Lehrer is a traitor to his country. I am merely pursuing justice." He gave one of his soldiers a nod.

"He's not a—" Michel protested.

The barrel of a gun pressed against his head.

Arlette looked suddenly unsure. She glanced at Michel.

"It's your choice, Fräulein. I presumed you cared for this man. Obviously I was mistaken." Holm shrugged. "Perhaps I should kill him now. If you refuse to honour our agreement, why should I keep my promise?"

"Let Michel go, and I'll deliver the English spy." Arlette's voice wavered. "I'll do whatever you want me to." Her shoulders slumped. "I was so careful. They shouldn't have found me… us."

"A wonderful decision, my dear, although I think it might be for the best if we keep Michel for a while longer." Margarete smiled. "Standartenführer Holm is quite right. Why should he keep his promise when you haven't kept yours? However, despite that, he has still offered you another chance. This way there is still a small probability your friend might live. Isn't that right, Herr Holm?"

Holm stood, walked around the front of his desk, and handed Arlette an envelope. "Deliver this to Herr Doktor Lehrer. A soldier will escort you to Cyrville-sur-Mer."

"I said I'd give you the Englishman. I don't know any Dr Lehrer. I'm afraid I can't help you."

"Oh, I'm sure you do." Margarete nodded towards the envelope. "I'm also certain *Kit* Lehrer can be persuaded to do the right thing and give himself up. Be sure to tell him that we have his *close* friend." She gave Holm a nod. "I'll escort you myself to make sure this nice soldier treats you properly. After all, we women need to look out for each other, don't we?"

The soldier marched Arlette from the room at gunpoint. She glanced back at Michel and mouthed, "Je suis désolée," but he ignored her.

Kit was still free. Whatever the contents of Holm's note, he had to stay safe. Michel's life wasn't important. He wouldn't let himself be used to… oh God.

The invasion was close. If he could hold out for a few more days…

"Take him away," Holm said, "and tell Reiniger to come to my office. I wish to speak with him."

The soldier saluted. "Yes, Standartenführer." He shoved his gun in Michel's back and pushed him towards the door.

Ken started to follow, but Holm shook his head.

"Not you, Herr Lowe. I wish to speak with you. Our conversation was interrupted last time, and we still have much to talk about." Holm smiled. "You've said nothing since your arrival. Let's see what we can do about that, hmm?"

"We don't have anything to talk about, Herr Holm," Ken said. "There is nothing left. It's all been said."

Michel turned at the door and caught Ken's eye. Ken gave him a brief nod. The door closed between them, and Michel was led away.

CHAPTER FIFTEEN

"Where are they?" Kristopher glared at his watch again. It was well past curfew, and neither team had returned.

He and Liang had reached the bush a safe distance from the cottage, stayed there until dark, and then made their way to the church. Esser had left the area shortly before dusk, leaving half a dozen men standing guard.

"Stop pacing," Liang said. "It's not going to make them get here any faster, and it's more sensible to save your energy in case we need to make a run for it."

"Cécile's keeping watch outside the church. So far it appears as though only the one safe house has been compromised." Nicolas pursed his lips. "If your friends do not return soon, it doesn't bode well. Either they have been caught, or they know we've been betrayed. I want to know how they'd know. Were they lucky like you were, or—"

"Our friends are not traitors." Kristopher didn't want to argue about that now. "Something's wrong. I know it is."

"They might be waiting until it's safe to return. If the safe house isn't the only place crawling with soldiers, it would be sensible to find somewhere to hide and stay there for a while." Liang glanced over at Théo, who was focused on his radio set. He'd been attached to the thing night and day since the message about the invasion had been broadcast on the BBC. "How well do you know Sébastien?"

"Surely you don't think he's a traitor?" Kristopher didn't know Sébastien that well, but his gut feeling was that he could be trusted.

"I've worked with Sébastien since we formed this cell," Nicolas said. "I trust him, and Arlette. I haven't seen Michel in years, and I know nothing about you and your American friends. What proof do I have that you're not double agents?"

It seemed Sébastien had shared what he'd discovered, which explained why no one from the cell had asked many questions. There was no need to if they already knew.

Théo looked up from his radio. "Sébastien wouldn't betray us." Although he spoke French, it appeared he knew more German than he'd let on, or he wouldn't have been able to follow their conversation.

"Unless we work together, we won't have to wait to be discovered. We'll betray each other," Kristopher said. "Théo, how much German do you understand?" Arlette had implied he knew very little.

"Enough. *They* transmit in German, after all." Théo narrowed his eyes. "You know more French than you claim to. I've seen you listening to our conversations."

"I know enough." Kristopher's French had improved a lot over the past few weeks, although he understood more than he spoke.

"Let's pick a language and stick to it," Liang suggested. "I can translate in either direction if there are any problems. Perhaps French as we are in France and guests of your cell?"

"I have no intention of speaking German unless I have to," Théo said.

"Fine, that's sorted, then," Liang said quickly, "at least for now. Once our friends return, it would be easier to speak German as their French is not as good."

"You can translate." Théo turned back to his radio.

"I think I liked him better when he didn't say much," Liang muttered in English.

Kristopher shook his head and gave Liang a look of disapproval. Théo had told them he didn't speak English, but he might understand it. Until they discovered who the traitor was, they'd need to be careful.

Had coming to the church been a good idea? What if Cécile had offered to keep watch so she could more easily betray them to the men hunting them? It would be easy to lead their pursuers directly to this room beneath the church. There were only two exits—the stairs and the trapdoor. Easy enough to block off the door at the top of the stairs, and she'd know where the tunnel at the end of the trapdoor led to as well.

Kristopher massaged his temples. Surely if that were the case, she wouldn't betray her husband? Nicolas would be caught with the rest of them.

"Headache?" Liang asked. When Kristopher nodded, Liang gave him a sympathetic nod. "Hopefully we will—"

A series of knocks at the door interrupted him.

Nicolas put his fingers to his lips, signalling silence, and sprinted up the stairs leading to the church. He rapped a simple rhythm on his side of the door, then drew his gun. A moment later, there was a reply from the other side—a code Kristopher and the others hadn't been told about.

"Wonderful," Liang said. "So if it had been us, they wouldn't have let us in."

"It's a wise precaution." Kristopher swallowed, edging closer to the bottom of the stairs. *Please let it be Michel.* He had to be all right.

As soon as the door opened, Matt pushed past Sébastien

and scanned the room. "Where's Ken?" he asked. "Have you heard anything?"

Nicolas shook his head. He pressed back against the wall so Matt and Sébastien had room to pass him.

"The Germans were waiting for us." Sébastien followed Matt down the stairs. He sounded tired, and his shirt was splattered with mud. "We had to walk back and hide in a ditch to avoid a patrol near the safe house. I thought they'd never leave."

"The other team hasn't returned yet." Kristopher's stomach clenched. If it wasn't only the safe house that had been compromised, and Michel was still out there... *Please no.* "If Holm knew where you'd be, there's a good chance he had men waiting for them too." His voice shook. He forced himself to calm. They could be hiding somewhere, waiting.

"They also knew about the truck." Matt's voice sounded husky, as though he was fighting to keep his emotions under control. "What makes you think these men are working for Holm? Cécile told us the safe house was compromised and that you barely escaped capture."

"If you hadn't insisted we return here instead of the safe house, we would have been caught too," Sébastien said slowly.

"Esser was there," Liang said. "Remember him? He told you he was on his way to report to Holm when he stopped our truck outside Bétheny. Then you said you saw him again at Pont-Audemer when Jacques was arrested. I could have sworn he saw us, although he didn't call his men. I'm still trying to figure out what the hell he's playing at."

"Wait a moment." Sébastien held his hand up for silence. "Ken is Marcel's real name? Oui?"

"Oui," Matt confirmed. Denying his slip now wouldn't achieve anything. He glanced at Kristopher and Liang. "It looks as though we have a traitor. You're right, Benoit. This was too well thought out," he said grimly. "If they were at the safe house too, we have to think about the possibility that the whole mission was compromised. Ken's team took out the secondary target, so they should be back by now. My guess is that they're either in hiding or were arrested shortly afterward."

"I'm sorry," Kristopher murmured. "I should have listened to you in the first place. I must have been wrong about why you were nearly caught when—"

"Your reasoning was sound," Liang said, "and we've had several successful missions since we started using your tactics. Feeling guilty isn't going to help anyone."

"Perhaps now would be a good time to tell us why the SS is after you." Sébastien moved towards the bottom of the stairs, blocking the way out.

"If our operation has been completely compromised, why isn't the church already overrun with soldiers?" Matt spoke slowly and watched Sébastien carefully. Did he think Sébastien was going to turn on them?

"My guess is because the traitor has decided to keep this location safe for some reason," Nicolas said. "Keep *himself* safe while he betrays the rest of us." He levelled his gun at Matt.

"We need to work together." Matt shook his head. He raised his hands slowly in a sign of surrender. "We're wasting time, and this is probably what our enemies want. Why spend resources finding us if all they have to do is wait for us to make a mistake and reveal ourselves because we're too busy squabbling?"

Sébastien snorted. "It doesn't dismiss the fact that someone has betrayed us. I think we need to find them and hand them over. Perhaps even trade them for our own people. After all, this Holm wants your team for a reason." He narrowed his eyes. "Or perhaps not all of your team?

After all, Esser saw Alexandre and Benoit and didn't arrest them. Perhaps that is because *they* are the traitors?" He glanced at Matt. "And it was *your* decision to avoid the safe house. Was that because you already knew it was compromised?"

"That's ridiculous," Liang said. "If we were traitors, we wouldn't be here having this conversation. You'd all be in custody, and the church would be surrounded."

"You could be waiting for Arlette's team to return first." Nicolas had edged across the room as they'd talked so he now stood on top of the trapdoor, blocking the other exit from the room. "Your friend Holm wouldn't have to worry about finding them later, then, would he?"

"We don't have time for this," Kristopher snapped. "I'm not going to stand around arguing while Holm or Reiniger could be doing God knows what to M—our friends."

Matt stepped in front of Nicolas, and his gun. "My name is Captain Matt Bryant, and I'm part of a joint operation between the SOE and OSS to smuggle important information out of occupied Europe." He indicated Liang. "This is Zhou Liang, and—" Matt turned to glance at Kristopher. "—Paul Reichel. Ken Lowe is a sergeant in the US Army."

"Reichel is a German name." Nicolas eyed Kristopher suspiciously.

"I already told you I was German," Kristopher said evenly. It was better that Matt hadn't given Kristopher's real name. Although they needed these men to trust them, it would be foolish to tell them too much. He moved to stand next to Matt, as did Liang at the same time to flank Matt's other side. "There are many of us who do not agree with what Herr Hitler and his men are doing. I'm fighting for my country, as you are for yours."

Nicolas reholstered his gun. "Arlette is convinced you're an English spy, but I don't believe her. You're taking more of a risk claiming to be German, so I'm inclined to think you're speaking the truth."

"Thank you." Kristopher couldn't rid himself of the feeling that, although they'd achieved this small victory, something was still terribly wrong.

"We can't tell you the specifics of our mission. It's classified, but it is very important to the war effort." Matt lowered his arms. "If this information falls into the hands of the enemy, it won't matter how close the Allied invasion is. This victory will be a short one, and many people will die."

"Do Michel and Ken have this information?" Sébastien asked.

"No, but—" Kristopher knew what Holm would propose if he did have Michel.

Matt put a warning hand on Kristopher's shoulder. "We need to find them. That is not open for negotiation. If they're in custody, I'm not leaving them there for any longer than I have to."

"I can't risk my team, especially this close to an Allied invasion," Sébastien said. "If your men do not have the information, they are not essential to your mission, oui? I'm sorry, and I'm not happy about leaving Arlette to the mercy of those pigs either. However, she would not want us to jeopardise our operation to rescue her, and I'm sure your men wouldn't either. We need to collect what we can from here and find somewhere safer. If the Germans do not know where we are now, it is only a matter of time before they do."

"To hell with whether they're essential or not." Kristopher grew cold. If he gave himself up, it wouldn't stop Reiniger from torturing Michel, just because he could. He couldn't let the plans fall into the hands of the Nazis, but he wasn't prepared to lose Michel either. "I'm not leaving—"

"Paul," Matt said. "You are *not* going after them. We'll find a way. I'm not leaving any of them. I know what Holm and

Reiniger are capable of. I…" His voice shook. "We'll find a way, whatever it takes. I promise."

"I wasn't suggesting *I* go after them." Kristopher didn't bother to hide his anger. "I know the importance of this mission as much as you do. Perhaps more so. But that doesn't mean—"

He froze midsentence when someone knocked on the door.

Matt already had his gun in hand. So did Sébastien.

"Grab what you can," Matt whispered urgently, "and get out through the trapdoor. We'll be right behind you."

Another series of knocks sounded. This time it was a familiar rhythm—the code they'd used on their first visit to the church.

Matt frowned, and then hope danced in his eyes. "They're here at last."

"We don't know that," Sébastien pointed out. "Cover me." He ran up the stairs and rapped a response. It wasn't one Kristopher had heard before. A couple of long moments later, someone responded. "Who's there?"

"Arlette. You have to let me in. Please." Arlette sobbed the words.

When Sébastien opened the door, she half fell into his arms. He held her, stroking her head. "Je t'ai, ma chérie. Tu es securité maintenant."

Matt ran past them and peered outside. "Where's Ken? Where are Ken and Michel," he asked urgently. "Where the hell are they?"

Arlette looked up at him with tear-soaked cheeks. "It was awful. We were caught by the Germans and delivered to a SS officer. I managed to escape. They didn't. I'm sorry."

"You've led me on quite the chase, Herr Lowe." Holm stood so close Ken could feel the heat of his captor's breath on his cheek. "You have also lost me two prisoners. I cannot allow that to go unpunished. After all, my superiors grow impatient for results."

Holm was mistaken if he thought his threat would get a reaction. Ken stood staring straight ahead and didn't reply. It hadn't been a question, and he wasn't foolish enough to think Holm would be satisfied with any answer he was given.

He had to stay calm and not give Holm anything he wanted.

Matt was still free. He needed to stay that way. Holm hadn't mentioned any other prisoners, so Ken could let himself think Matt was safe. Right?

Don't try to rescue me. Don't try to rescue... Don't try—

Ken gasped and tasted blood. He tried to wipe the side of his mouth, but remembered too late that his hands were cuffed behind him.

Holm smiled. "So you are still with us? That's good to know. I don't like it when people are distracted. It's so rude. I'm sure your father didn't raise you to disregard your manners." Holm walked around Ken and yanked at his restraints, the rough motion sending a wave of pain through his arms. "We know where your priest is hiding." Holm hissed in Ken's ear, then let the linking chain of his handcuffs drop again.

Ken took a sharp intake of breath, berating himself as soon as he'd done so.

"Hmm," Holm said. "As much as I regret it, it appears that dear Fräulein Huber might have a point. Friendship is a weakness. Those we trust are often the very people who betray us, don't you think?"

Ken gritted his teeth. He'd never forget finding Matt in that cell after Holm had finished with him. Matt had been so raw and vulnerable. His physical scars had faded, but his emotional ones probably never would. He'd cried out in his sleep for weeks afterwards until he finally felt safe in Ken's arms to let himself relax enough to sleep properly.

"Bastard," Ken muttered.

"As I said," Holm said, a slow smile turning up the edges of his thin mouth, "friends have a tendency to betray us."

"If you're trying to get me to betray mine, you're wasting your time." Continuing to stay silent wouldn't help him now. Ken had heard that Holm refused to stop an interrogation until he'd gotten the results he wanted.

This was going to take a while. Ken knew he could be stubborn—Matt had told him that often enough—but Holm also had plenty of practice on his side.

Holm pulled up a chair and pushed Ken into it. He then returned to his own chair so the desk was between them and glanced up at the guard. "Leave us, and make sure we are not disturbed."

"Yes, Standartenführer." The soldier saluted and then left the room.

Ken figured what Holm would bring up next so saved him the trouble. "I'm sorry your father died in the last war. So did mine. People kill each other during a war. Neither of us knows exactly what happened, so I don't see the point in discussing it further."

"An interesting theory." Holm seemed to consider it for a moment, then shook his head. "No, I don't think so. I've always believed people should be made to pay for their crimes. And you're wrong. There were witnesses. My father surrendered to yours in good faith, and then your father shot him."

"Shit." Ken closed his eyes for a moment. He wanted to argue that his father wouldn't have done such a thing, but he couldn't. He'd never met Patrick Lowe. All he knew about him came from the stories his mother told him. She'd wanted him to be proud of who he was, but how well had she known the man who had fathered her child? Patrick hadn't married her, although he'd promised he would when he returned from the war. Men promised a lot of things before they went to war. She'd named him on Ken's birth certificate, but no one from Patrick's family had ever made contact. Either he'd never mentioned them, or they'd turned their backs on Cho Tsukino and her son.

"Either you didn't know, or you're like your father and have a gift for deception." Holm sounded thoughtful. "Never mind, it doesn't matter."

"I never met my father." Ken wondered why he was wasting his time defending his reaction.

"A pity. There is a strong resemblance between the two of you. I thought you were your father the first time I saw you. Foolish of me, considering he is dead." Holm opened a folder and shoved a photograph across the desk.

Ken leaned forward so he could see it. His mother only had one photograph, which was faded and crinkled with age. This was much clearer, and for the first time, he could see the resemblance. Patrick's hair seemed much lighter in colour than Ken's, although it was difficult to tell from the sepia photograph. If Ken squinted and looked at it from an angle, he supposed he and his father could be mistaken for each other, but he suspected Holm had seen what he wanted to.

Several emotions chased each other—curiosity, sadness, and regret. Although he'd taken his father's name when he'd joined up, and to avoid the internment camps, Ken had always thought of himself as Tsukino. His father was a story, a name on a birth certificate, a man only his mother talked about. When Ken asked his maternal grandparents about his father, they shook their heads and told him the past was where it needed to be and he should focus on his future.

"I'm surprised your Chinese friend is still working with you." Holm retrieved the photograph and placed it carefully in his folder, which he closed again. "He was most surprised to hear that you were half Japanese, as was I."

"I'm not. My mother is half Japanese." He frowned. If Liang had known, he hadn't mentioned it. Surprising, considering how often he spoke of his own family and what had happened to them at Nanking. Liang tended to confront the truth head-on and didn't waste time sugarcoating anything.

A memory rushed to the surface. When Ken and Michel had rescued Liang in Stuttgart, Liang had hugged him—an uncharacteristic response both men had vowed never to speak of again. He'd also said he hadn't believed what Holm had told him, but refused to say what that conversation had been about.

"Oh." Ken said the word before he realised he'd done so.

Holm smiled. "I wouldn't count on a rescue attempt by Herr Doktor Zhou. You've been keeping secrets. I do hope he hasn't told your friend the priest. Oh yes, Matt. That's his name, isn't it? I have information he's in the area. It won't be long before he's caught. His reaction will be most interesting, won't it?"

"He already knows." Ken wasn't about to let Holm bring Matt into this argument. "It doesn't matter what happens to me. It's only a matter of time before you're finished, Herr Holm."

"That's an interesting idea." Holm chuckled. "Do you really think an Allied invasion is close at hand?" He seemed amused by Ken's shocked expression. "Come now, of course we're aware of the broadcast. How foolish, thinking your leaders would broadcast their invasion plans over the BBC?

The very idea is ridiculous. No, I think it's safe to assume rescue will not be coming anytime soon." Holm wiped the smile from his face. "We've had enough of niceties. You have the opportunity to confirm the information I possess, and I advise you to cooperate. After all, we already have one hostage. We do not need two."

"I will not tell you what you want to know." Ken kept his voice even. The hardness in Holm's eyes made him shiver.

Holm picked up his telephone receiver. "Send in Leutnant Beutel. I have a task for him." He replaced the receiver in its cradle and studied it for a moment before addressing Ken once more. "You are surplus to requirements, Herr Lowe, but I am not an unreasonable man. I am giving you a chance to cooperate. Whether you do or not is your decision. However, I, unlike your father, am a man of my word. I will at least give you the chance to live once you've surrendered. I want you to tell me the truth. Do you understand the choice I've given you?"

Yes, he understood. Ken didn't have a choice. He wouldn't give anyone else up to this asshole. Holm had done enough to Matt already. This wasn't about getting information or finding Kristopher. Holm had Arlette for that.

This was about revenge.

"Herr Lowe?" Holm prompted.

Ken nodded. His mouth felt dry. He didn't dare answer aloud. He wasn't sure he could. Holm had no reason to keep him alive. He already had Michel. He didn't need Matt. Kristopher was his target.

Or at least he was *supposed* to be.

I'm sorry, Matt. Stay safe. Survive this war. Live your life. Please.

"Ah, Beutel." Holm nodded when the Leutnant entered.

Shit. He *was* the German who had attempted to rape Jacques's daughter in Pont-Audemer.

Ken swallowed. He bit his lip.

Don't react. Keep Matt safe.

He bit his lip again, hard. Blood dribbled down his chin.

Don't react. Focus on the pain.

Don't react.

"This man has the audacity to continue to lie to me about something I already know to be true," Holm continued. "Do what you need to ensure his cooperation."

"Whatever I need?" Beutel looked at Holm in surprise.

"Yes, Leutnant, whatever you need. That is an order." Holm returned to studying the files on his desk. "Take him away. I'll check on your progress later. Oh, and Beutel?"

"Yes, sir."

"He's a friend of the man who posed as a German officer in Pont-Audemer. I'm certain I don't need to remind you what that incident cost you, do I?"

Beutel smiled. "No, sir. You do not."

"Where are they?" Matt asked Arlette. He'd given her some time to compose herself, but couldn't wait any longer. Holm only needed one hostage and wanted revenge for his father's death. Ken was running out of time… Once Holm had finished doing God knew what to him…

Matt shivered. An image came into his mind of Holm using that whip on Ken, of bare skin splitting open, blood dripping, and… Ken wouldn't scream. He'd retreat into himself and say nothing. He'd never beg for Holm to stop. He'd—

"Where the hell are they?" Matt asked Arlette again. "We need to find them before it's too late. I don't have time for this. He… Please, Arlette."

Sébastien sat next to her, his arm around her shoulders.

Despite Arlette's constant flirting with Michel, Sébastien was clearly sweet on her. She leaned into him as though seeking comfort, although she kept glancing at Kit and away again.

Surely she didn't know who he was and his importance to their mission?

"She's been through a lot," Sébastien said. "I'm sure she'll tell us what she can when she can."

Matt opened his mouth to remind Sébastien that he'd been prepared to leave her in the hands of the enemy only a short time ago, then decided against it. He needed all the help he could encourage Arlette to talk, and focusing Sébastien's anger at Matt and his team wouldn't achieve anything.

"Please, Arlette." Kit looked pale, and his voice shook. "You've already told us Holm has them. Surely you must know where you escaped from. You don't have to come with us. Just give us directions."

"You're not coming with us," Matt reminded him. He took a step back after the glare Kit gave him. "You know why," he continued softly.

"I'm not leaving him—them—there. You know as well as I do what Holm and Reiniger are capable of." Kit bit his lip. "Arlette?"

"I'm more interested in how she managed to escape." Liang was watching Arlette closely. "Holm is not a fool. Everything he does is calculated. How could she have escaped without help? And if she did, why leave Michel behind?" He glanced at Kit before continuing. "I know you have feelings for Michel, Arlette. You wouldn't have left him. What aren't you telling us?"

Sébastien flinched, yet he kept his arm around Arlette. "Maybe she did have help."

Usually Matt would have intervened and berated Liang for being so direct, but he was tired of waiting for answers.

"So you had help," he prompted. If someone had helped her, perhaps they could approach him or her, and it would be a way in, a chance to rescue their own.

Relief chased fear across Arlette's face. "Yes. I had help. A very kind German woman smuggled me out."

"What was her name?" Kit asked sharply. "What did she look like? How did she get you past the guards?" He took a step closer. Matt put a warning hand on Kit's shoulder. As much as he wanted to shake the truth from Arlette, it wouldn't help. They needed to gain her trust, especially after everything she'd claimed she'd gone through.

Arlette replied as sharply. "We can't get in the same way. She won't—can't—help."

For a moment, Matt saw real fear in her eyes. "Answer the question." A nasty suspicion formed in his mind. He wondered if Kit had come to the same conclusion.

"I've already told you, we're not risking our cell to rescue your men." Sébastien squeezed Arlette's hand. "But yes, I do agree with you. Answer the question, Arlette. You know as well as I do that having the name of someone whom we might be able to approach would be helpful."

"I don't know where they are being held," Arlette answered an earlier question instead. "We were taken there in the back of a truck, and I hid in the boot of a car when I was smuggled out."

"Margarete Huber." Kit spoke the name quietly. "She would be the only woman with access to the prisoners. There are only a few people Holm would trust."

"I wouldn't trust that woman with anything," Liang muttered.

"Holm doesn't either," Kit said, "but unfortunately he doesn't have a choice. Her grandfather has influence and money."

"She was very kind, and yes, that was her name." Arlette

hesitated before adding, "They're somewhere by the sea, but that's all I know. I heard the ocean, and the smell was unmistakable."

"That really narrows it down, given how close we are to the coast." Liang didn't look impressed. "Do you at least know how long you were travelling for?"

Arlette shook her head and said nothing.

None of the information she'd given them was particularly helpful—was that deliberate or because she truly had no clue?

"How do you know this woman?" Sébastien stood and took a couple of steps closer to Kit. "You have a lot of information about an officer of the SS too." He shook his head. "I get it now. You're the traitor! It's because of you this has happened."

Kit stood his ground. He lowered his gaze, his pallor turning slightly green.

Matt stepped in before Kit said something they'd all regret. In an indirect way, Kit was the reason this had happened, but Matt wasn't about to let him take all that guilt. Holm was responsible for this, not Kit. "Arguing about all of this isn't going to save our friends."

"You might not answer me, but your expression reflects your guilt." Sébastien glared at Kit. "Although I'm tempted to hand you over to the Germans, I won't. Unlike you, I still have some honour, and I'll be damned if I let you take that from me." He spat at Kit. "Traître!"

Kit pulled a handkerchief from his pocket and wiped his face. He didn't say anything, just bit his lip again.

"Accusing him isn't helping. He's not the traitor." Liang shook his head.

Sébastien snorted. Arlette caught his arm as he turned to walk away.

"Stop! You can't abandon Michel." She spoke quickly, her

words falling over each other. "He's already hurt. You don't understand. Holm will kill him unless—"

Kit looked like he'd been punched in the stomach. "Unless what?" He swore under his breath. "Scheisse."

Michel was hurt? What about Ken? Arlette was playing games with them. She knew where Ken and Michel were. Liang was right. This wasn't a simple lucky escape.

"Unless what?" Matt echoed Kit's question through gritted teeth, although he already had a nasty feeling what the answer would be.

Arlette reached into her skirt. "I have a note."

"Give me that!" Sébastien grabbed it, ripped it open, and scanned it. He frowned. "Who's Kristopher Lehrer?"

Kit snatched the note from him and read it quickly. He glared at Arlette, his eyes bright with anger. "Du verdammte Schlampe!" He took a step towards her, his fist balled, then turned on his heel and walked away.

<h1 style="text-align:center">CHAPTER SIXTEEN</h1>

Kit slumped into a chair on the opposite side of the room, burying his face in his hands. Liang and Matt exchanged a worried look.

"I'll talk to him," Liang said before Matt could offer.

"I'm guessing Holm offered him a deal. Even if he trades himself for Michel, there's no guarantee Holm wouldn't kill Michel anyway." Matt leaned in closer to Liang and spoke quietly so no one would overhear. Matt might have been hiding his reaction a little better, but his voice was strained, and he kept clenching and unfurling one fist.

"That's my guess too." Liang didn't think he'd be able to say anything positive, but he wasn't about to remind Matt that Ken's situation was even more dire than Michel's. If the note wanted Kit to exchange the information he carried for Michel, it probably meant Holm had already decided he only needed one hostage.

"My German isn't that good. I couldn't read much of the note," Sébastien said, "but I'm guessing Paul—if that's really his name—has whatever this Holm wants."

Liang nodded. They'd need to know exactly what was in

the note before they could begin to find a way out of the situation. He walked over to Kit, pulled up another chair, and sat next to him. "We'll do what we can. I'm sorry, Kit." He didn't see the point in using Kit's assumed name, and it was obvious Sébastien had already worked out who Kit was. "We need to see the note."

"I can't…" Kit looked up, his face pinched. He handed the note to Liang, his hand trembling. "Holm will kill him. Not only that, but he'll hurt him, no matter what I do. I always said I'd never let that happen. Why did I make a promise I couldn't keep?"

"We all make those." Liang skimmed the note and shook his head. No wonder Kit had sworn at Arlette. He put a brief hand on Kit's shoulder before standing and rejoining Matt and the others.

As much as they wanted to save their friends, rushing in wouldn't help. Difficult as the decision was, they'd need to wait and plan their next move carefully.

Matt read the note quickly, but thankfully not aloud. "Holm's obviously finished with Arlette. He's named her as his informant, and probably thinks we'll deal with her so he doesn't need to. That figures."

"I didn't tell him about the church." Arlette hadn't spoken since Kit had read the note, but instead sat quietly in the corner. Nicolas stood guard over her in case she attempted to escape, and given his angry expression, he was looking forward to any excuse to put a bullet in her. "I wasn't followed. I was careful. It's still safe here."

"How am I supposed to believe anything you say?" Sébastien snapped. "I trusted you! We've worked together for months. I…" He turned his back on her in a deliberate gesture. "Don't worry. I'll deal with her. I trusted her, so I will do it."

"If she *had* told Holm about the church, he'd be here by

now. We're all here. He has no reason to wait." Kit scrubbed at his eyes, then stood and crossed the room to join them. "I need to do something. To know I've at least tried."

"You can't take part in any rescue," Matt said. "To hell with giving Holm what he wants. If you give yourself up, Michel's still as good as dead. I figure as long as we don't wait until after the deadline he's given you, Holm still has a reason to keep him alive."

He didn't mention Ken. All they could do was hope and pray he survived long enough to be rescued too.

"What else was in the note?" Sébastien glanced at Arlette again. "I know I said several times that I won't risk my team to help, but she was one of ours. This is now a question of honour. We will do what we can to help."

"I'm Kristopher Lehrer, and the note was for me. I... I have the information Holm wants, information that could win the war." Kit wasn't telling Sébastien anything he wouldn't have already figured out. "Holm has proposed a deal. If I give myself up before curfew tomorrow night, he will consider letting Michel live. He knows we are friends and that I..." Kit bit his lip. "I offered my cooperation once before in exchange for Michel's freedom. It was seven months ago, and Michel and I had only just met, but Reiniger —and Holm—wouldn't have forgotten it. I should have never... even if I could give Holm what he wants, it wouldn't save Michel. I can't watch..."

Matt put a hand on Kit's shoulder. "I know," he said softly. "We'll do what we can. I promise. I'll do whatever it takes to save both of them or..."

He trailed off, but Liang still heard the unspoken words.
Or I'll die trying.

Nicolas whistled. "Information that could win the war? That is quite a burden you're carrying, mon ami."

Kit managed a shaky nod. He held himself together well, considering the situation. Liang knew how he'd be reacting if given the choice between his own life and Juliane's. However, this wasn't only about Kit and Michel—and Ken. If this weapon was built, it would kill so many more.

"That's typical of Holm." Liang snorted. "He always makes it sound as though he's not the one making the decisions when he is the only one with the power to do so. Kind of him to give you time to consider it too." Waiting only made it harder not to give in to the temptation to accept the so-called offer, and Holm would be well aware of that. "Bastard."

He obviously thought there was a good chance Kit would give himself up. What the hell was Margarete Huber's part in all this? She had to be involved, or why would she make sure Arlette escaped with the note? Had she figured out what Michel truly was to Kit?

Liang remembered what she'd said to Michel in Stuttgart —*"I told Herr Holm that if he found you, he'd soon have Lehrer."* If this offer was her idea, she deserved whatever harm came her way.

"It sounds as though you speak from experience," Sébastien said.

Théo looked up from his radio. Although he hadn't said anything, he'd been following their discussion closely. Liang rather hoped he'd keep out of the conversation. Given the nature of it, his abrupt and less than witty repartee would only add to the already tense atmosphere.

"Liang and I have both had the misfortune of being guests of Herr Holm." Matt's tone suggested he would not answer any more questions on that particular subject. Liang didn't blame him. He didn't want to talk about it either.

"There is nothing in the note about your other friend?" Sébastien asked.

"No." Matt spoke so quietly Liang almost missed his reply.

"I'm so sorry," Kit said. "Perhaps if I—"

"No! We are not making deals with Holm. He's taken too many lives already. This stops now." Matt strode over to Arlette, pushed Nicolas out of the way, and yanked her to her feet. "Get her out of here. We need to make some difficult decisions, and I don't want her here, even if she won't be able to pass on the information afterward." He glanced at Liang and Kit, his expression grim. "We all know what Sébastien has offered to do. If anyone has an issue with it, speak now." He turned to Sébastien. "I know you had feelings for her. If you want me to—"

"She was under my command. Therefore she is my responsibility." Sébastien drew his gun and gestured to Arlette to start moving towards the stairs. "Nicolas. Go check on Cécile and make sure this area hasn't been compromised. I do not wish to be interrupted." He waited until Nicolas had left before continuing. "This is the only way we will be safe."

"I was only trying to keep Michel safe." Arlette glared at Kit. "This is your fault. Call yourself his friend? I love him. I—"

"You're a fool," Liang told Arlette. "Michel does not love you. His heart belongs to another." Had she truly believed her feelings for Michel were reciprocated? "You've betrayed his *friendship*, and there is no way back from that after everything you've done."

"I know he doesn't love me." Arlette replied to Liang, but she kept looking at Kit. "I heard you talking. You were planning to stay in France. With him." She took a deep breath before continuing. "I knew about François. I thought Michel had learned to do the right thing, but then I saw that he was about to make another mistake, and I had to save him. Don't you see? He'd be in terrible danger if anyone found out."

"He's in danger now," Matt said quietly.

"This is no one's fault but your own, Arlette." Sébastien glanced at Matt and his team as though still giving them the opportunity to voice their disagreement. If he'd worked out what Arlette was referring to, he didn't comment on it.

Kit studied the ground but didn't say anything.

Liang shrugged. He had no sympathy for Arlette. Although she'd acted in some misguided effort to save Michel, all she'd achieved was her own death sentence—and most likely his.

"Thank you," Matt said.

Théo stood and stretched. "I need some air." He pushed past Arlette, glanced at her for barely a second, then sprinted up the stairs.

"I—" Arlette started to say something, but Sébastien cut her off.

"It's too late for words now." He escorted her up the stairs and kicked the door shut behind them as they left.

Matt gave Kit a brief hug. "I know you want to go after Michel. I want to wrap my hands around Holm's neck and throttle the asshole. If I find him, I'll do it for both of us."

"A bullet between the eyes might be easier, but probably not as satisfying." Liang should have been disturbed by the easy manner in which they were discussing another man's death, but after everything Holm had done, and now this… The situation felt a little surreal, and he half expected to wake up and find none of it had happened.

"We just agreed to an execution, and I didn't say anything to stop it." Kit still looked ill, but he was regaining some of his colour. "All I could think about is Michel and what Holm is doing to…" He stilled and shook his head. "Oh God."

"I know," Matt said softly. "Believe me, I know."

"Verdammt." Kit met Matt's eyes. "This is not easy for you either. I wish—"

"That we could talk about what we really want to?" Matt suggested. "Don't worry, Kit, I know, and I'm guessing you know as well."

Liang cleared his throat. "Right, so now we *all* know, let's get on with the matter at hand, hmm? You can talk about what you know later, when your… friends… are safe."

Matt paled. "You know?"

"None of you are as careful as you should be," Liang said. "Arlette wasn't the only one who figured things out, although I suspect it was in part because she already knew about François, whoever he is." Given Kit's expression, he'd already known about François, but thankfully he didn't try to explain. "I hope for your sakes no one else finds out, and you take more care once this mission is over. Don't worry. I'm not going to tell anyone." If it had been in any other circumstance, he would have chuckled at Matt's shocked expression. But for now, he wanted to believe his friends still had a future with the person they loved, and he'd continue to do so until he had proof to the contrary. Once they lost that hope, what was the point of any of this?

"I've already had that conversation with him," Kit said dryly. "Michel—"

He flinched at the sound of the gunshot above their heads. To a passerby, it would have sounded like a car backfiring, but they all knew what it was.

A coded knock at the door interrupted the strained silence that followed. Liang opened the door. Sébastien looked pale, and his shoulders were slumped.

"It's done," he said.

~

Kristopher's head pounded. He'd tried to sleep but couldn't. When he closed his eyes, he saw Michel broken and bleeding with Reiniger standing over him. In the end, he'd headed outside to get some fresh air.

Holm had given Kristopher until curfew the following day—Monday—to surrender. It would take until then to put everything in place and to get the uniforms and false identity papers ready, so it wouldn't leave them with much time to make their rescue attempt.

Nicolas found them some blankets before he and Cécile headed home for the night. Sébastien had taken first watch, Théo the second. Kristopher didn't recognise the woman who relieved Théo, although she clearly knew Matt and his team were now a part of their cell. She'd warned him not to go far and suggested a small alcove behind the church so he couldn't be easily seen from a distance.

A few minutes later, Matt had joined him. "Couldn't sleep either, huh?"

"I'd prefer not to." Kristopher kept telling himself they had more chance of rescuing Michel and Ken if they waited, yet it was getting harder and harder to believe it.

"I want to storm that bunker and do whatever I need to keep Ken safe." Matt put an arm around Kristopher. "We're doing the right thing by waiting," he said softly. "Getting ourselves killed or captured isn't going to help either of them."

"I hope you're right." Kristopher didn't shake free of Matt's loose embrace. "Watch the sunrise with me? If I start talking about any of this, I'm afraid I won't be able to stop. Not only that, but it will make it real."

"I wish it wasn't real either, but yes, I know what you mean." Matt grew silent for a moment. "If we don't get through this, it's been a privilege knowing you, Kit."

"And you, Matt."

They'd stayed there until dawn and then quietly returned to their hiding place beneath the church. That morning neither spoke of their conversation the night before, focusing instead on what needed to be done. Keeping busy helped, and Kristopher went over their plan several times, working through all the possible scenarios he could think of.

It had a good chance of succeeding.

It had to succeed.

The rest of their team had headed out a short time ago, leaving Kristopher alone with Théo. Nicolas kept watch in the church above them.

Kristopher rapped his fingers on the table, replaying one of Bach's fugues in his mind, forcing himself to analyse the chord progressions. The music in his head grew louder as his attempts at distraction failed, and Michel cried out in pain above it.

He winced, gritted his teeth, and began to pace. *C major, a passing note leading to the dominant—*

Théo turned to Kristopher, his eyes shining with excitement. He'd spent the night at the church too, although he must have slept for some of it, as he looked much brighter than Kristopher felt. "They're broadcasting the second part of the code!" He turned the radio up so Kristopher could listen.

"D'une langueur montone."

Kristopher caught the last part of the broadcast. Excitement bubbled up inside. This was the distraction they needed to rescue Michel and Ken.

"It's a good thing we didn't wait for this, oui?" Théo grinned.

They'd discussed waiting, but both Matt and Kristopher were adamant that if they did, it would lessen Michel and Ken's chances of survival. Sébastien's contacts had discovered Holm's current whereabouts, and a truck had been seen pulling up there the evening before, so it had to be where Ken and Michel were being held.

The command post near the coastal battery was heavily guarded, although the Resistance had a contact on the inside willing to help. Matt and Sébastien would pose as German soldiers delivering a prisoner to Standartenführer Holm. It was a calculated risk, as Holm would be expecting Kristopher. Liang had suggested acting as their prisoner and pretending he had given himself up in order to betray his colleagues after he'd discovered they'd been working with a Japanese man without his knowledge.

Matt hadn't been happy with the idea but admitted it sounded realistic and would hopefully be enough to get them into the building. After all, lies worked best when there was some truth to them.

Once inside they would split up. Matt insisted he'd look for Ken, while Liang and Sébastien found Michel. The Resistance contact had promised a diversion to aid their escape, yet too much of the plan depended on him being trustworthy rather than it all being an elaborate trap.

No one had any idea who he was, only that he was a German with some serious reservations about the methods Holm used to get results. With an invasion so close, perhaps he had decided it was time to take one last chance, especially considering what was at risk? Nicolas had suggested he take Sébastien's place, but Sébastien would hear none of it. He had introduced Arlette to the cell and accompanied her on the mission to get Matt and his team to Normandy safely. This was his responsibility, and he would complete his mission.

Kristopher realised Théo was expecting an answer. "Oui, although the broadcast only means the invasion is imminent. It doesn't mean it will happen tonight. This could be all over before any Allied troops set foot on

French soil. I don't like waiting. I'd feel better if I was doing something."

If the Allies were arriving soon, he was running out of time to disappear. Although Michel had told Kristopher how to contact people who could help, he wasn't sure how they'd react to the news that Michel was in custody.

"Apart from pacing?" Théo shook his head. "There is nothing we can do but wait. Nicolas is keeping watch upstairs. We should be safe here until it is all over."

Since everyone else had left, Théo had suddenly found his voice. Perhaps it was because he hated waiting as much as Kristopher did?

"I hope Sébastien was right about the church still being safe." Unfortunately Arlette knew about all their safe houses, so if Holm and his men had been told about the church, they probably had been given information about anywhere else they could hide too. "I'll be relieved when this is all over."

"Hopefully your Allied friends will evict all the German scum from France and we won't have to worry about it. Vive la France!" Théo raised his hand in a victory signal. "We've waited a long time for this."

"Perhaps, but I doubt it will be as simple as that. Even if the invasion is successful, a lot can happen in a few hours."

Kristopher couldn't shake his growing feeling of dread. Although he'd reasoned that Holm didn't know about the church, he'd been wrong before. He sat for a few moments and then started to pace again. At least there was the trapdoor if they needed to leave, although he had no idea where they'd go.

If Matt and the others had already been caught, Holm's men could be on their way now.

What if Michel was already dead, or worse? Kristopher swallowed a lump in his throat and closed his hand around the gun in his coat pocket. He knew what he needed to do if it looked as though he would be caught. Holm could not get his hands on the information Kristopher carried. He hoped he'd find the courage to do what he had to.

At least if he were dead, there would be no reason for Holm to keep Michel alive. Better a quick death than long, lingering torture.

Kristopher stifled a sob. He'd been so naive when he'd first fled the institute. He'd only thought of the risk to himself, and already so many good people had lost their lives. How much longer could he go on like this?

Théo tilted his head to one side. "I thought I heard something," he whispered.

A loud crash sounded above them.

Both men froze.

"You cannot commit this sacrilege," Nicolas yelled. "This is a church!"

Something shattered on the floor directly above Kristopher's head. It was quickly followed by a gunshot.

Théo began shoving his radio equipment into a small suitcase. "Get the trapdoor open," he hissed. "I'm not leaving this here for them to find."

Once he had the trapdoor open, Kristopher grabbed a chair and headed for the stairs. If he could shove something under the door handle it would give Théo more time.

"Open this door!" A man yelled in German, then kicked at the door. When it didn't open, he put more force behind it. The wood began to splinter.

Kristopher dropped the chair, sprinted across the room, grabbed Théo's sleeve, and yanked him towards the trapdoor. Once they were both through, he reached up and closed it, slamming the bolt shut. Locking it might slow their pursuers but wouldn't stop them.

He turned on his torch and shone the light around. The tunnel was narrow, but although Kristopher was able to stand upright, he didn't dare run. A few minutes later, it split into two.

"Take the left." Théo was breathing heavily. "It comes out in a hall at the end of the street. Climb the stairs and you should find the back door open. I'll be right behind you."

Wood cracked behind them. Their pursuers had found the trapdoor. It wouldn't be long before they were in the tunnel.

The left tunnel led to a dead end. A wooden ladder stood propped against the wall, a trapdoor above it. Kristopher climbed quickly and pushed it open. With men in the tunnel behind them, there was nowhere else to go. Once out of the tunnel, he crouched down to help Théo haul the radio out. He slammed the door shut, and Théo helped him to drag a heavy box over the top of it.

"I need to find Cécile and warn her. There are others working with us too. We're all in danger." Théo picked up the suitcase holding the radio. "It's almost curfew. We need to find shelter quickly."

Kristopher nodded. He followed Théo onto the street, forcing himself to slow down to a walk. They needed to look as though they were ordinary citizens going about their normal business. Where could they go? Anyone who gave them refuge would put themselves at risk, and also Kristopher had no idea whom he could trust.

They'd barely crossed the road when two soldiers approached them. Kristopher fought to hide his panic.

"In here." Théo ushered Kristopher into a doorway and handed him the suitcase. "I'm going to lead them in the opposite direction. Bérénice who owns the bakery on the other side of the square works with us. You can trust her, but make sure she hasn't been compromised. Tell her you need to purchase two bagels for your wife's anniversary and give her the radio. She has a good hiding place for it, and she will also be able to help you get out of Cyrville-sur-Mer."

Kristopher nodded. "Be careful."

Théo gave him a curt nod. "And you." He yelled at the soldiers in French, waited until they'd all turned in his direction and then started running. They quickly gave chase.

Kristopher waited until they were out of sight, and keeping his head down, began to walk towards the square.

CHAPTER SEVENTEEN

The Gefreiter glanced at Matt's identity papers, then scanned a document on his desk. "I have no record that you are expected."

Getting past the guard outside had seemed a little too easy. He'd studied Matt's and Sébastien's identity papers, saluted, and pointed them to the narrow flight of concrete steps that led down to the command bunker.

Liang tried not to shiver. This place with its narrow tunnels reminded him too much of a rat trying to find its way out of a maze. The map Sébastien had managed to secure showed another two exits off the personnel shelter. That bloody map had better be right.

While Matt talked to the guard outside, Liang had distracted himself by listening to the sound of the waves crashing against the shore below. It did nothing to quell his anxiety, despite telling himself it was better to be heading into the bowels of the earth than standing close to the edge of a cliff.

On reaching the bottom of the staircase, they'd found themselves in a decent-size room. A series of tunnels connected each room with a long corridor leading to the command building. According to Sébastien's contact, that was where Michel and Ken were being held. All they needed to do was get past the armed guards. Good thing they weren't here to destroy the artillery battery itself, as *that* was surrounded by barbed wire, soldiers, and land mines.

"There is definitely nothing here," the Gefreiter repeated. He moved one hand to his holster, ready to draw his weapon.

"Oh, I'm sorry," Liang said. "I seem to have forgotten to make an appointment. That's the thing with betrayal. Often it is spur of the moment rather than planned."

The Gefreiter blinked a couple of times and relaxed his stance, replacing his look of suspicion with one of confusion. Often all it took was a flippant remark to throw a man off guard.

"I am under orders from Standartenführer Holm to deliver Herr Doktor Zhou to him personally, as he has information regarding Herr Doktor Lehrer," Matt said. "I hope I misheard you. I wouldn't want to have to tell him you questioned his orders."

"No, Herr Hauptmann. Of course not, sir." The Gefreiter checked the document again, frowning. "There is a note that he is expecting a Herr Doktor Lehrer, sir."

Liang smiled. "There you go, then. Unfortunately Herr Doktor Lehrer was unable to keep the appointment, so I'm here instead. It looks as though whoever was on duty before you forgot to pass along that information to you." He leaned in and lowered his voice. "You must excuse my earlier comment. I'm nervous about meeting Herr Holm. I do hope we can keep this between ourselves."

"Of course, Herr Doktor Zhou." The Gefreiter gestured to the man standing guard nearby. "Keep watch while I—"

Sébastien drew his gun and shot him, the silencer masking the noise of the bullet. The Gefreiter fell forward, blood smearing the papers on the desk from the bullet wound in his head. The guard levelled his weapon at them.

"Drop your weapons, or I'll—" He cried out and dropped to the ground, clutching his leg.

"Quiet!" Matt ordered, "or I'll aim for somewhere that will hurt a lot more." He turned to Sébastien. "There was no need for that. You'd better find somewhere to hide the body." He threw Liang a pair of handcuffs. "Take his weapon, restrain him, and find something to gag him with."

"He was reaching for the telephone." Sébastien shrugged. "If he'd told Holm we're here, we'd be finished." He began to move the body, stopped, and rearranged some of the papers on the desk so they covered the bloodstain. "There. Now he looks as though he's sleeping."

Liang closed the handcuffs around the guard's wrists, used the man's handkerchief to gag him, and then forced him to his feet. The man stumbled and gasped in pain through his gag. "Why don't we leave him here?" Liang suggested. "We're wasting time, and he can't walk far. Trying to find somewhere to hide him will only draw attention to ourselves."

Where the hell was the Resistance contact? Liang wasn't happy about pretending to betray his friends although it gave him a better chance of making it out alive if the plan went to pot than playing prisoner and having to wear handcuffs.

"If you've changed your mind, this is your last chance to leave." Matt spoke to Sébastien, but he looked at Liang as he said the words.

And be the one to tell Kit they'd decided to leave Michel in custody? Liang shook his head. "We'd better split up before someone finds these two. Sébastien?"

"Good hunting, mon ami." Sébastien nodded to Matt, waiting until he'd headed into the tunnel ahead of them before speaking again. "Remember your role in this," he told Liang. "Do not let anyone know you are armed. It is better for them to see you as a civilian and therefore less of a threat."

"I'm not an idiot," Liang muttered. He'd refused to walk into the lion's den without a weapon.

"I never said you were. If anything, I think you are brave, especially as it is very obvious that you have not had much in the way of training."

"Thank you. I think." Liang followed Sébastien down the tunnel to the radio bunker. Thankfully the tunnels widened out substantially almost immediately, so it was easier to pretend he was in a corridor in a building above ground.

A couple of minutes later, he heard voices.

"In here." Sébastien shoved Liang into a small darkened office and followed him inside. Liang pressed himself against the wall while Sébastien quietly pulled the door towards him until it was only slightly ajar.

"I am impressed with your technique, Beutel, but there is still much you could learn." Reiniger sounded pleased with himself.

"Thank you, sir." Beutel's tone was a mix of respect and pride. "I appreciate this opportunity. It has been most satisfying, although I must admit the prisoner is extremely stubborn."

Reiniger laughed. "They always *think* they are, Leutnant, but everyone breaks eventually. It's important to remember that and to exploit any weakness." He paused. "Meet me outside the traitor's cell after you've had your meal break. Fräulein Huber should be finished with him by then, and I can teach you some of what I've learnt from watching the Standartenführer. He is an excellent interrogator, and I'd be happy to demonstrate some of his methods for you."

"Yes, sir. Thank you, sir."

Liang grimaced. Those bastards needed to pay for what they'd done. "He can lead me to Michel," he hissed at

Sébastien. If they'd miscalculated where Michel was being held, at least this way one of them would find him. "You stick to our original plan. I'm going after Reiniger."

It took Kristopher longer than he anticipated to reach the square. He didn't dare run and draw attention to himself, although he was aware it would be curfew soon. If he were caught out on the streets after that, the Gendarmerie wouldn't need an excuse to arrest him. Already there were fewer people around. An older couple nodded to him as they passed, and he returned the gesture, as it would have been rude not to.

The bakery was where he remembered it. He picked up his pace, relieved that he'd soon be somewhere safe. Hopefully Bérénice would have news about Cécile as she would have been on her way back to the church when the soldiers had arrived. Kristopher had already decided he wouldn't impose on Bérénice any longer than he had to. Once he knew Michel's fate, he'd either wait for him or ask Bérénice to help him organise safe passage to Bernay to meet with their contacts there.

A truck rumbled past him, and he ducked out of sight into a nearby alcove. The truck stopped outside the bakery and soldiers climbed out. One of them strode up to the front door and banged on it.

"Open in the name of the Führer!" The soldier—an SS Unterscharführer—gestured to two of his men, who headed around the back of the shop.

A few minutes later, a woman answered the front door. Kristopher strained to hear and edged as close as he dared without risking being seen.

"I do not know what you are talking about," she

exclaimed. "There is no one else here. I live alone and have done so since my husband and son presented themselves for national service."

Men pushed past her. Glass smashed, and heavy objects hit the floor with a thud. Bérénice—Kristopher guessed it must be her—protested, and the Unterscharführer slapped her across the face.

"You work with the Resistance. You know the penalty. However, if you can tell me the whereabouts of Herr Lehrer, I might be persuaded to show some mercy."

"Herr Lehrer? I don't know anyone by that name. Nor am I involved with the Resistance. How dare you suggest such a thing!" Bérénice held her head up high.

"We'll see." The Unterscharführer gave one of his men a nod. The soldier entered the truck and a few moments later dragged another man from it.

Théo's mouth was bleeding, and his hands handcuffed behind him. The soldier forced Théo to his knees.

"Now, Fräulein," the Unterscharführer said, "I will ask you again. Do you work for the Resistance?"

Bérénice shook her head.

"In that case, this man is of no further use to me. I had thought he might persuade you to cooperate, but I see he will better serve as an example." The Unterscharführer shrugged, then drew his gun and shot Théo. He fell forward, twitched, and then stilled.

Bérénice put her hand to her mouth. "Meurtrier! I will not help you." She spat at the Unterscharführer.

Scheisse.

Kristopher's stomach churned. The Unterscharführer had asked for him by name before killing Théo without a second thought.

"We'll see." The Unterscharführer shrugged, took Bérénice by the arm, and ushered her back inside the bakery.

How long would it be before they found others who knew of the Resistance? How much did the SS already know? Kristopher didn't know whom he could trust, and if he approached anyone, he'd only be signing their death warrant.

His heart sped up, and he forced himself to think. Panicking wouldn't solve anything. He shoved his hand into his pocket. He still had his gun. His fingers closed over the small cyanide capsule he'd wrapped in his handkerchief.

He couldn't see a way out. If he were Holm, he'd have roadblocks on all the roads out of the area. Reaching the bunker by Holm's deadline now wasn't an option. Holm would have realised Kristopher wasn't coming and would be setting up his next move. With Holm there was always a next move—he'd never given up and wouldn't do so now. The only chance Kristopher had to win this game would be to do something Holm wouldn't expect. He'd go to the one place he should be staying the furthest away from.

Matt and the others could already be in custody or dead. Kristopher couldn't rely on help from them.

He took a deep breath. To hell with waiting to be caught. At least if he took action, he'd die knowing for sure that he'd done what he could. If his attempt to rescue Michel failed, he'd use either his gun or the capsule to ensure he wouldn't be persuaded to reveal the formulae to Holm—or anyone else.

Either way he'd be killing Michel—if he wasn't already dead—but at least this way, Holm would have no reason to torture him. Better a quick death than a long, horrible, lingering one.

"I'm coming, Michel," he whispered. "Whatever happens we'll be together soon. I promise."

～

Matt saluted the two soldiers when they passed him and kept walking as though he was meant to be there. Unsurprisingly the soldiers returned his salute and did not stop to question a superior officer.

The closer he got to the hospital bunker, the colder he felt inside. What if he was already too late and Ken was dead? He'd worked through several scenarios, yet as soon as he reached the part where Ken was—Matt couldn't get his mind to go any further.

Despite that, a part of him did acknowledge the possibility. His initial anger over what had happened gave way to… nothing. He couldn't give in to his emotions. He'd made a promise to see this mission through, whatever it took.

He paused at another fork in the tunnels, recalling the map he'd memorised. He had to keep going straight ahead. Sébastien's contact had said one of the prisoners was being kept in the hospital bunker, the other somewhere else, but he wasn't sure where.

Matt had taken the chance that Holm would keep Michel closer. It also made sense that Michel's location would not be as well known, as he could be used to negotiate with Kit. It wouldn't do for him to disappear at the crucial moment, after all.

Taking down the radio bunker with a few well-placed explosives should provide enough distraction to get to both hostages and free them.

He hoped.

Whoever Sébastien's contact was, he had kept his identity a secret and stayed well out of this. Matt understood the need for self-preservation, but he would have appreciated a little more help about now.

Unless the whole thing was an elaborate trap?

At this point, Matt really didn't care. He wanted to find Ken and get out of here. If Ken was already—Matt would cause as much damage as he possibly could and go down fighting.

Damn it, these walls all looked the same.

At least the place was well lit.

A sign on the wall indicated he'd entered the section of the bunker where he needed to be. Matt clenched one fist. His skin felt clammy. He swallowed.

Ahead of him two soldiers looked up. They stood in front of a door and were very obviously standing guard.

"I'm here to see the prisoner," Matt said. "Standarten-führer Holm wishes me to speak to him in the hope I can get some answers out of him."

The men glanced at each other. "Leutnant Beutel told us to keep guard until he returned," one of them said.

Beutel? Holm had ordered *Beutel* to interrogate Ken?

"I need to see the prisoner." Matt struggled to keep his voice calm. "Why doesn't one of you check with Leutnant Beutel while the other stays here?" He hardened his tone. "I'd think carefully about doubting the word of a superior officer before you do so."

"I still need to check with the Leutnant, sir." The Gefreiter swallowed but held his ground. "Obersturmführer Reiniger told us only to let him or Leutnant Beutel enter the room."

Matt nodded. "I understand that, Gefreiter, but the sooner one of you confirms my orders, the sooner we'll all be able to get back to our duties." He paused for effect. "And, as I said, they come directly from Standartenführer Holm."

"Yes, sir. Sorry, sir." The Gefreiter who had argued the point strode away and was soon out of sight. He wouldn't be gone long.

"Sorry," Matt murmured to the remaining soldier.

"Sir?" The Gefreiter didn't have the chance to say anything else. Matt's fist connected with his jaw, and he slid to the floor.

Matt kicked the door. He heard a low moan inside the room. The stupid door didn't open. He shoved his shoulder against it, putting his weight behind the action. The door burst open. Matt dragged the unconscious man's body inside quickly and looked around.

Piles of boxes filled the room. The moan sounded again from his left. Matt pushed past the boxes, not caring when some of them fell to the floor.

A small area had been cleared at the back of the room—square in shape and about the size of a cell.

Ken sat slumped forward on a chair in the centre of it. His arms were bound behind him, and he wasn't moving. Blood spotted the floor around the chair. Ken's shirt was ripped, and ugly bruises covered his chest.

"Ken!" Matt whispered. He sprinted across the room. Was he already too late? "Ken? Please be alive. Please be alive."

He'd heard a moan before. That meant he was still alive. Right?

Ken looked up, eyes unfocused, staring at Matt. "Be safe," he whispered. "Don't come for me." He yanked at his restraints, rough rope chafing already raw wrists.

"I'm real. I'm here." Matt kissed Ken's forehead. "God, what have they done to you?" He'd kill the bastards.

Get Ken out of here. Worry about that later.

Matt crouched down behind Ken, pulled out a knife, and cut through the ropes holding him to the chair. "I'm here to rescue you. You didn't think I was going to leave you, did you?" He kept his tone light, knowing if he let himself think too hard about anything, he'd be no use to Ken at all.

Ken was alive.

"Oh hell." Ken spoke in a hoarse whisper. "You can't be here. You're supposed to be safe. I don't... I... You can't be here."

Matt sawed through the final piece of rope and pulled Ken into his arms. Ken flinched when Matt touched his skin.

Ken's stomach and chest were covered in bruises, one eye almost swollen shut. He took a breath and let out a grunt of pain. He probably had at least one broken rib, maybe more.

"I'm rescuing you whether you like it or not." Matt leaned in and kissed Ken on the lips. "I love you, and I don't want a life without you." He helped Ken to his feet and wrapped an arm around him to steady him. "We're getting out of here. You can tell me I'm an idiot later."

"You're an idiot, and I love you too." Ken hissed in pain. "Waste of time arguing with you." He tried to stand on his own and nearly fell over. "Need to help me," he said through gritted teeth.

"I am going to kill the fucking asshole who did this to you."

"Oh God." Ken tried to shove Matt behind him.

Matt looked up and saw what—or rather who—Ken was looking at.

"Herr Bryant." Holm shook his head. His expression suggested he'd tasted something nasty. "This explains so much. You're… I'd say it was quite the touching reunion if I wasn't so disgusted by it." He aimed his weapon at both of them. "I have no use for either of you. The question is, who do I kill first?"

"You fucking bastard." Matt stepped in front of Ken and drew his own weapon. Holm couldn't kill both of them with one bullet. Matt would get him first, whatever it took.

Holm smiled. "I don't think so." His finger tightened on the trigger.

The ground shook under them. Boxes wobbled, then fell. Matt ducked to avoid them at the same moment Holm fired. Ken hit the floor with a thud. The lights died, plunging the room into darkness. Matt reached out, frantically trying to find Ken. His hands hit cardboard, then metal. He pushed them aside, only to grasp at air.

"Ken!" Matt didn't dare fire his weapon. "Ken?"

Please no.

Someone grunted. Was it Ken or Holm? Had the noise come from behind him or in front of him?

A siren wailed its warning too late. Air raid.

Matt coughed.

Smoke.

Something was on fire. He almost hoped for a flame, anything to be rid of the darkness. He hated the dark—it felt too much like the familiar panic and dread of his nightmares.

This wasn't a dream. This was real.

He wasn't alone. He almost wished he was.

CHAPTER EIGHTEEN

Kristopher parked the stolen car a few hundred metres away from the command post and took one last look at himself in the rearview mirror. He adjusted his fedora and then climbed out of the car.

It had taken a few tries to find an unlocked car, and he'd almost been caught while he'd bypassed the ignition in an attempt to get it started.

The hat and coat completed his persona. He had to look the part he was playing, or he'd never get past the guards. Someone dressed as a Frenchman would only further raise suspicion, and he was taking a big chance as it was.

A couple of deep breaths and Kristopher began walking. He could do this. He had to do this.

The barbed wire on either side of the trenches surrounding the artillery battery did nothing to set his mind at ease. Escape that way would be impossible. Even if he wasn't caught on the barbed wire, he doubted he'd escape the blast of a land mine.

He caught a whiff of the ocean—a reminder that the cliff

face wasn't far away. Whoever had chosen this location had thought of *almost* everything.

Only one guard stood in front of the narrow tunnel that led into the command bunker.

Kristopher strode up to him. "Good evening, Gefreiter," he said pleasantly. "I am Herr Doktor Gage and here at the request of Standartenführer Holm." He pulled out his identity papers and gave them to the guard. "And before you ask, yes, I was born here, but my mother is German, and my home is in Berlin."

"I have no—"

Kristopher interrupted him before he could speak further. "It's good to see someone being so thorough." He reached into his pocket for the note Holm had sent and showed it to the Gefreiter. He'd already folded it over so that the first half of it couldn't be seen. "See, it says there that he requests my presence here before curfew. I'm sure you recognise his signature."

"It doesn't have your name on it, sir." The Gefreiter glanced between the identity papers and the man in front of him. Unfortunately Kristopher only had access to his papers for Benoit Gage on such short notice, but it was better than trying to bluff his way into the command bunker with no papers at all.

"That part of the note is classified, so I can't show it to you." Kristopher shook his head. "I see my earlier appraisal of your efficiency was a misjudgement on my part." He took back the note. "Not only do I have to deal with my car breaking down, which is why I'm late, but now your insubordination." He gave the soldier a look of distain. "I wish to speak to your superior officer. I'm sure he will treat me with the respect I deserve. What was his name again? We spoke on the telephone earlier. Oh yes. Obersturmführer Reiniger."

The Gefreiter paled. Reiniger's reputation hadn't lessened since his time at the institute in Berlin.

Kristopher glanced at his watch. "This is important. Herr Holm asked for me specifically, and my identity papers are in order, are they not?" He studied the Gefreiter and altered his expression to one of extreme annoyance. "I don't remember you from the institute. Are you a new addition to Herr Holm's staff?"

"Yes, sir." The Gefreiter seemed suddenly unsure. He wasn't that old, probably twenty if that.

"Ah. I worked there directly under Herr Doktor Kluge and Herr Doktor Lehrer. Brilliant men. Both of them. I was extremely distressed over the whole business." Kristopher shook his head sadly.

The Gefreiter barely managed to hide his concern, although it was probably for himself rather than Kristopher. "I'm sorry to have held you up, sir." He stood to one side to let Kristopher pass. "Have a good evening, sir."

"Thank you, Gefreiter." Kristopher paused at the doorway. "What is your name, Gefreiter? I'll be sure to put in a good word for you."

"That's fine, sir, and totally unnecessary." The Gefreiter saluted. "There's a room at the end of this first tunnel. The soldier there will check your papers again and then call someone to take you to Herr Holm."

"Excellent." Kristopher didn't smile. He walked past the Gefreiter without another word. He couldn't believe his ploy had worked so well. But then, his father had been a master at bullying his employees to ensure he got the results he wanted.

I'm playing my father.

Aren't I?

Kristopher's mouth felt dry. Surely he hadn't ever been as abrupt and obnoxious as his father used to be? A memory of when he'd looked in the mirror after he'd first dyed his hair a darker shade caught him unawares, and his step faltered. He'd seen a glimpse of his father in himself then. Merely a glimpse, and only in looks.

I'm nothing like him, and I don't intend to be.

Paul Lehrer had embraced Hitler's ideals and wanted to be rid of the Jews and others he thought of as undesirables.

What would he have thought of Kristopher risking his life to save the *man* he loved?

Kristopher didn't have the luxury of worrying about that now. He had to find Michel or at least what had happened to him. Then he'd decide what to do next.

To his surprise, the guard he expected to be on duty at the front desk was nowhere in sight. Another man lay sprawled across the desk. Either asleep or…?

Kristopher let out a sigh of relief. He'd been prepared to have to repeat his story and to an audience who would be much harder to convince. He hesitated. This was too easy. The man at the desk wasn't moving at all. He peered closer. Was that blood?

A muffled grunt came from under the table. Kristopher ducked his head to take a look and met the angry gaze of a soldier. The man was restrained, and there was dried blood on his leg. Apart from that, he seemed unharmed and would have to stay there until someone else found him. Hopefully it wouldn't be for a while yet. Kristopher had memorised the map for the bunkers and their connecting tunnels when Matt and Sébastien were formulating their plan. He'd head for Holm's office and start looking in the storage rooms nearby.

"Is this *your* doing?" Oberscharführer Esser stepped out of the tunnel ahead, blocking Kristopher's path.

"I found them like this." Kristopher thought quickly. Esser must know who he was. "I'm here to see Herr Holm as he requested." If he could distract Esser for a moment, he could maybe… God, he'd have to kill him. It was the only way out of this. "I'm—"

"I know who you are, Herr Doktor Lehrer." Esser seemed surprised to see him but didn't draw his weapon. He gave Kristopher a nod. "Emil Esser."

"I know who *you* are, Oberscharführer. You seem like an educated man. Let's keep this civil, hmm?"

"You misunderstand me, Herr Doktor. Nun muss sich alles, alles wenden."

"*You're* the Resistance contact?" Despite Esser using the code phrase, Kristopher took a step back. "You really expect me to trust you?"

"I saw you and Herr Doktor Zhou at the safe house, and I said nothing." Esser indicated the tunnel. "We should walk or someone might be suspicious. I'm sure neither one of us wants to be here when these men are discovered."

"I didn't kill that man," Kristopher said evenly. Something about Esser's tone made him think the man spoke the truth.

"I also warned Jacques Dubois's family in Pont-Audemer. I fight for our country, Herr Doktor, as I believe you do, but I will not be party to Holm's methods. I will tell you where your friend is, and then I will leave. I suggest you do the same. The Resistance is finished in this area. Holm knows who they are, and he is sending his men to round them up tonight."

"How do I know you're not delivering me to Herr Holm?" Kristopher didn't want to reveal his weapon until he was sure he could win any altercation, and he didn't have a silencer on his gun like Matt and the others did.

"You don't. At least not yet." Sébastien stepped out of the shadows, his gun aimed at Esser, who raised his arms. "You're not supposed to be here," he told Kristopher.

"The church was compromised. Théo is dead, and I think Nicolas is too. I hope Cécile is safe, but Théo was going to find her when he was caught. There was nowhere else to go."

"So you figured you'd go down fighting?" Sébastien shook his head. "You play a dangerous game, mon ami." He cocked his head at Esser. "Eine Kugel kam geflogen."

Like the first, it was another quote from a poem by Uhland.

"Ich hatt' einen Kameraden," Esser replied.

Sébastien lowered his gun. "You could have found out the code phrase you used earlier through torturing members of the local Resistance, but only one person besides myself knew the correct response to that one. This man can be trusted. He is my contact."

"How long have you been listening?" Kristopher asked. "Where's Liang?"

"He's gone after Reiniger. Michel wasn't where we thought, so I was heading back. I've set the explosives on a timer, so if we're going to find him, we'd better do it quickly."

"He's gone after Reiniger?" Kristopher's stomach sunk. "Reiniger will kill him! You have to find him. I'll search for Michel—"

"He is being held in a cell off the storeroom by the ammunition tunnel," Esser said quickly. "The cell is not included in the original plans, and Holm has only trusted a few men with its location, which is why it's taken me this long to discover where it is."

Kristopher raised an eyebrow. "Holm doesn't trust you."

"Not only that, but I think he grows suspicious, so I won't be able to help you for much longer. Reiniger will be inspecting the mess shelter. I know the route he will have taken. If Sébastien and I intercept Reiniger, it will give you some time to get to your friend."

"Hopefully Liang hasn't confronted him yet." Kristopher thought about telling Esser he'd be able to surrender to the

Allies soon but decided to keep that information to himself for now. He'd find out soon enough, and Kristopher planned to be well away before the Allied troops arrived. He wouldn't be caught by either side.

"He said he hoped Reiniger could lead him to Michel," Sébastien said. "He didn't say anything about confronting him."

"If the opportunity presents itself, he'll take it." Kristopher knew what he'd do if he was in Liang's position. "Good luck." He nodded his thanks and turned to walk away.

The ground rocked.

Kristopher grabbed for the wall.

"Air raid." Esser swore under his breath. He took a step back towards the entrance.

Then the lights went out.

Liang followed Reiniger at a discreet distance. He kept his head down and was careful to avoid eye contact. The couple of soldiers he passed had encountered Reiniger first, and then seemed in a hurry to leave his presence as soon as they could. Liang could understand that. He had no intention of confronting the man unless he had to.

As Reiniger neared the commander's office, the door opened. Liang ducked into a side room and pressed himself against the wall. There were a few empty rooms in this tunnel, several of which had been converted into storerooms. Liang grabbed a torch from the pile in a nearby box and shoved it into his pocket. At least now if he had to hide in another darkened room he'd be able to see.

He heard familiar voices from the corridor outside his hiding place—Reiniger and Holm. Liang couldn't quite make out their conversation as both men spoke quietly, but he caught the words "Lehrer" and "matter of time." Neither boded well.

Damn it. He needed to get closer. Laing peered through the crack between the hinges of the open door, hoping for some visual clues.

Sébastien walked past, only pausing to salute both men. They returned the salute and continued with their conversation. Whatever information Arlette had given them, she hadn't betrayed Sébastien, as neither man had seen him as any more than the soldier he pretended to be.

After what seemed forever, Reiniger saluted and continued on his way. Holm watched him, a minute smile on his face, and then walked in the opposite direction, turning left at the end of the corridor.

Damn it. Matt, get out of there.

The last thing this rescue needed was for Holm and Matt to come face-to-face. Unless Matt got the upper hand and killed the bastard. Liang wouldn't have an issue with that in the slightest.

Not after everything Holm had done.

The corridor empty once more, Liang slipped out of the room and hurried to catch up with Reiniger. Hopefully by the time he found Michel, Sébastien would be finished in the radio room and they could all leave together. They still had plenty of time between the end of this shift and the beginning of the next.

Reiniger turned right, towards another section of the bunker. This corridor led to the water storage tank. Given his route, it looked as though he was checking supplies, although Liang thought Reiniger would have delegated tasks like that. Maybe he'd decided to stretch his legs after hours of doing God knew what—not something Liang wanted to dwell on.

Finally Reiniger began to retrace his footsteps but,

instead of leading Liang somewhere useful, he entered the personnel building, supposedly heading for his quarters. He'd told Beutel to meet him where Michel was being held. Why the hell wasn't he heading there now? He'd given Margarete plenty of time to work her so-called charm on the prisoner. Not that that would do her much good. Michel was too smart to fall for any of her tricks. At least Liang hoped he was. Men didn't always think clearly when tortured. Hell, Liang still couldn't remember what he'd told Holm that day over three months ago. Truth be told, he didn't want to remember.

Bloody hell. Liang had had enough of this. He'd already wasted too much time. Michel and Ken had rescued him from a cell he'd thought he'd never get out of alive. It was time to return the favour. If Reiniger wouldn't tell him where Michel was, at least Liang could put an end to this nightmare.

Reiniger had left the door to his quarters unlocked. Liang drew his gun and slipped inside, then closed the door quietly behind him. Reiniger had taken off his holster and placed the weapon on a side table.

"I left orders that I wasn't to be disturbed." Reiniger sat at a desk with his back to the door. His eye patch lay on a pile of papers. Reiniger sounded annoyed, and his shoulders slumped as if he was tired.

Liang moved silently, waiting until he was between Reiniger and his weapon before speaking. "I've never been good at obeying orders."

"Verdammt." Reiniger turned and reached for his gun in one motion.

Liang shook his head. "I have the power this time, Herr Reiniger, not you."

Reiniger glared at Liang through one eye. A jagged scar ran from his forehead through his closed eyelid to his cheek.

Ragged skin that had been stitched closed was all that was left of his right eye.

"I hope that eye still gives you trouble. It's the least you deserve for everything you've done."

"At least I'm still alive," Reiniger sneered, "which is more than I can say for your pilot friend. He died begging for his life, showing himself to be the coward he was."

Liang snorted. "You tell yourself that. We both know that wasn't the case." Leo Dawson had sacrificed himself to save the rest of their team. It would have taken one hell of a lot of courage to light that dynamite, knowing he was sentencing himself to death as well.

"If you've come to kill me, get on with it." Reiniger shook his head. "You're a scientist, Herr Doktor Zhou, not a soldier. I don't believe you have the courage to pull that trigger." He stood. "I'm going to collect my gun, and then I'm going to arrest you. Let's see how determined you are once you're in custody. You remember what being in custody was like, don't you?"

"Sit down!" Liang barked. He'd had enough of this shit. "Where's Michel?"

Reiniger laughed. "You've come to rescue him. Is that it? You repaying the favour you think you owe him? You're too late. All you've done is hand yourself over to Standarten-führer Holm." He took one step towards the side table.

Liang shot him in the leg. Twice.

Reiniger crumbled to the floor and gasped in pain. "You shot me!"

"I'm not the same man I was, Herr Reiniger. What you did to me changed that." Liang shook in head in disgust at the man on the floor at his feet. "If Michel is dead, you're of no use to me." He raised his weapon.

Reiniger's mouth trembled. The bully who had caused others so much pain was now little more than a scared man in fear for his life. "You won't kill me." He didn't sound convinced.

Liang tightened his grip on the gun. His knuckles were white. He'd waited so long to kill the man who had captured him and made his life hell.

This was his chance to finish this, to get revenge. To hear Reiniger beg for mercy.

His hand shook.

Damn it.

Liang wanted to kill him. Why couldn't he? He didn't want to spend the rest of his life looking over his shoulder. But this Reiniger wasn't the man from Liang's nightmares. If he shot Reiniger now, he'd be no better than his tormenter.

No point in swapping one set of nightmares for another.

"No, I won't kill you." The bullets had caused little more than a flesh wound, though they would still hurt like hell. Keeping his weapon aimed at Reiniger, Liang looked around for something to restrain him with. "Use your handcuffs on yourself. I know you still have them."

Reiniger hesitated. Liang aimed his gun at his other leg.

"If you don't, I'll shoot you again. *Your* choice, Ober-sturmführer. Whatever you decide, you and your precious Standartenführer Holm are finished. You're not my problem anymore."

Once Reiniger was restrained, a quick search of his belongings supplied the belt and a couple of ties needed to finish the job. Liang stood back to admire his handywork.

The ground shook. The lights went out.

Liang heard a thud in front of him. Luckily he'd already had his back against the wall so hadn't lost his balance. He retrieved the torch he'd found earlier and switched it on. Reiniger lay on his side, still strapped firmly to his chair. Liang couldn't help but smile grimly when Reiniger glared at him and muttered something through his gag.

"I'm guessing that was a close hit by some of our chaps in the RAF." He whispered in Reiniger's ear to ensure Reiniger could still hear him through the howling siren. "It looks as though the Allied invasion has started. With any luck, they'll be the ones to find you, as your men are going to be busy saving themselves."

He headed for the door, leaving Reiniger alone in the darkness.

Keep calm. Keep calm.

Matt repeated the words silently. His heart pounded, his skin felt clammy.

Darkness and fire.

A life without Ken.

Ken could already be dead.

Of those realities, Matt knew which one he preferred. Fuck this. He steeled himself. If Ken was still alive but died because Matt couldn't fight the fears that had ruled him for far too long, he'd never forgive himself.

He almost jumped when something brushed against his leg. Matt tightened his shaking hand on his gun. Another touch. This time stronger, familiar, and from behind him.

Relief flooded Matt, but he couldn't give in to the emotion now. Ken was alive. Matt felt behind him, ran his fingers across Ken's hand. Ken caught Matt's hand and squeezed it before letting go. Ken shifted so his back was against Matt's.

He must have dropped to the floor when Holm had fired, and shuffled backwards, using the siren to mask the sound of his movements. Ken had always thought quickly under fire. Because he was so unsteady, the floor was the safest place as there was nowhere left to fall. Staying together back to back also meant they knew where they both were.

Where the hell was Holm?

If Holm had any sense, he'd stay still and not reveal his whereabouts. No point trying to hit a target in the dark. They'd have to keep quiet and wait for the lights to come back on. Why couldn't he see the fire? Damn it. Where was the door?

Outside the room, men shouted. Matt flinched at the unmistakable sound of a fire extinguisher. Ken must have heard it too—he briefly rested his hand on Matt's thigh.

The siren stopped wailing. The fire must be out, but for how long?

If this had been an air raid, the bombers would be aiming for the battery artillery. If they hadn't gotten it the first time, they'd try again.

Matt tried to get his bearings, but it was hopeless. Even if he managed to find the door, he'd need to get past Holm.

The asshole was probably biding his time and waiting for Matt to make a mistake. Why put himself in danger and reveal his position when he didn't need to?

Great. Was this the way his life was going to end? In a standoff with an SS officer?

Matt blinked against the sudden rush of light.

The door slammed shut.

Behind him, Ken turned and pushed Matt down in one action. Something whizzed through the air past Matt's head.

He looked up. A pile of boxes balanced precariously above his head, the top one edging over.

Ken dragged Matt back in time, but Holm dived out of the way, too late, and his leg was trapped under several boxes. He let out a noise that was part anger, part pain. His gun fell from his hand to the floor just out of reach. He tried to crawl to it but couldn't pull himself free.

Matt grabbed the gun. He slid it across the floor behind him to Ken.

"You haven't won, Priest," Holm said. "Neither of you will get out of this bunker alive."

"Neither will you." Matt levelled the gun at him. "I told you what I'd do if you hurt Ken. I always keep my promises."

"You're finished," Holm spat. "We'll win this war. Kill me, and someone will take my place." He looked past Matt to Ken. "At least I'll die with honour. You, like your father, take the coward's way out. You're not the one pulling the trigger. You're getting your deviant *lover* to do it for you."

"There is nothing honourable in anything you've done." Matt met Holm's gaze. There was no sign of the gentleman Holm had once pretended to be. "The Allies are invading. Germany will fall. I promise you that."

"I am not my father," Ken said quietly. "I'm not killing you because I promised your sister I wouldn't. Matt made another promise. I'm not going to stop him."

"My sister?" Holm's defiant expression shattered. "But she's—"

Matt didn't wait for the rest. "Goodbye, Herr Holm. I hope you rot in hell." He pulled the trigger.

Holm slumped forward and lay still.

Matt lowered his gun and walked over to Ken. "Lean on me. We're getting out of here together." He helped Ken from the room, only pausing to shut the door. Neither of them looked back.

CHAPTER NINETEEN

Michel closed his eyes. Everything hurt.

He didn't want to die.

He bit his lip. He wouldn't show weakness, wouldn't be tempted to betray the person he loved. He managed a laugh, but it came out like a hoarse, twisted pretence of sound. Margarete had presumed her gloating would break him. Instead it gave Michel the hope he thought he'd abandoned hours ago.

Had it only been hours? He'd lost track of time. Margarete had left when the lights had died. He wasn't sure how long ago that had been either.

Kit hadn't given in to Holm's demands. He was still free.

Mon cher. I'm so sorry.

Michel had hoped Kit would never have to make the decision to sacrifice one life to save however many this bomb would take.

It was selfish, but in a way Michel was relieved he hadn't had to make the choice. He hated that Kit had, but Kit was strong, much more so than he gave himself credit for. If Michel had seen Kit tortured and hurt in the same way he'd been, he would have screamed at Reiniger to stop and given him anything he wanted.

He still had nightmares about Kit getting shot. This would be so much worse.

Michel let his head fall forward. He was tired. He almost wished Margarete would return and finish this. It would be a mercy. Kit wasn't coming. There was no point in keeping him like this.

Merde.

What if Margarete wasn't coming back? What if she intended to leave him to die here?

Panic rushed through him. Michel yanked at his restraints, fire screaming through his arms. He moaned and blinked back tears. He wouldn't give any of these bastards the satisfaction of thinking they'd broken him.

Je t'aime.

He heard Kit in his mind. He could almost feel Kit's fingers brushing his face. "Ich liebe dich auch," he whispered. He wanted to let go. He had nothing left.

Footsteps. Was Margarete coming back to gloat? Or…?

No.

Kit would be far away by now. Safe.

"Michel?"

Michel opened his eyes. When had the lights come back on? He'd given up trying to hear anything outside. Reiniger had made a point of reminding Michel that no one would hear him—or find him. His world had shrunk down to his makeshift cell and everything in it.

He tried to focus on the person standing in front of him. "Arlette?" He must be dreaming. Why dream about her, of all people?

"Yes, it's me." Arlette made an apologetic noise. She stretched up and yanked at the chains that held him suspended from the ceiling, his feet not quite touching the floor.

He gasped in pain. "Please…"

"I'll be quick, I promise. It's difficult to reach the lock." Arlette had keys in her hand. She tried one and then another. "Mon Dieu, what have these bastards done to you?"

Finally the chains loosened, and he fell into her arms. She stroked his face and held him. He flinched. Had she…? He'd imagined Kit's touch. Had it been Arlette's?

She kissed him on the lips, gently brushing her mouth against his.

"I… I'm sorry, Arlette. I don't love you." Michel knew it probably wasn't the wisest move to upset a woman who had obviously risked much to find him, but he'd let this go for far too long.

"I know that. I betrayed you. I'm being foolish, but I had to steal a kiss, just once." Arlette helped Michel stand. "We can talk about this later. If you want to."

"This has nothing to do with that. My heart belongs to another."

"A good man who loved me gave me a second chance." Arlette cupped his face in her hands so he had to look into her eyes. The regret and sadness quickly gave way to determination. "I'm passing on that chance to you. I made a mistake. I'm sorry."

Someone clapped their hands from the doorway in a slow round of applause. "How touching." Margarete Huber shook her head. "Both of you in love with someone who doesn't return the sentiment, yet here you are together, despite everything you've done. It's poetic in a way. Or should that be pathetic."

"Let her go," Michel said. "She's already been useful to you."

"Or you'll what? You're hardly in a position to make

demands." Margarete gestured at the doorway. "As I said before, dear Kristopher isn't coming. It appears he doesn't love you after all."

"Go to hell," Arlette told her.

"This is tiresome." Margarete aimed her gun at them. "Neither of you are of any more use. The bunker is under attack. There was always the chance Kristopher might be foolish enough to try to rescue you, and I'd be able to finish *all* of my business here, but it appears he considers his own welfare more important." She shrugged. "How disappointing, although it does mean you are no longer needed. I do so dislike leaving loose ends."

"No!" Arlette launched herself at Margarete.

"Tsk tsk." Margarete neatly sidestepped and fired.

Arlette crumpled to the floor, blood pooling beneath her.

Michel's breath hitched. "You bitch!" Despite everything she'd done, Arlette had been a friend once. He dropped to his knees. He felt numb. He knew he should feel *something*, but there was nothing left.

Margarete levelled her gun at him again. "Give my love to Kristopher when you see him again. I figure if I can't have him, then he can't have you. Goodbye, Michel."

Michel closed his eyes. He would accept this without a fight. He'd had enough of fighting.

I'm sorry, Kit. I love you.

A shot fired. A woman screamed.

Wait. What? He wasn't dead. How?

Michel opened his eyes. Margarete lay on the ground, a figure standing over her. "Go on," he said roughly. Whatever sick joke this was, he'd had enough. "Kill me now. Finish it."

"Michel, it's me." Kit looked down at him. The gun wavered in his hand. "Don't you recognise me?"

This couldn't be Kit. Michel felt a sudden rush of panic. It had to be a trick.

But what if it wasn't? He couldn't let Kit shoot him and kill the slim hope they could still have a future together.

Michel got to his feet slowly, not quite hiding the gasp of pain when he moved, and forced himself to take a step back. "Put the gun down."

Please let it be him. Let this be real.

"Michel. Scheisse. What have they done to you?" Kit ran to Michel and pulled him into a rough embrace. "I thought… I couldn't let her shoot you." He sounded horrified.

"Kit." Michel kissed Kit's face. "It's you. It's you. What are you doing here? I thought… I thought you were safe."

"Neither of us is safe now." Kit brushed one finger over Michel's face, his expression growing angry when Michel flinched. "Come on. I'm getting you out of here. Can you walk?"

Michel nodded. "I think so." He had to at least try.

"There's a dead soldier outside. Arlette must have killed him. We'll borrow his jacket. I'll take you out of here at gunpoint."

"Kit—" Michel started to protest, but Kit put one finger over Michel's lips.

"The Allies have begun their attack. The men out there will be more worried about that than something they expect to see. I know a way out, but we need to hurry. The bunker wasn't seriously damaged this time, but I'm not sure what will happen if it's hit again."

Ken gritted his teeth. Any sudden movement hurt, but he didn't have time to give in to that now. He'd shoved Holm's gun into the waistband of his pants at his back and draped his shirt over it. As Matt still wore his German uniform, he'd given Ken his jacket. They'd already passed a few injured men, so no one questioned another.

The repaired lighting was dimmer than usual. If this was an Allied attack, it was only a matter of time before they targeted the battery again.

"We need to find Michel," Ken said.

"I'm getting you out first, and then I'll go back for him." Matt didn't sound happy.

"It might be too late then." Ken paused to catch his breath. "At least let's check any rooms we pass in case he's there."

"Depending on how long it takes us to get out of here, it *will* be too late. Do you have any idea where they were keeping Michel?"

Ken shook his head. "They kept us separate." He started to walk again. Matt slipped an arm around Ken's waist when he swayed on his feet. "I don't know what state he's in or if he's still alive."

"I'll do what I can for him, but I can't help both of you at once, and I'm not risking you for him when he might already be dead."

"You're not only concerned the Allies are going for round two, are you?" Ken asked. A horrible thought struck him. "Is Arlette still working with you? You can't trust her. She's—"

"She's dead—executed as a traitor." Matt spoke without any inflection. They'd talk about it later. "And yes, it's not just that."

"Better to get out of here, then." Ken guessed what Matt wasn't saying. They'd have hardly gone to the trouble of getting into the bunker without causing some damage on their way out. If the Allies didn't get them, whatever explosives Matt's team had set would finish the job.

Matt hesitated when they reached the end of the corridor. "Stay here." He ducked around the corner.

The ground lurched. Ken grabbed at the wall. The siren began to wail again.

A loud crack was followed by shouting and coughing. Ken peered into the corridor on his right. Dust filled the air. He coughed. Oh God. Matt had just gone that way. Ken reached for his weapon when a dust-covered figure ran towards him.

"Change of plan." Matt cleared his throat, spitting up dust. "We're getting out the way we came in. A section of the ceiling has caved in. It's passable but most of the men are heading for the personnel shelter. They know this bunker is done for. It's a narrower tunnel out this way, so only the men working close by will try to use it."

"You hope, and they're more done for than they realise," Ken muttered. That hadn't been an explosion from inside the bunker. The Allies had dropped another bomb.

"Straight ahead to the end of this corridor, through one room, and up the steps. Think you can manage?"

Ken nodded grimly. "I'll be right behind you." *I hope.*

Matt shook his head. "Together, or not at all." He wrapped his arm around Ken again and half helped, half dragged him through the corridor.

The office at the end stood empty. Ken hoped like hell Michel had managed to get out. They couldn't do anything for him now.

Matt let go of Ken when they reached the steps leading to the surface. "Only room for one." He shoved Ken in front of him.

He only got a glimpse of the night air before Matt tackled him, slamming them both to the ground as the underground bunker exploded behind them.

Ken coughed, trying to catch his breath. Luckily most of the explosion had been trapped inside. The ground shook a couple of times and then was still. The siren stopped abruptly as though its throat had been cut.

He sat up, shivering. "Matt? Matt!"

"I'm here," Matt said hoarsely. He gave Ken a brief hug, breaking it quickly at the sound of someone approaching.

"You made it." Sébastien seemed pleased to see them. Ken looked past him and froze.

"What the hell is *he* doing here?" Ken ground out. He and Matt both drew their guns and pointed them at Esser.

"He's one of the good guys, believe it or not." Liang pushed past Sébastien and strode over to what was left of the steps. "I left Reiniger in there. He's… I didn't leave him to die."

Matt put one arm briefly over Liang's shoulder. "He deserved everything he got." He turned to Sébastien and Esser. "We didn't find Michel. You managed to get him out, right?" He paled. "You did find him?"

"I'm sorry." Sébastien shook his head. "We found Liang a few moments before the second siren sounded, and we got out together through the personnel shelter. It was too dangerous to stay any longer."

"Oh hell." Matt closed his eyes. Ken wished he could take him into his arms and hold him.

Damn this all to hell.

Liang started to head down the steps.

Matt caught his arm. "You can't go down there. There's nothing left. I'm sorry."

Liang struggled against Matt's grip, but Matt held him tightly. "Kit's still in there. Sébastien saw him. He was going to find Michel."

"He was supposed to stay at the church. He was supposed to be… All this and for…" Matt let go of Liang's arm. His shoulders slumped.

"We've all lost good people today." Sébastien sighed. "I'm going to go find the rest of my cell, if there is anyone left alive. The invasion is only beginning, and this fight is far from over."

Esser gave Matt a nod. "I need to surrender myself to you, as the senior Allied officer here."

"I'll put in a good word for you," Matt told Esser. "Go help Sébastien. You can surrender once we make contact with the Allied troops." The Allies would have dropped troops by parachute behind enemy lines to help with the sabotage ahead of the invasion—the Germans wouldn't give up France that easily. "Be careful. This night is going to be a long one."

Sébastien gave Matt a salute. "It's been an honour working with you. All of you." He indicated the bunker. "Perhaps they have survived. If they got out beforehand or got to the shelter…"

Matt shook his head. "I doubt it. Merci. Adieu, mon ami."

"Adieu." Sébastien gave each of them one last nod, and then he and Esser walked away.

Kristopher stepped out of his hiding place as soon as Sébastien and Esser were gone. He'd hated letting his friends think he and Michel were dead, but he didn't have a choice.

Liang looked up, disbelief quickly giving way to a mix of relief and anger. "You're alive!" He rushed over, studying both of them in turn, the anger in his expression growing as he looked closely at Michel. "I thought… Don't scare me like that again." He turned to Matt. "Holm *is* finally gone?"

"Holm is dead," Matt said evenly.

Michel squeezed Kristopher's hand. Now they were out of the bunker, he'd stopped hiding his tiredness. He winced when Kristopher touched him, yet leaned in close to him as though he didn't want to let go. Kristopher had told him that

Matt knew about their relationship. This would be the last time either of them would be able to be so open with anyone else, and it seemed right that their last time as a team would be without secrets.

They were safe here for the few minutes they needed to finish the mission they'd started all those months ago.

Anyone with any sense would be either trying to flee the bunker from the other exits or staying well away. With the Allied invasion force on their way, there were two options—escape or surrender.

"We barely got out in time," Kristopher said. The second siren had howled as they'd reached the personnel shelter. By the time they'd made their escape through one of the exits, men were already heading into the shelter from the other side. Kristopher had slammed the door shut behind them, and they'd run, not stopping or looking back until they knew they were clear.

"I'll tell London you were in there when it was destroyed," Matt promised. "Do you still have Benoit's identity papers?"

Kristopher handed them over. Finding a body to claim as his wouldn't be a problem. Not everyone would have made it to the shelter in time.

"I don't have mine," Michel said.

"Not a problem." Matt shrugged. "I never knew your real name, and although I didn't find you, I have no idea where you are."

"If you're going, you need to do it now before you're seen by anyone else." Ken held out his hand. "Keep your heads down and survive this damned war."

Michel shook Ken's hand. "It's been an honour working with you. All of you. Thank you."

"Our so-called simple mission turned into anything but, didn't it?" Matt gave Michel a loose hug when it was his turn to shake hands.

"I always thought you were overly optimistic, and now I know you better, I'm convinced of it." Liang shook Michel's hand, then gave Kristopher a hug. "I'm expecting a card after the war. Don't disappoint me," he whispered.

"I won't." Kristopher exchanged a hug with Matt. "One year after the war. Talk to Liang," he murmured. "Au revoir, my friends. Stay safe, and thank you."

He turned away, blinking back tears. Although they'd arranged to meet, he'd never see them again. It was safer that way. If someone had told him before all this had started that he'd be standing outside a bunker in Normandy saying goodbye to a British man and two Americans, he would have never believed it. They'd all been thrown together, and grown into not only a team, but a makeshift family.

Michel leaned in and kissed him softly on the cheek. Matt put his arm around Ken. Even Liang seemed subdued.

"Thank you," Michel said softly. He offered his hand to Kristopher. "Come on, mon cher. We need to go."

"I know," Kristopher said quietly, slipping his hand into Michel's. He'd hold on to it for as long as he could.

Kristopher Lehrer was dead. He wouldn't use that name again. It was the way it had to be.

He looked back over his shoulder once more, then followed Michel into the new life they would build together.

EPILOGUE

Kit drew his bow over the strings of his violin, his fingers swaying back and forth in a gentle vibrato. He closed his eyes, losing himself in the melody of the Brahms Lullaby. Over the violin, the counterpoint played by the flute added to the richness of the music, both instruments complementing each other yet coming together in unison for the final note.

Instead of lowering his instrument immediately, Kit stood for a few moments, lost in memories of not only the music, but the man sharing the duet with him.

"I never tire of playing music with you." Michel smiled. He put his flute on the table, then carefully returned it to its case.

"That was beautiful. You promised me a duet not long after we met, but you've given me so much more."

"More than one duet, and many more to come, I hope." Michel took Kit's violin and set it down. He then pulled him close and kissed him gently on the lips. "I still remember that first time we played together. We were both very out of practice."

Kit chuckled. "I'm sure your cousin wondered if she'd done the right thing giving me her violin."

"Even out of practice, you were still a better player than she ever was, and she knew it." Michel rested their foreheads together. "There were too many moments when I thought we'd never reach this point in our lives."

"Too many close calls, mein Schatz." Kit wrapped his arms around Michel's waist. "I worried every time you went on a mission, but I knew you had to do what you could to help finish the war."

After leaving Cyrville-sur-Mer, they'd spent most of the following year moving around France, helping the Resistance when they could, yet not staying too long in one place. Neither could, in good conscience, find somewhere to hide and sit out the rest of the war. They'd been careful, though. Kit had done his bit behind the scenes, never placing himself in a position where he could be compromised or caught, while Michel took a more active role.

Finally, after France had been liberated in May, they'd come home to Melun. Michel's parents had welcomed Kit into their family, introducing him as Kit, a distant cousin from Switzerland. Although he spoke French fluently now, the story covered his German accent, which he would never completely lose. He'd settled into life as a farmer, the hard work bringing him a sense of peace he'd never thought he would have.

One day Michel would inherit the farm from his father, but in the meantime, Jérôme Faber had told them to make one of the smaller worker's cottages their own. It gave them some privacy and a safe place to be open with each other about their relationship. Michel had told his family of Arlette's death, of how she'd died trying to save him. People knew she'd been sweet on him, so they presumed that in his grief he'd decided to remain a bachelor. It made sense for the distant cousins—and close friends—to share the cottage, especially as Kit had lost his family during the war and had nowhere else to go.

"We both did what we could," Michel said softly. He always knew when Kit was thinking of the friends they'd made, and lost. "We *all* did."

Although it was a year after the war had finished, being back in France brought back memories Matt preferred to forget. He'd been surprised to get the letter from Liang—they hadn't been in contact since the news that the bombs had been dropped on Japan and the war was well and truly over.

Not that the letter had said much. Nevertheless, Matt and Ken had decided to keep the appointment with Liang, so here they were, sitting in Le Café Magalie, off Avenue des Champs-Élysées. The owner of the café—a middle-aged Frenchman who introduced himself as Brice—had directed them to a group of tables near a large window looking out onto the street.

The café's decor was simple, yet welcoming. Round wooden tables were placed at intervals around the room, covered with pale yellow tablecloths, and each decorated with a vase with a single flower. The walls were a paler shade —a few brushstrokes suggesting the illusion of sheaves of wheat rather than confirming it. A radio provided background music, its volume carefully chosen not to intrude on conversation.

Their tables had been booked, Brice had told them with a smile, and it was his mission to ensure their visit to Le Café Magalie would be a pleasant one. Matt had thought it an odd turn of phrase and attempted to continue the conversation in French in case it was a translation problem. However, Brice had chuckled and suggested they speak English if that was more comfortable. His English was excellent—he'd had a good teacher—although his German still was not.

"Quit being so nervous," Ken said. "They'll be here. We were early."

"Sorry. I keep having to remind myself the war is over." Matt was being foolish. He was fine—more or less—at home in Pennsylvania, but this was different. He'd spent so many months thinking of it as enemy territory.

The other patrons had given them a few looks when they'd first spoken, no doubt noticing their American accents, then returned to their own meals and conversation.

"I know," Ken said softly. "Me too. Although it's been a year since the war ended, coming back to France makes it feel like yesterday. Part of me wants to find a quiet table in the corner and stay out of sight." He smiled at Matt. "Any regrets? About being here, I mean. Not the rest of it."

"Not about here, too many about the rest of it, but none about what we have now." Matt brushed his hand against Ken's, careful not to linger long enough that it would be noticed. He loved the life they'd made together, although to everyone else, they were war buddies who shared an apartment over the automobile repair shop Matt owned. Ken had found his niche building and repairing radios and had set up a business nearby. He also helped Matt out in the shop on occasion—Ken had always been interested in how things worked.

"You're easier to live with than I thought you'd be." Ken grinned. He was far more relaxed than he used to be, although his sense of humour hadn't improved any.

"Thanks. So are you." Matt glanced over at the door again. Where the hell had Liang gotten to? He'd said he'd be at Le Café Magalie by noon. It was almost one.

Brice placed two cups of coffee on the table.

"We didn't order these," Matt said. They'd finished one each and decided to wait for Liang before ordering more.

"Compliments of the house. Dr Zhou left a message he'd be running late as his wife needed to make a detour on their way here."

"Thanks." Matt waited until Brice had walked away before continuing. "It sounds as though married life is agreeing with Liang."

He'd sounded happy in his letter, more settled than Matt remembered. Of their original team, he'd been the least prepared for life in the field. A brief stint at basic training for something he'd never volunteered for hadn't been enough, but then with the way the mission had gone, all of them had quickly been dropped into a situation they hadn't expected or been prepared for.

"More than he told us." Ken nodded towards the door.

Juliane Zhou looked around the café, her face lighting up when she saw them. She scurried over to their table. Matt stood and pulled out a chair for her. "It's good to see both of you again. Liang will be here shortly. I didn't want to interrupt his conversation, but I needed to sit." She took the offered seat and rested her hand on her stomach. "I'm afraid this child already has a mind of his own. Much like his father."

"And his mother," Ken murmured.

Matt kicked him under the table. "It's good to see you again too, Juliane. I didn't know you and Liang had gotten married until I received his letter."

"He invited me to Cambridge to find him once the war was over." She chuckled. "You should have seen the look on his face when I showed up. I don't think he expected me to take him up on it." She sobered. "There was nothing left for me in Germany. My family is gone, and Liang and I are happy together. His grandparents have made me feel very welcome."

"I'm sorry about…" Matt wasn't sure what to say exactly. He'd killed her brother.

Juliane shook her head. "We don't choose our families, Matt. Karl was a driven man, and I didn't agree with what he did. If you hadn't shot him, someone else would have. I'm sorry for what he did to both of you."

Liang walked up behind her and kissed the top of her head. "I hope my wife isn't boring you with pregnancy stories. It's good to see you again. You're both looking well."

"It's been too long." Matt hadn't seen Liang since they'd parted ways in London. Matt and Ken had continued to serve in the military until the end of the war—in separate units—while Liang had returned to his academic life at Cambridge.

The debriefing after D-Day hadn't been pleasant, although they'd all been careful to word their statements so their superiors were left thinking their mission had been a failure. They'd returned from Europe without the formulae for the atomic bomb and the scientist who had helped develop it.

He and Ken had been horrified when the bombs had been dropped on Hiroshima and Nagasaki. It had taken Ken over a week to get news of his grandparents, but luckily they'd decided to visit family in Iwaki a few days beforehand.

"It has." Liang looked apologetic. "I'm sorry I didn't return your call last August. I… the whole thing was a little too close to home with everything we'd been through."

"You didn't fail," Juliane said softly. "It could have been far worse, and they didn't get the information to make that terrible thing because of you. Remember that."

"I hope K—" Liang stopped and sighed. "He wouldn't have been happy."

Matt hoped Michel had been with Kit when he'd heard about it. Knowing Kit, he would have felt responsible, although he wasn't. They all still had nightmares about the war, to some degree. Matt wondered if they would ever be entirely free of them.

"You said you'd heard from them?" Matt was careful not to use names. Although the war was over, there would always be someone out there wanting to use Kit's knowledge for their own agenda.

"Yes." Liang reached into his pocket and pulled out a playing card. It was a four of hearts with the name of the café written on it in Kit's handwriting. "Oh hell. Wait there. I told them only a few minutes and it's been longer than that." He jumped up from his chair and strode over to the back door of the café.

A few moments later, he returned with two people. An older woman and a younger man. The man walked with a pronounced limp and used a walking stick.

Matt frowned, not recognising either of them at first. They'd changed so much.

"Dr Lehrer!" Ken exclaimed.

"Clara, please." Clara Lehrer looked at least ten years older than when they'd seen her last. Matt had tried to trace her after the war, but with no luck as the trail went cold after she'd been sent to one of the camps. "Juliane contacted me and asked if I was interested in seeing you again. Of course I said yes. Trevor insisted on accompanying me."

Trevor Palmer pulled out a chair for her, then took a seat himself. "I met Juliane by chance in Berlin a few months after the war, and we found Clara together, through some of Juliane's contacts. Clara's still practicing medicine, and I thought I could do some good there, so I stayed." He too looked much older since they'd last seen him almost three years ago, although he was still only in his early twenties.

"Leg was never right again after that bastard shot me. He broke it to try and get me to talk. Waste of time, but he didn't listen."

"Reiniger never did," Liang said quietly. Juliane took his hand in hers and caressed it with her thumb.

"I was hoping you had news of my brother." Clara sounded hopeful.

Matt shook his head, feeling bad he had to lie to her. "He's—"

"He's still alive. They both are. That's part of the reason Clara is here." Liang lowered his voice. "Kit asked me to find her. I didn't expect either of our mutual friends to show up, but I'd hoped there might be a way to get word to them as they arranged this meeting. I know they survived the war, but that's all I know. I have no clue where they are."

"Dr Zhou?" Brice brought over two bottles of wine and a tray of glasses.

Matt eyed him suspiciously. "I hope those aren't compliment of the house as well."

"My nephew described all of you extremely well." Brice chuckled and indicated the playing card. "The wine is from him and his… cousin. I have a letter for you. If you wish to reply, I can make sure they get it." He handed Matt a note. "It's a pleasure to finally meet you, Monsieur Bryant."

"Merci, you've been a gracious host." Matt frowned. "Your nephew?"

Brice placed two extra glasses in the middle of the table and, instead of answering, gave them all a nod and returned to his work.

"Michel had an Uncle Brice," Liang said slowly. "Kit told me that once, I'm sure of it."

"Oh," Clara said. "So the letter could… Read it. Please."

Matt opened the letter with shaking hands. He recognised the handwriting immediately, and began to read aloud.

. . .

"I hope this finds you all well. I can't tell you much, but I can say that we are both alive and happy with our life. I'm sorry we couldn't be with you today, but I'm sure you understand why. Please give my love to my sister and tell her I'm sorry. If you wish to reply, B will make sure we receive it. We miss you all, our dear friends. K and M."

Ken filled their glasses, then raised his. "To absent friends," he said, breaking the silence.

Of those who couldn't be with them today, at least Kit and Michel had been able to send word. Too many people had lost their lives and given themselves bravely so others could live.

Elise Schuster.

Ed Walker.

Leo Dawson.

Jacques Dubois.

The members of the Resistance who had helped them both in Germany and France.

They hadn't heard from Sébastien again. After Cyrville-sur-Mer had been liberated from the Germans, he hadn't many friends left alive to go back to either.

Matt glanced at Ken, then frowned as something—or rather someone familiar—caught his eye outside. No, it couldn't be.

"Matt?" Ken asked.

Matt looked back out onto the street, but whomever he'd seen was gone. If they'd been there at all. He filled the two empty glasses before raising his own. "To absent friends."

"To absent friends," Liang echoed. "Lest we forget."

~

Kit lowered his head when Matt looked up. It had been a foolish idea coming to Paris, but he'd wanted to see their friends one last time.

He and Michel had a good view of the café from across the street, and Kit had thought that would enough. Then Clara had arrived, and he'd needed to see her, to make sure she was all right. He missed her terribly, yet it would be too dangerous to meet directly. Brice had a second letter for her, in case she had come, and offered to act as go-between so they could at least stay in contact that way.

Michel waited until they were a good distance from the café before he spoke. "I miss them too," he said softly.

"There was so much I wanted to put in that letter." Kit wished he could rest his head on Michel's shoulder like they were free to do at home.

"I know." Michel grew quiet. He led Kit to a discrete spot where they wouldn't be overheard. "Any regrets? Not only about today or the letter."

"I regret a lot of what I've done." Kit smiled. "Do you remember the evening by the pond at St. Gertrud's?"

"I've never forgotten it. We talked about the future we both wanted, and when I asked you whether you were happy with the choices you'd made in life, you couldn't answer me."

Kit nodded. "I'd imagined a future in which we'd just played a duet, and after we finished, you put your arms around me, kissed me, and asked me that question."

"I liked that future, and I still do." Michel brushed his hand against Kit's arm, the most intimate touch he could risk out in the open. "Kit," he said softly, "can you answer that question now?"

"I think so." Kit spoke slowly. Although he'd given it a lot of thought, he wanted the words to be perfect. "I've made a lot of mistakes, but I don't regret any of the choices I've made since I met you. Although the weapon I'd hope would never be built was used, I at least know it wasn't because of me. I don't think anyone goes through life without regrets, so instead of berating the past, I want to focus on what we have now. We're together, and I thought we'd never have that. It's enough. So yes, I have regrets, but I'm happy with my life as it is now."

"As am I. Whatever happens, we'll face it together, mon cher. That's all anyone can ask for. Ich liebe dich, Kit."

"Je t'aime, Michel." Kit smiled. "You're mine just as I am yours. The two of us. Making our future together."

ABOUT THE AUTHOR

CONNECT WITH ANNE

Contact me at:
annebarwell.wordpress.com
darthanne@gmail.com

Anne Barwell lives in Wellington, New Zealand. She shares her home with Kaylee: a cat with "tortitude" who is convinced that the house is run to suit her; this is an ongoing "discussion," and to date, it appears as though Kaylee may be winning.

In 2008, Anne completed her conjoint BA in English Literature and Music/Bachelor of Teaching. She has worked as a music teacher, a primary school teacher, and now works in a library. She is a member of the Upper Hutt Science Fiction Club and plays violin for Hutt Valley Orchestra.

She is an avid reader across a wide range of genres and a watcher of far too many TV series and movies, although it can be argued that there is no such thing as "too many." These, of course, are best enjoyed with a decent cup of tea and further the continuing argument that the concept of "spare time" is really just a myth. She also hosts and reviews for other authors, and writes monthly blog posts for Love Bytes. She is the co-founder of the New Zealand Rainbow Romance writers, and a member of RWNZ.

Anne's books have received honourable mentions five times, reached the finals four times—one of which was for best gay book—and been a runner up in the Rainbow Awards. She has also been nominated three times in the Goodreads M/M Romance Reader's Choice Awards—twice for Best Fantasy, once for Best Historical, and once for All-Time Favourite M/M Author.

Shadowboxing
Complete their mission or lose everything.

Berlin, 1943

An encounter with an old friend leaves German physicist Dr Kristopher Lehrer with doubts about his work. But when he confronts his superior, everything goes horribly wrong. Suddenly Kristopher and Michel, a member of the Resistance, are on the run, hunted for treason and a murder they did not commit. If they're caught, Kristopher's knowledge could be used to build a terrible weapon that could win the war.

For the team sent by the Allies—led by Captain Bryant, Sergeant Lowe, and Dr Zhou—a simple mission escalates into a deadly game against the Gestapo, with Dr Lehrer as the ultimate prize. But in enemy territory, surviving and completing their mission will test their strengths and loyalties and prove more complex than they ever imagined.

Winter Duet

Who do you trust when no one is who they seem?

Germany 1944

Fleeing German physicist Dr Kristopher Lehrer and his lover, Resistance fighter Michel, are caught up in an Allied bombing campaign. Separated from Michel after discovering an injured RAF pilot in the Black Forest, and pursued by the SS for the information he carries, Kristopher is frantic to reunite, unaware that Michel has been recruited by the Allies for a rescue mission.

Time is running out. The Gestapo is closing in. How can they decide who to trust, when the dagger pointed at Kristopher's back could be wielded by a friend?

www.ingramcontent.com/pod-product-compliance
Lightning Source LLC
Chambersburg PA
CBHW061017120726
47910CB00006B/1984